A TEMPTATION OF ANGELS

A TEMPTATION
OF ANGELS

BY MICHELLE ZINK

DIAL BOOKS FOR YOUNG READERS
An imprint of Penguin Group (USA) Inc.

DIAL BOOKS

An imprint of Penguin Group (USA), Inc.

Published by The Penguin Group

Penguin Group (USA) Inc., 375 Hudson Street, New York, NY 10014, U.S.A.

Penguin Group (Canada), 90 Eglinton Avenue East, Suite 700,
Toronto, Ontario M4P 2Y3, Canada (a division of Pearson Penguin Canada Inc.)

Penguin Books Ltd, 80 Strand, London WC2R 0RL, England

Penguin Ireland, 25 St. Stephen's Green, Dublin 2,
Ireland (a division of Penguin Books Ltd)

Penguin Group (Australia), 250 Camberwell Road, Camberwell, Victoria 3124,
Australia (a division of Pearson Australia Group Pty Ltd)

Penguin Books India Pvt Ltd, 11 Community Centre,
Panchsheel Park, New Delhi - 110 017, India

Penguin Group (NZ), 67 Apollo Drive, Rosedale, Auckland 0632,
New Zealand (a division of Pearson New Zealand Ltd)

Penguin Books (South Africa) (Pty) Ltd, 24 Sturdee Avenue, Rosebank,
Johannesburg 2196, South Africa

Penguin Books Ltd, Registered Offices: 80 Strand, London WC2R 0RL, England

Copyright © 2012 by Michelle Zink

The publisher does not have any control over and does not assume any responsibility
for author or third-party websites or their content.

Book design by Jasmin Rubero

Text set in Perpetua Std

Printed in the U.S.A.

10 9 8 7 6 5 4 3 2 1

CIP is available.

ALWAYS LEARNING   **PEARSON**

For Steven Malk,

who never stops believing.

A TEMPTATION
OF ANGELS

ONE

Though it was late, it was not the sound of arguing that woke Helen in the dead of night.

She lay in bed for a long time after retiring, listening to the rise and fall of voices coming from the library. It was a familiar sound, comforting rather than worrisome. Her mother and father often met with the others, though the meetings had become more frequent and heated of late. Yet, there was something about this night, the cadence of these voices— however familiar—that made Helen's nerves tingle, as if they were humming too close to the surface of her skin.

At first, she tried to decipher the words drifting through the vents set into the floor of her chambers, especially when they sounded in her father's familiar baritone or the strong, clear voice of her mother. But after a while, Helen gave up, opting instead to let her mind wander as she stared at the canopy above her head.

Her thoughts settled on the morning's fencing exercises and her argument with Father. It was not the first time she had rebelled against the recent addition to her curriculum. She still failed to see how fencing could contribute anything to her schooling, but Father's word was law when it came to her education. He knew well that Helen's prowess lay in the strategy of chess, in the logic problems and cryptographs she could solve faster than he, not in the agile movement required of her on the ballroom floor where they practiced fencing. Still, he pushed. Using the foil out of deference to her inexperience was his only concession. Were Father working with one of his usual sparring partners, he would, without question, have used his saber. Now, in the muffled quiet of her bedchamber, Helen vowed that in time Father would use a saber with her as well.

She didn't remember slipping into the emptiness of sleep, and she did not awaken gently. It was the sound of hurried footsteps down the hall that caused her to sit up in bed, her heart racing. She did not have time to contemplate the possibilities before the door was thrown open, candlelight from the sconces in the hall throwing strange shadows across the walls and floor of her sleeping chamber.

Scooting to the headboard, she pulled the coverlet to her

chin, too frightened to be ashamed for her childish behavior.

"You must get out of bed, Helen. Now."

The voice was her mother's. She moved into the darkness of the room, the strange shadows disappearing as she crossed to the dressing table. She fumbled with something—the glass jars and scent decanters atop the vanity clinking noisily together.

"But . . . it's the middle of the night!"

Her mother turned then, and a shaft of light from the hall illuminated the valise in her hand. The realization that her mother was packing, packing Helen's things, blew like a hurricane through the confusion of her mind. Her mother was across the room in seconds, leaning over the bed and speaking close to her face.

"You're in grave danger, Helen." Her mother pulled the coverlet from Helen's shivering body. Her nightdress was twisted around her thighs, and the cold air bit her skin as her mother's hand encircled her arm, already pulling her from the warmth of her bed. "Now, come."

The carpets were cool under Helen's bare feet as she was led to the wall next to the wardrobe. Her mother reached into the bodice of her gown, pulling from it a chain with something dangling at its end. It caught the light spilling in from the hall, glimmering faintly in the darkness as her mother removed it from her neck. Fear coiled like a snake in Helen's stomach as her mother pushed aside the large mirror in the corner, bending to the paneled wall behind it. She continued speaking as she worked something against the plaster.

"I know you won't understand. Not yet. But someday you will, and until then you must trust me."

Helen was oddly speechless. It was not that she had nothing to say. Nothing to ask. She simply had so many questions that they washed over her like waves, one right after the other. She had no time to formulate one before the next carried it away. She could not make out what her mother was doing, bent forward in the darkness, head tipped to the wall, but she listened as something scratched against the wallpaper. A moment later, her mother straightened, and a door swung outward, revealing a hole in the plaster.

Even in the dark, Helen saw tenderness in her mother's eyes as she reached out, pulling Helen roughly against her body. In her mother's hair, Helen smelled roses from the garden, and on the fine surface of her mother's skin, the books to which her head was always bent. They were a memory all their own.

"Helen . . . Helen," her mother murmured. "You must

remember one thing." She pulled back, looking into Helen's eyes. "You know more than you think. Whatever else you discover, remember that."

Voices erupted from downstairs, and though the words themselves were indistinct, it was obvious they were spoken in anger or fear. Her mother dared a glance at the door before turning back to Helen with renewed fervor.

"Take this." She thrust a piece of crumpled paper into Helen's hand. "Take it and sit very quietly, until you know they're gone. There is a stair that will lead you beneath the house and back up again farther down the road. Join with Darius and Griffin. The address is here. They will take you to Galizur. You have everything you need, but you must be silent as you make your escape. If they hear you, they will find you." She paused, forcing Helen's chin up so that she was looking straight into her eyes. "And this is important, Helen: If they find you, they will kill you."

"I won't *leave* you!" Helen cried.

"Listen to me." Her mother's voice became firmer, almost angry as she grabbed hold of Helen's shoulders. "You *will* do this, Helen. You will get out of here alive, whatever else happens. Otherwise, it's all for nothing. Do you understand?"

Helen shook her head. "No! Mother, please tell me what's happening!" But she already knew her mother would not. Already knew, somehow, that they were out of time.

Her mother lifted the chain from around her neck, placing it around Helen's. A key at the end of it fell to the front of her nightdress.

Holding her daughter's face between her hands, Helen's mother leaned in to kiss her forehead. "Lock the door from the inside. Use the pendant to light your way—but don't make a move until you are certain they won't hear you. And be safe, my love."

Helen was shoved into the hole in the wall, the valise pressed against her until she had no choice but to wrap her arms around it. She ducked, stumbling through the small doorway, trying not to smack her head. Her mother paused one last time, as if reconsidering, and then, without another word, she began to push the door closed. She became a smaller and smaller sliver, disappearing bit by bit until she was gone entirely in the small click of the door.

"Lock it, Helen. Now." Her mother's voice was a hiss from the other side of the wall. Helen fought a surge of panic as she heard the wallpaper smoothed over the keyhole, the mirror dragged over the opening to her hiding place.

It was worse than dark inside the wall. It was as if she had fallen into nothingness. She set the bag down, feeling for its clasp in the darkness. She had no idea what was on the piece of paper her mother had given her, but it was damp with the sweat of her palm. She couldn't read it now if she wanted to, and she pushed it inside the bag.

She reached for the chain around her neck until she found the key at its end. Grasping it in one hand, she fumbled around the edge of the wall in front of her with the other, trying to locate the lock she knew must be there. Her hands shook with rising panic. The door cut into the wall was almost seamless, making it nearly impossible to find in the darkness. She was on her third pass when she finally felt a slim line in the plaster. Running her fingers slowly over it, she felt for the keyhole. It seemed like far too long before she finally came upon it.

She was trying to fit the key in the lock when noise burst from somewhere beyond the chamber. She could not fathom its direction, for she was wrapped in the muffled cocoon of wood and plaster that was her hiding place. Still, she strained to decipher the sound. She thought she heard shouting . . . weeping. And then a crash that caused her to startle. The key dropped from her hand, falling with a clink to the floor. She hesitated only a moment.

Whatever was happening was going to get worse before the night was over.

Feeling along the floor for the key, Helen tried to ignore the noise from the rest of the house. Her hiding place was not large, and it only took a few moments for her fingers to close around the chain attached to the key. She grasped it carefully in one hand and felt again for the keyhole. This time, it didn't take long.

Using both hands, she lined the key up with the hole in a couple of tries, turning it quickly and scooting away from the hidden door until her back stopped against a solid block of wood. She had only a few moments, a few precious moments of silence, before she heard the thud of boot steps.

At first the footfalls were distant. Helen thought they would pass her chamber completely, but it wasn't long before they grew louder and louder and she knew they were inside her room. She had a flash of hope. Hope that it was Father coming to get her. To tell her that whatever danger had been in the house had gone. But she knew it wasn't him when the boot steps slowed. There was no rush to the door of her tiny room to free her from its darkness.

Instead, the footsteps made a slow pass of her chamber before stopping suddenly in front of the hiding place.

Helen tried to slow her shallow breathing as she waited for the footsteps to move away, but they didn't. Whoever had entered her chamber was still there. She held as still as possible, attempting to calm her mind with the knowledge that she had spent many hours in the room, and there had never been any hint of the secret door, even during times of bright sunlight. Surely this stranger would not be able to see the opening in the dark of night and with her great dressing mirror pushed in front of it.

For a few seconds, it worked. She began to breathe a little easier in the silence.

But that was before the room outside exploded into riotous noise. Before she heard the dressing table cleared of its bottles and jars, the glass thudding against the carpets and shattering against the wood floorboards. Before she heard the bureau overturned, the armoire pushed over. And yes, before she heard the heavy carved mirror guarding her hiding place tipped to the floor, the glass shattering into a million pieces.

TWO

In her mind's eye, Helen could see her pursuer survey-ing the newly destroyed room, scanning the floors and walls for the hiding place that was hers. She heard the breathing, raspy but unlabored, even through the wall.

Somehow, she knew it was a man, though she could not have said why. Perhaps it was the heavy boot steps, which had now fallen silent. Or the aggressive energy probing the space between her chamber and the inside of the wall, where she hid, crouched and still.

Whatever it was, she *felt* the man searching on the other side.

She cursed her stupidity for not having located the staircase before he arrived, if only to give her some hope of escape. Now she had no choice but to be quiet. To wait as Mother had instructed her to do.

She remembered the game she played with Father when she was small. It was called Find the Way Out, and on any given outing, be it to the park, a museum, or a restaurant for tea, Helen's father would command her to locate both the nearest and least obvious of exits. She had enjoyed the challenge in the safety of Father's company.

There was no such safety here.

Something scraped the outside of the wall, and Helen's head jerked up in response to the sound. It seemed impossible that the man on the other side of the door could not hear her breathing. That he could not feel her cowering as she felt him seeking.

The sound became fainter, and she imagined him circling her chamber, running his hands over the walls. He was completing his circle, the sound coming back around, when the footfalls of another interrupted his progress.

"Where is she?" The voice was garbled, but Helen could still make out the words. She tried to place their direction, deciding that whoever spoke them was likely standing in the doorway of her bedroom.

She held her breath in the pause that followed, waiting for her pursuer to answer. The seconds stretched, and she could not help wondering if perhaps the man knew exactly where

she was hidden. If he was simply toying with her for his own amusement.

His voice, when it came, was younger and clearer than Helen expected, even muffled as it was from outside her hiding place. "She's not here. They must have moved her before we arrived. What of the others?"

She held her breath, waiting to hear the fate of her parents and their colleagues.

"Taken care of." The breath caught in Helen's throat as she frantically tried to decipher the meaning of so simple a phrase. She did not have long to ponder the matter before the other man asked a question of his own. "What should I do now?"

Helen's whole life was suspended in the pause that followed. It crashed to the floor with the answer.

"Burn it."

The words were almost impossible to comprehend. Surely they did not mean to burn the house in its entirety. Surely she would not be trapped in the wall as the house fell in flames around her.

It was a comforting brand of denial, and she clutched the valise more tightly to her chest as the boot steps on the other side of the wall turned and made their way from the room. The house grew silent, and her brain settled into an oblivious lethargy. She remained very still even after the first tendrils of smoke drifted up through the floorboards and her forehead began to bead with sweat, the temperature slowly rising within the walls.

It was not until something crashed beneath her, followed by the unmistakable crackle of flames from her chamber, that she was shaken from her stupor. Her mother's words drifted on the smoke that seeped with ever-increasing thickness through the floor and walls.

There is a stair that will lead you beneath the house and back up again farther down the road. . . .

She had told Helen to wait until the house was silent, but Helen knew it would never be silent again. Not until it was ashes. She was already fighting the urge to cough and gasp, the smoke filling the small room as her nightdress stuck to her skin in the heat of the fire.

Letting go of the valise with one hand, she reached around her neck for the pendant that had been hers since her tenth birthday. She had a flash of her parents, their smiles tinged with something like awe as she had removed the pendant from its elaborately wrapped gift box. Her mother had knelt beside her, leaning in for a bone-crushing embrace.

It's an important heirloom, Helen. Never remove it. Never.

Her eyes shone in the candlelight from the elaborately set dinner table, and Helen had nodded with a lump in her throat, though she did not know if it was from worry or affection. She had placed the strange object—a rod with a translucent prism glittering at one end and a filigree metal crown at the other—around her neck.

As her mother had instructed, she had not taken it off since.

She reached for it now, unable to contain her retching as a cough burst forth from her throat. She had no idea how the pendant could help her. As far as she knew, it was nothing more than an exotic piece of jewelry. But her mother had told her to light the way with it, and she had nothing else to trust save those instructions.

Grasping the necklace in her free hand, Helen waved it in the dark. There was no light, only a chilling cold that spread from her palm, up her arm, and to the outer reaches of her body, quelling even the heat from the quickly enclosing fire. Still, it was not the heat alone that was her enemy. The smoke stung her eyes and throat, and a series of hacking coughs burst too loudly into the small space around her. It was when she recovered her wits a moment later that she thought she could make out the floorboards beneath her feet and perhaps even the wall in front of her. Squinting into the darkness, she wondered if it was her imagination. If perhaps she was simply becoming used to the dark. But no, the room *was* becoming lighter, and when her eyes followed the light to its source, she understood why.

She had been holding it wrong. The pendant glowed from the translucent crystal held inside her fist. Once she flipped it around, holding it by the metal crown, the other end glowed like a tiny beacon, an eerie green light illuminating the wall in front of her and the ones to her right and left. Now she could see the smoke filling the room. It dipped and swirled in the light. She scooted away from the wall at her back, gagging and choking as the smoke filled her lungs and knowing the space behind her was the only hope for the stairs Mother had promised.

At first, it seemed only a wall—a solid span of timber that had sheltered her back as she listened to the footsteps of the man stalking her from within the bedchamber. But when she followed it with her eyes to the place where it should meet the other wall, she realized it didn't quite connect. Crawling toward the gap while clutching her bag in one hand and her pendant in the other was neither easy nor quiet, but she had long since given up remaining silent, despite her mother's warning. If the creaking and crackling of the fire were any indication, her scuffling across the floor of the hidden room was the very least of her concerns.

It took only seconds to reach the break in the wooden wall. The gap was larger than she first thought, and she leaned forward, peering around to the blackness on the other side.

The stairs were just as Mother said they would be. They descended in a tightly packed spiral into utter darkness below, but the burning in Helen's eyes and lungs was a reminder that she had no choice. Mother had said they would come and they had. She had said the stairs would be here and they were. She had said Helen would escape—and she would.

She hesitated at the top of the stairs as the groaning of the house grew stronger, the smoke thicker. She saw the fear in her mother's eyes in the moment before they had been separated. Helen retched, her lungs burning, even as the resolve to return for her parents solidified.

Leaving her mother and father to this dark fate was impossible.

She started back for the door to her hiding place but stopped short when her mother's voice echoed through her mind.

"You will get out of here alive . . . Otherwise, it's all for nothing."

Something fell with a crash somewhere below, and the floorboards quaked under Helen's feet. She didn't know what was happening or why, but one thing was certain: Her parents wanted her out of the house alive, and they had been willing to sacrifice their own lives to see it done. If she went back now and was killed, her mother would be right: It would have been for nothing.

She would find Darius and Griffin and enlist their help. Then, she would come back for her parents.

Looping the valise's handle over her shoulder, Helen scooted back to the stair, holding the pendant in front of her to illuminate the way. She wasted only seconds fumbling for a handrail before realizing that it was futile. There wasn't one. The stairs were placed right up against the walls of the house. They would have to be her guide.

Wherever they led, it was the only way out, for the crashing of the house grew around her until she was certain the roof itself was falling. The heat and smoke was still overwhelming, and she was surprised every moment when the stairwell did not cave in on her completely.

Time lost all meaning in the blackness floating above, below, and around the staircase. She focused only on the next step, pushing aside the feeling that she was descending into hell itself. To a place where there was no comfort, no safety. A place where she would be alone, if she were to survive at all.

Then, all at once, a smooth expanse of floor stretched in front of her. She stepped onto it, relieved to find a stone wall to one side and a tunnel heading in the other direction. Whoever had made her escape route had made certain there would be no doubt which way she should go.

She had not noticed a decrease in the smoke and heat on her way down the stairs, but as she made her way through the tunnel, her head began to clear. The air was cold and damp. She sucked it greedily into her lungs while trying to blink the soot away from her eyes. For a time, she walked into the dark without a thought as to where she was going, relieved simply to be away from the smoke of the house.

It was only when she fell against the stone wall that she realized her exhaustion. It was a sudden, bone-deep fatigue that settled not only into her body but also into her consciousness. Her very will to go on. The pendant's green light flickered in the darkness, and she stood straighter, worrying suddenly about being stuck in the tunnel with no light. It had never occurred to her that the light of the pendant might be limited, and she pushed off against the wall, continuing down the tunnel with as much speed as she could muster in her weakened state.

She almost ran into the wall before seeing it.

The tunnel ended abruptly, and she felt a surge of claustrophobic panic in the moments before she noticed the rough-hewn door set into the wall. Even with the pendant's diminished light, she could see the simple iron handle, but tugging on it did no good. The door was locked.

Her legs buckled, and she slid to the ground, back against the cold stone of the wall. The light dimmed further and she clasped her hand more tightly around it, willing it to stay lit. As she tugged on the pendant, it was the chain, cool against her neck that reminded her of the key.

Forcing herself to stand, she reached inside her nightdress, pulling out the key her mother had used to open the hiding place in her wall. The key Helen had used to lock the door behind her.

However dim the remaining light of the pendant, it was enough to light the keyhole. She pushed the key into it and turned, feeling a bolt disengage from somewhere inside the door. Letting the key drop back against the bodice of her nightdress, she reached for the handle, then hesitated, wondering what was on the other side.

But she knew that she had no choice. She had to open the door and step through it. The only thing that awaited her at the other end of the tunnel was the surely burned ruins of her childhood home and the men who hunted her. She turned the handle and pushed.

THREE

She was well past surprise when the door swung wide, revealing another staircase. This one wound upward, a faint light coming from somewhere above. She allowed the pendant to fall back against her chest, relieved to have a free hand as she ascended the stairs. She didn't stop climbing until the stairs abruptly ended, opening directly onto a rain-wet street, weak yellow light seeping from a streetlamp near the curb.

Daring a look back, she took note of the wall through which she had emerged. The door was gone, the brick wall at the bottom of the staircase unbroken. She blinked a couple of times to be certain and in the end could only add the disappearing door to the catalog of unexplainable things that had happened this night.

Turning her attention to the street, she glanced left and

right, trying to get her bearings. The long descent from the house and the winding journey through the tunnel had been disorienting, but one look at the elaborately lettered sign quickly clarified the matter.

Claridge Hotel.

The windows and door beneath the sign were familiar and lit from the inside. It gave her an odd sort of comfort. It could not be a coincidence that her escape route led to the hotel where she so often accompanied Father to high tea. It was some kind of message, some kind of sign, and this one led her to thoughts of others.

Leaning against the brick wall of the hotel, she opened the valise. She felt past the clothing and other personal items her mother had packed until her hand closed around the crumpled piece of paper. The ink was already faded, and she slanted the paper toward the light spilling from the hotel windows, trying to make out her mother's script.

It was a name. Two names, to be exact, and an address.

Darius and Griffin Channing. 425 Oxford.

She knew the streets surrounding Claridge's well. She and Father had often strolled the neighborhood after tea. Still, it was a different matter entirely to walk alone and unaccompanied in the dark of night. She hurried through the streets as fast as her bare feet would allow.

The gas lamps lit her way, smoke swirling eerily near the flames as it had before the light of the pendant. She felt a moment's self-consciousness as the cold seeped through the fabric of her nightdress, but her soot and dirt-smudged arms were oddly comforting. With any luck, she would pass for a common street urchin with nothing to steal. Nothing to lose.

Of course, that was now truer than she was prepared to admit.

In any case, the streets were empty, save an occasional drunkard, and she made her way carefully over the wet cobblestones until she came to the right address. Her gaze traveled upward, taking in the imposing structure. It rose into the night sky, carved marble gargoyles and unnameable beasts flashing pale in the dark above her, as light flickered from behind the curtained windows. She stood for a moment, gathering her wits. Who were Darius and Griffin Channing? And why would Mother and Father send her to strangers for shelter? The questions found no answers. She was alone, and if ever anyone had been without answers, it was her. It was not courage but desperation that finally led her up the steps leading to the great front door.

There was simply nowhere else to go.

She had just reached the top of the steps and was lifting her hand to knock when the door opened. A young man about her age stood in the light of the porch lamp, blinking as if he was surprised to find her there, despite the fact that he had opened the door without prompting. Even in the faint light, she could see the flecks of yellow in his green eyes.

"G-good evening. I'm looking for . . ." She made a show of glancing down at the paper, just so he would know someone had sent her. "Darius and Griffin Channing."

Something moved behind his eyes. She thought it was, perhaps, an understanding of the situation in which she found herself. A situation even she didn't fully comprehend.

"You're younger than I imagined," he said.

Helen didn't know how to respond. The very idea that he had imagined her of any age was so beyond her grasp that she didn't even attempt to inquire about the particulars.

"I'm Griffin." He stepped back from the doorway. "You must be cold. Please come in."

She hesitated for a moment. It was more than unseemly to enter a gentleman's home in the dark of night. Even she, with her limited social experience, was aware of such rules.

Yet, Mother and Father had sent her here. And this was no ordinary night.

She stepped into the house. "I don't know who you are or why my parents sent me to you, but I need your help. They're in great danger. We must—"

"You can't go back," the man interrupted. "I'm sorry, but it's impossible."

His eyes were kind, but that did not prevent her frustration from bursting forth. "You don't understand! If you just let me explain—"

He held up a hand to stop her. "I don't know the details, but I imagine your parents' lives were threatened, and they worked quite hard to see that you remained alive. Is that right?"

"Yes, yes. But they . . . that is, we . . ." She stumbled over the words, unable to distill everything that had happened to a few sentences that would make the man listen to her.

She flinched as he reached out, touching a hand gently to her arm. "I know you're upset and frightened, but you must trust me; your parents sacrificed themselves to ensure your escape. If you go back now, their bravery will have been for nothing. Do you understand?"

His words were an echo of her mother's. Helen could only nod around the lump in her throat.

"Good." Griffin shut the door. His tawny hair fell across his forehead as he turned to face her. "May I take your bag?"

His words did not make sense until she followed his eyes to the valise in her arms. It was all she had left.

"No, thank you."

He nodded. "This way. We need to see my brother, Darius."

There was nothing to do but follow. She trailed after him as he made his way down the marble hall to a massive door on the left. He turned to her before entering the room. She breathed a little easier when she saw the compassion in his eyes.

"Listen, I'm sure you'd like to clean up and change, but Darius won't allow you to stay until he has cleared you. All right?"

"Yes . . . No . . . I don't know." The nod of her head turned into a shake.

He smiled. "It will be fine, you'll see."

He turned without waiting for an answer, and she followed him into a darkly paneled library.

At first it seemed they were alone. Helen took advantage of the moment to reach up and smooth her disheveled hair. It was the first time all night that she had thought of her appearance, but it somehow seemed important to impress Darius, whomever he was and however impossible a task it might be, given her dirty nightdress, bare feet, and sooty skin.

"That cannot be her." The voice, deep and low, came from a chair in a shadowed corner.

Griffin stopped in the middle of the plush carpet, very like the ones in her own home. She had an image of the rugs in her chamber burning, the carved bed aflame, the paint melting across the portrait of her mother in the parlor. A spasm of loss and grief almost brought her to her knees.

"It is," Griffin answered. "At least, I believe it is."

"Have you even prepared for the possibility that it's not?" There was steel behind the question, though Helen had no idea what the man meant.

Griffin sighed. "She's just a girl, Darius. And she's cold and tired."

"I should hope she is anything but a simple girl. Otherwise, you have let a stranger into the house at great risk to us both." The shadow that was Darius continued without waiting for an answer. "Never mind. Bring her here."

She saw the apology in Griffin's eyes as he prompted her forward with a nod of his head.

Lifting her chin, Helen moved toward the chair. Dishevelment aside, she did not intend to be bullied.

"I have no idea who or what you think I am, but I can assure that I am, in fact, *just a girl* as your brother claims." She was relieved to hear the anger in her voice. To feel it trickle through her bloodstream in place of the numbness she had felt since escaping her burning home.

The figure in the chair rose to his feet, his face still in shadow. She felt him survey her in the silence that followed. "She's too young."

The simple pronouncement fueled her annoyance. "If you have something to say about me, kindly afford me the respect of saying it *to* me, will you?"

Darius did not answer right away, and Helen wondered if she had gone too far. Anger seemed to flow outward from the shadow where he stood.

"Fair enough," he said, his face directed toward hers. "You're too young."

She shook her head, feeling as if she had landed in some kind of alternate reality. "Too young for what?"

"Too young to be who you're supposed to be and too young to be of any use if you are."

"And who exactly am I supposed to be?"

She saw the tip of his head, even in the shadows, as if he was considering his answer. When he stepped into the light

of the desk lamp, she saw that he was taller than Griffin, with a fine scar running from his right temple nearly to his chin. She thought him striking, and not as old as he sounded when shrouded in darkness. His eyes, identical to Griffin's, flashed yellow-green when he answered.

"One of us."

FOUR

I'm *not* one of you."

She had no idea what Darius was getting at. Still, she was certain that she was not anything approximating *one of them*.

"You're getting too far ahead, Darius. You'll frighten her." Griffin's voice came from her left, irritation evident in the look he shot Darius before turning to her. "Come. Sit down."

Helen allowed Griffin to lead her to the sofa, scolding herself the whole way for cowering in the face of Darius's questionable authority. Father always said that people only had the power you gave them. She had already given Darius too much.

She surveyed him from the sofa as he crossed to a cabinet against one of the walls. He poured clear liquid into a crystal tumbler, and she took in the sandy hair, cut too long for a gentleman. She saw the resemblance between brothers in the eyes and the strong set of their jaws, but in every other way,

Griffin seemed a gentler version of his brother. He sat at the other end of the sofa, tipping his body toward her.

"Why don't you start with your name?"

She was suddenly unsure about divulging her identity, despite the piece of paper that had led her to them. "Why don't you tell me? You already seem to know who I am."

She caught a trace of admiration in Griffin's smile. "It doesn't work that way. They didn't tell us your name. And with good cause. We've been kept separate for a reason, though it doesn't seem to have helped."

She didn't understand the meaning behind his words, but it was obvious that they would all be here for a very long time if someone didn't start talking. Somehow Helen knew it would not be Darius.

She sighed. "My name is Helen Cartwright. My parents are Eleanor and Palmer Cartwright and they were taken or . . . something earlier this evening."

"What do you mean they were taken 'or something'?" Darius narrowed his eyes, as if trying to gauge her truthfulness.

She shrugged. "I don't know. One minute I was in bed and the next my mother was packing up my things and hiding me in the wall. I . . . I think the house was on fire."

"Why would your mother hide you in the wall?" Even as

Griffin asked the question, it seemed he knew the answer.

"They were meeting with their colleagues, a group of business associates that often came to the house for evening meetings." Helen looked down at her hands. "They became noisy or . . . upset, and then my mother told me to hide and not to make a sound or I would be killed. She gave me this." The piece of paper was still crumpled in her hand, and she held it out for Griffin and Darius to see.

"May I?" Griffin asked.

She hesitated before handing it to him. It was the last thing her mother had touched before closing the door between them.

He opened the piece of paper, tipping it to the light of the desk lamp before looking at Darius. "It's our names and address."

Darius's face betrayed no emotion. When he spoke, his words were directed at Griffin. "There's only one way to know for certain who she is."

Griffin nodded, reaching into the neckline of his shirt at the same time Darius reached into his trouser pocket. When their hands emerged, they were each holding pendants.

"Does this look familiar?" Darius asked.

They were not identical to hers. Not exactly. She could see

even from a distance that the scrolled crown at one end of their pendants had a slightly different pattern than the one that hung from the chain around her neck. But there was no mistaking it.

"It's . . . It's almost like mine."

"What do you mean?" Griffin asked, though she heard relief in his voice that told her he already knew the answer.

Helen swallowed hard, hesitating only a second before pulling her own pendant from the neckline of her nightdress. She held it up without removing the chain from her neck.

"Like this. Only it seems yours is different on the end," she said softly.

Darius stood, his eyes locked on the pendant in her hand, as still as one of the statues outside the house. Finally he turned toward the bookcase lining one wall. In his voice was a new resignation.

"Show her to a room. Then, we go and see Galizur."

The house was even bigger than it seemed from the street. She followed Griffin up an elaborately carved staircase and down a series of richly carpeted halls.

Darius did not accompany them. He had not, in fact, even turned around after instructing Griffin to show her to a room.

She had been dismissed, and though she gave a moment's thought to refusing the room on principle, reason quickly settled in.

"Here we are." Griffin stopped at a large wooden door. As he leaned in to open it, his face was contorted in the gleaming brass of the knob.

Following him through the doorway, she was surprised to see a clean nightdress folded on the bed and a tub of steaming water standing in the middle of the room. She had not seen a single servant. Yet it seemed someone besides the brothers knew that she was here.

"Helen?" Griffin's voice shook her from her thoughts.

"Yes?"

He studied his feet before meeting her eyes. "I'm sorry. About your parents, I mean. It is . . ." His voice caught in his throat, and he turned away for a moment before composing himself and looking back. "It's no easy thing to lose your parents in such a manner. It's something Darius and I know a great deal about."

His pain collided with her own until all she heard was the unspoken message in his statement. She swallowed her despair. She was not ready to consider her parents lost. Hope that they were still alive was all she had left.

"Did they . . . did they take your parents, too? Do you know what happened to them?"

She heard the desperation in her voice and felt sorry for her selfishness. She *did* want to know what had happened to Griffin's parents. But more than anything, she hoped that knowing what had happened to Griffin's would tell her what had happened to her own.

His throat rippled as he swallowed. "You should bathe and rest. We'll talk more later."

Her face grew hot with anger. "Why don't you trust me?" She opened her arms. "Look at me. I'm just a girl in a night-dress."

He shook his head sadly. "We'll explain everything in the morning, Helen." Turning to leave, he stopped when he reached the door. He did not look back when he spoke again. "Please make yourself at home. There's a bell by the bed should you need anything."

And then he was gone.

It took her a while to calm down. She was unused to feeling helpless and did not care for the sensation at all. Still, after standing amid the luxurious chamber in her filthy nightdress, she began to realize the futility in simply being angry. There was obviously more at work than she understood, but fuming in filth was not going to get her answers, to say nothing of the exhaustion seeping into her bones.

First, a bath. Then, sleep. Tomorrow, answers.

She was preparing to strip off her nightdress when she caught her reflection in the looking glass over the bureau. Crossing to it, she looked at the girl staring back at her. At the soot-smudged face and dark, tangled hair. She was almost unrecognizable. It was only her eyes, so deeply blue she was often told they were violet, that were familiar.

She stepped away from the glass, not wanting to see the hollowness in them, and began removing her nightdress. She left it on the floor, trying not to remember putting it on earlier in the evening. Trying not to remember her last moments at home.

She was naked and shivering in the center of the room. It was strange to be without clothing in someone else's home, and she crossed quickly to the copper tub, lowering herself into the still-hot water. Using a delicate bar of soap, she washed from head to toe. Once she had rinsed the soap from her skin and hair, she lay back against the tub. She closed her eyes and allowed herself a moment to let go of all that had happened, as the faint scent of roses drifted up from the steam.

When her thoughts came back to her parents, to the men who had burned her home, she simply pushed them away. At the moment, denial was her only friend.

Then, out of the rose-scented steam, she remembered something her mother had said in the frenzied moments before the door had closed on the hiding place in the wall.

Join with Darius and Griffin. They will take you to Galizur.

Helen's eyes opened with the memory, and all at once, she was in denial no more.

FIVE

It took her a few minutes to dress and find the staircase lead-ing to the main floor.

The house was eerily quiet as she made her way through the halls. She was used to the rushed voices of her parents, the ticking of the grandfather clock, the scuffle of the servants above and below stairs. Even in the dark of night, her home had rarely been silent.

Here, there was not a sound until she reached the bottom of the stairwell.

Murmuring drew her down the hall to the library door. The marble was cold underfoot, but she was glad she had left her shoes behind. They would have made too much noise on the hard floor.

The voices grew louder as she came closer to the library. She stopped just before reaching the doorway. The hall, spare and without furnishing or ornament, did not leave many places to hide. Glancing around, she settled for a deep shadow in the corner where the hallway met the entrance to what looked like the kitchen beyond.

Aided by the utter silence of the house, she picked up snippets of conversation from the library.

"She has the pendant. She's one of us, Darius. Why are you denying the obvious?"

She could hear the frustration in Darius's voice, even from afar. *"Because I don't want it to be true. She'll be nothing but a burden. She hasn't even reached Enlightenment."*

"It doesn't matter. We have to protect her."

"We can hardly protect ourselves, Griffin. She would be safer in hiding while we find out who's responsible." There was a shuffle from within the room, and she leaned farther back into the shadows, still listening as Darius continued. *"Let's go see Galizur. He probably already knows, but we should be sure."*

Boot steps sounded across the carpet, and she pressed as far back into the shadows as she could, holding her breath and willing herself to become invisible, yet again.

The brothers crossed the threshold of the room, turning, and passing her without a glance. They did not head toward the front door but to the back of the house. She waited a few seconds before following in their footsteps. She had never followed anyone before, but it seemed only wise to keep as much distance between them as possible.

The click of the door somewhere beyond her line of vision freed her from the shadows, and she hurried through the doorway which did, indeed, lead to a cavernous kitchen. There was only one exit. She made her way to it with as much speed as possible. It would not do to lose the brothers in her worry over being caught following them.

The door opened to the back of the house. She had the sense of a garden or grounds beyond, but it was too dark to make out anything other than the steps leading downward. Taking them as quietly as possible, she continued down a pathway at the side of the house. She could not be certain this was the direction Griffin and Darius had traveled, for they were already out of her line of sight. But the only other possibility was the backyard, and she was quite sure the brothers were not taking tea in the garden.

The path led her to the front of the house. She saw the streetlight under which she had stood some time ago, trying to decide whether or not to ring the bell, and stood back from it, not wanting to be seen. She had a moment's panic as she surveyed the streets, black save the pools of light seeping from the streetlamps. What if she was too late? What if they were already out of sight?

But no. As she looked to the right and spotted the brothers making their way down the smoky walk, relief flooded through her. She followed them down the street, trying to maintain enough distance that they would not see her shadow or hear her footsteps, though this was likely an unnecessary precaution. She noted with satisfaction that her bare feet made nary a sound on the stone.

It was not easy, trying to keep up with the long-legged stride of the two men while trying to mind landmarks so that she would not be lost on her way back to the house. She was skirting a light post when a dark figure appeared out of nowhere, standing in the shine of the lamp.

"Oh, my goodness!" She clamped a hand over her mouth even before the words had escaped entirely.

"You must be joking." Her shock at the sudden appearance of the figure was outdone only by her surprise at the dry—and now slightly familiar—voice that came from its direction.

She leaned toward him, peering through the fog. "Darius?"

He sighed, tipping his head so that she could make out his features. "You shouldn't sound so surprised, given that *you* were following *us*. Unless you're in the habit of following strangers?"

She shook her head. "But you . . . I . . . That is, I was following you."

"I think that has already been established." The voice came from behind her. She knew without turning that it belonged to Griffin.

She blinked a few times, trying to clear the fog that seemed to have drifted from the street to her mind. "I was *following* you. That means you were in front of me."

Darius folded his arms across his chest, his expression growing as dark as the streets around them. "That's generally how following someone works." His gaze drifted to Griffin. "She *is* a clever one, brother."

"No need to be snide," she snapped. "You know what I mean."

She looked up the street where they had been walking only moments before. She *knew* they had been there. She had seen them. And yet now Darius was right beside her as if he had appeared out of thin air.

Griffin sighed. "Listen, we'll explain everything later. You really shouldn't have followed us. It isn't safe."

She placed her hands on her hips. It was the only act of

defiance she could muster, other than her words, which never failed her. "I'm not going back. Whatever you're doing, wherever you're going, it concerns me as well. I'm not a child and I won't be ignored like one."

"Any other time, I might like to argue that point." Darius stepped from the lamplight. "As it happens, we don't have time to debate the issue, and I'm quite sure you don't know how to jump yet. You'll have to come with us now, though you may very well wish you hadn't, when all is said and done."

He walked ahead without another word as Griffin gestured her to follow.

"Come. And stay close. It's a very dangerous time for those of our kind."

She lost track of their progress through the darkened streets. She didn't know why she should trust the Channings after so short a time, but she no longer worried about finding her way back to the house alone. She somehow knew that at the end of the night, she would return with the brothers to their great, silent house.

They passed through the wealthy neighborhoods surrounding Claridge's and into a less desirable part of the city. She wasn't afraid, though Griffin's face remained taut, his hand on a strange-looking object hanging from his belt. She couldn't make out Darius's expression, for he continued his pace well ahead of them. In any case, it didn't matter. She doubted anything could change his angry countenance.

She was beginning to wonder where they were going when Darius stopped walking. She lifted her head, taking in the crumbling warehouse before them, certain that Darius had made a mistake. But when she looked to Griffin, he didn't seem surprised.

"Where are we?" Her voice rang too loud into the darkness.

Darius was already stepping toward the large iron door at the front of the building. He didn't look at her when he spoke.

"Calling on one of the only people in London who can help us."

SIX

Darius stood at the door in silence, as if he expected it to open on its own. Helen resisted the urge to ask him why he didn't knock. Her mere existence seemed to annoy him, and she was too tired and cold to buffer herself against his obvious dislike for her.

A moment later, the door was opened by a pretty, doe-eyed girl, and Helen was relieved that she had not suggested knocking. She already felt dim around Darius, though she had only known him a couple of hours.

The girl standing in the doorway seemed no more surprised to see them than Darius and Griffin were to see her open the door without prompting.

"Come. Father is working," she said. "He has been quite busy of late, as I'm sure you can imagine." She cast a smile

Helen's way. "If you don't mind, we'll make our introductions later, once we're safely inside."

Helen nodded as Darius stepped through the door. Griffin gestured for her to go ahead, waiting for her to pass before entering the house and shutting the door behind them. They followed the girl down a gritty, crumbling hall. There was nary a candle for light, but even in the dark, the girl's hair glimmered gold and copper.

Helen was forced to an abrupt stop as Darius halted suddenly in front of her. Peering around his shoulders, she fought the press of claustrophobia when she saw that they had come to a large metal door. The hall seemed to contract, and she noticed for the first time that, other than the closed door in front of them and the one through which they had entered, there were no windows and not a single additional door. Helen glanced at Griffin. He seemed to sense her fear, and his teeth flashed white in the darkness, casting more strangeness into the already bizarre night.

The clink of metal on metal drew Helen's attention from the hall, and she stood on tiptoe to see around Darius's broad shoulders. The girl had produced a ring of large, strangely scrolled keys from which she plucked one, almost without looking. She fitted it smoothly into a complex opening that looped and curved unlike any keyhole Helen had ever seen. The door swung wide and soundless.

The girl glanced past Helen and Griffin toward the front door, hurrying them forward with a wave of her hand. "One cannot be too careful, especially now."

As Darius stepped past her, he stiffened, careful to avoid touching her. The girl did not seem to notice, smiling warmly as Griffin and Helen followed Darius into a high-ceilinged room stacked with crates. She closed the door, and a bolt somewhere within fell into place on its own volition.

"You haven't asked about the girl." Darius's voice was argumentative and directed at the young woman leading the way in front of him.

She spoke without turning, a smile in her voice. "Darius Channing, after all of this time, don't you think I trust you?"

Darius did not answer for a moment, but when he did, his tone had softened. "Even still," he grumbled. "You might be more careful. You're in danger, too, as I'm sure you're aware."

The girl stopped walking then, turning to look at him as she placed a small hand on his arm. When she spoke there was tenderness in her voice. "I'm well aware of the situation, but I have a responsibility to keep you and your kind safe and well. It's my purpose—one you and I have discussed at length. Let's not discuss it again when there's so much to do."

There were volumes unspoken in her words, and Helen wished suddenly for more space so that she might give them privacy. Clearly, theirs was an old argument.

Darius's shoulders relaxed the slightest bit, and there was regret in the small nod of his head. Helen caught a glimpse of the girl's forgiving smile as she turned back to lead the way.

They wound through several rooms, each as nondescript as the last. There was not a single candle. Helen was led only by the white of Darius's shirt in front of her and the occasional sound of the girl's voice. It was a comfort to have Griffin at her back, though she did not know him at all. He was a calm sea in the presence of his brother's tornado. One might rock you to sleep while the other would turn on you with a moment's notice.

She was nearly dizzy with disorientation when the girl stopped before another door. After producing a key like the others from the folds of her gown, she bent to the large iron door. It opened as suddenly and quietly as the one in the entrance.

This time, Helen did not need to be prompted. Stepping

through the frame, she was relieved to see light flickering from sconces set against the walls. Tables were scattered across the well-appointed room and yet more light spilled from several lamps sitting atop them.

The girl closed the door behind her, fitting one of the keys into another strangely shaped lock. Gears rumbled to life within the walls, followed by a series of creaks that ended with a solid bang she could only assume indicated a large and complex locking mechanism slamming into place.

The girl was just straightening when a high-pitched whine sounded from an adjacent room. She looked toward it with surprise. "I've forgotten the water! Wait just a moment, and we'll take tea with Father in his office."

She hurried toward the sound of the whistling kettle, disappearing through a doorway without another word. Darius seemed to relax, and Helen wondered why he seemed so ill at ease in the other girl's presence.

But Helen did not spend long contemplating Darius's mood. It was the first moment she'd had alone with the brothers since arriving at the strange residence. She wanted to make the most of it.

She turned to Griffin. "Where are we?"

"We're at the lab—"

"Griffin!" Darius interrupted his brother, forcing his name through clenched teeth.

Griffin's voice exploded into the room. "She's already shown us her pendant! What more do you need?"

Stubbornness radiated from Darius as he folded his arms across his chest. "Her story will be confirmed. *Then* we'll tell her."

"Fine!" Griffin threw up his hands in resignation. Helen knew the battle was lost when he avoided her eyes.

She had nothing to gain by letting her frustration loose on Griffin and Darius. It seemed answers would be forthcoming with the mysterious Galizur. She calmed her own rising temper by surveying the room.

If the meandering way into the building resembled an abandoned factory, the room in which she now found herself was a comfortable, aged parlor. Two sofas sat near a crackling firebox and several high-backed wing chairs were positioned near reading tables throughout the room. The wooden floor, though worn to a soft sheen, was glimpsed in between rugs not unlike those at home—or in the home that used to be hers.

She shook her head against the thought as the girl returned bearing a teapot and several cups on a silver tray.

"Shall we?" A smile touched the corners of her mouth as if it weren't strange that they hadn't been introduced yet. As if it weren't strange that they were standing inside a locked and barricaded fortress in the dark of night.

Darius moved to a door beyond her, opening it so that the girl could pass through with the tray. Helen felt her eyebrows lift at the show of chivalry, though she was quite certain no one noticed.

The girl smiled into Darius's eyes, and something moved between them.

Helen stifled her surprise.

She didn't know why it should seem strange that Darius fancied someone, but even as little as she knew him, it already seemed improbable, though not as improbable as someone fancying him in return.

Griffin nodded toward the door, and Helen followed the girl into a short hallway that opened suddenly into a large, dimly lit room. It was almost identical to the parlor from which they had just come except for the enormous carved desk dominating the room. The girl made her way toward it, setting the tray on its gleaming top and turning to call into the room.

"Father? Our guests have arrived."

Helen did not have time to register the expectation in the girl's words before a voice came from a set of stairs that descended to the left.

"Yes, I expect they have, Anna."

A silver-haired man appeared at the top of the stairs, wiping a pair of spectacles on a cloth held in his hands. He peered at them, squinting though he was only a few feet away.

"This is her, then? This is the girl?" His voice was gentle, and Helen somehow didn't mind his inquiring after her, though they had not been officially introduced.

Griffin nodded. "She's shown us the pendant."

She braced for another round of doubt from Darius, but he did not say a word while the man walked toward her, stopping when he was but two feet away. He studied her face with sadness in his eyes.

"Helen. Daughter of Palmer and Eleanor Cartwright."

The sounds of her parents' names spoken into the unfamiliar room took her by surprise. "I . . . Yes. But how did you know?"

Something fell from his eyes. She could not help but think it might be hope itself, though it made no sense at all in the present moment.

"Come, let us sit and have tea while I explain. I imagine

you've had quite a long night." He took her arm, leading her to one of the sofas near the blazing fire.

His gentleness nearly undid her. Perhaps it was simply because he reminded her of her father. Or perhaps it was because she knew what he would say. In any case, she sat on the sofa that was, upon closer inspection, quite tattered and worn. Though the Cartwrights' furniture had always been meticulously maintained, this place still somehow felt like home.

The girl named Anna poured tea as Griffin made himself comfortable on the sofa and Darius lowered himself into one of the chairs. It was obvious from the easy manner of the brothers that they had been here many times in the past.

Helen liked Anna's father even more when he brought over the delicate teacups, brimming with freshly brewed tea, holding his daughter's while she became situated on a chair near Darius. It was unusual to find a gentleman willing to wait on anyone. Helen had only ever seen her father do such a thing. It made her miss him with a vengeance.

"We have been forced to take great precautions, as you will soon understand, Helen." The older man spoke suddenly and without preempt. "They are necessary, yet I doubt they have allowed time for proper introduction. I am Galizur and this is my daughter, Anna. May I ask how you found your way to Darius and Griffin?"

"My mother. She gave me a slip of paper with their names and address just before she . . . before she hid me in the wall of my chamber."

Galizur nodded as if it was the most natural thing in the world to be hidden within a chamber wall.

"Was this when they came for them? For your parents and the others?" he asked.

She was stunned into momentary silence, unable to fathom how Galizur, a man she had never met, knew about the event she was still trying to process.

She swallowed around the sudden dryness in her throat as a sense of foreboding crept like too much sun across her skin. "How did you know?"

SEVEN

Galizur crossed the room to the enormous desk, stepping behind it to one of the bookcases that ran from the floor all the way up to the towering ceiling. Reaching toward the polished mahogany shelves, he pulled a burgundy-bound volume from its place. Helen thought he might give it to her. That it might hold some secret that would tell her what had happened to her mother and father. But he simply placed the book aside, reaching into the pocket of his trousers.

He removed a rings of keys, identical to the one Anna had used to open the doors leading to the hidden home of her and her father. The recess left by the book was shadowed, but Helen presumed it must harbor a keyhole, for Galizur plucked another looped and whorled key from the ring and lifted it toward the darkness shielded from view by the books still on the shelf. A moment later, the floor shook slightly, the fringe on the shades of the table lamps swinging to and fro as the bookcase shuddered.

Torn between fascination and a rising panic, she watched as the bookcase moved back, sliding behind the one next to it until she could make out a panel of brass tags set into the wall. She felt herself falling further into the abyss of utter strangeness.

Galizur peered at the wall of brass tabs, his eyes moving from one to the next until they came to rest near the top of the second row. Reaching out, he pulled one of the tabs and a long wooden box emerged from the wall.

He presented it to Helen with reverence. His dark eyes spoke of things she did not want to know.

She took the box.

"It's yours." Galizur's eyes met hers. "You may open it whenever you wish."

He held her gaze until she lowered hers to the box resting atop the skirt of her gown. The wood was not finished like that of the bookcase. It was rough and fresh-scented, as if it had been chopped and fashioned only hours before.

Lifting her hands to the top, she attempted without success

to separate the flat lid from the base. Her fingers told her there was no seam, no place where the top joined the bottom. When she held the box level with her eyes, she knew why.

Using her thumbs, she pushed back on the top. It slid away from the base, revealing its contents a little at a time until the lid broke free and she could see everything nestled inside.

The first thing she saw was the currency. There was a lot of it, and it took her a moment to notice the smaller objects lying amid the paper bills. There was a cameo necklace that had been her grandmother's in one corner of the box and an envelope in another. She knew as soon as she saw the narrow lettering spelling her name—*Helen*—that it was written in her father's hand. Something about it, about the slant of her name written by her father against some future circumstance, forced her to confront the truth.

She raised her eyes to Galizur's face. "My parents are dead, aren't they?"

"I'm afraid so," he said, gravely.

She dropped her gaze back to the box. She didn't understand how Galizur would have come into possession of the things inside—things obviously meant for her.

"Where did it all come from?" she asked him.

"From your parents, child. They knew what was coming.

We all did. They wanted to see that you were provided for, as all of the Keepers' parents did. I'm only sorry that so many of the boxes have been unclaimed."

She shook her head. "I don't understand."

"You'll have to show her the Orb." Griffin's voice was soft. She looked up, blinking at him in surprise. She had forgotten he was there at all. "Otherwise, she won't believe any of it."

"Yes, you're quite right." Galizur nodded her way. "Come along, then." He started for the stairs, stopping to look back when she didn't follow.

She looked down at the box in her hand, hesitant to let it go. She didn't know everything it held. Not yet. But she knew it was prepared by her parents. She knew it was all she had left of them.

Galizur's eyes softened. "It's as safe here as anything can be in these troubling times. You'll be back for it before the night is through."

She looked at Griffin, though she could not have said why his was the reassurance she sought.

He stood and crossed the room to stand beside her. "The box will be fine here until we come back up."

She rose to her feet, only vaguely registering his use of the word "up" as she turned to place the box on the chair before

plucking the letter from inside it. If she could leave the strange house with only one thing this night it would be her father's letter.

Galizur continued across the room, leading them to the stairway from which he had emerged when they first entered the room. Anna and Darius followed him down the stairs. Helen clung to the iron banister at the top.

"It's all right." Griffin's voice came from her right, and she flinched at the feel of his hand on hers. "Trust me."

His voice was gentle, and when she looked into his eyes, instinctively, she did trust him.

She braced herself against the fear that rose inside her as she stepped, once again, toward the unknown. At first, she could only hear the footsteps of the others in front of them, but as the dark closed in around her, she believed she could smell smoke all over again. Fighting the urge to cough with the memory, she kept her hand on the smooth railing, letting it lead her downward. It was only the sound of Griffin's boot steps at her back that kept her from returning to the top of the stairs.

She noticed the light before she reached the bottom of the staircase. Faintly blue, it reached to her from below. It was not bright, but soft and insistent, even when she finally stepped off the last stair to the cool stone floor. She wondered if they were near a window or door, for she was certain she could hear the wind rushing somewhere through the tunnel, empty save for her and Griffin.

"This way." Griffin's hand was light on her arm as he led her down a tunnel not unlike the one she had used to escape her burning home. But this passage, at least, was not dark. Torchlight flickered against the damp stone walls, casting shadows that licked toward the ceiling. She did not mind the stone against her bare feet. The ground here was as spotless as the rooms above.

Helen was surprised when a curve in the tunnel opened onto a large room where Galizur, Darius, and Anna waited. The ceiling now rose far above them, the space expansive in every direction. Hulking machinery lurked in the corners and against the walls, a low humming resonating from its steely forms.

But none of this, as strange as it was, is what commanded her attention.

It was the globe, enormous and rising all the way to the ceiling, that stopped her in her tracks. A perfect, massive replica of the Earth, the orb glowed from within, turning slowly in place on an invisible axle. The wind was not so much a wind as a breeze, and it was not rushing through the tunnel because of a draft. It moved softly *around* the globe through the sheer force of its size and movement. Helen's hair lifted in the current caused by its turning. She took a step back almost without realizing it.

"I . . . It . . . What *is* this?" She did not even have the presence of mind to worry about sounding like an idiot in front of Darius.

Griffin led her gently by the arm. "Galizur will explain."

She stumbled forward, even as she wanted to shrink in fear. In the end, her hesitation had no hope against the part of her that was drawn to the object as clearly as if it were calling her name.

It was beautiful, the azure oceans seeping into the green and gold landmasses that morphed slowly into ridged mountains. As the globe turned, the water seemed to undulate, the sand of the Sahara sifting from one side to the other. She caught the scent of salt water, wet earth, wind, and rain.

"It's the Terrenious Orb." Galizur's voice broke through the trance brought on by the object in front of her. "It's a measure of our world and how secure we are in it." He gestured at it with one hand. "And as you can see, things aren't going very well at the moment."

EIGHT

Galizur paced the floor in front of the globe before stopping, his gray eyes piercing hers.

"Let us begin with a story of sorts, shall we?"

Helen nodded. "If that will help me understand all this."

She didn't believe anything would help her understand everything that had happened in the last few hours, but clearly Galizur had information. And information was her only hope of making sense of it all.

"A long time ago, a group of lesser angels were—"

"Lesser angels?" Helen interrupted.

"They were not archangels," Griffin explained, "though they were of the same blood."

"Quite right." Galizur nodded, continuing. "In the beginning, three of these lesser angels were appointed to watch over the Earth. To keep it working, so to speak. Of course, the world quickly became too complicated for only three of them to manage, so that number grew, until finally, there were twenty, as there are today. Now known as Keepers, they're chosen before birth by a counsel of spiritual leaders known as the Dictata. The identity of each Keeper is kept secret—even from themselves—until they reach Enlightenment."

"Enlightenment?" Helen couldn't help repeating the word. It carried almost mystical connotations.

"At seventeen, the point at which the Keepers learn about their position," Galizur said. "After which they don't age, though they can still be killed by certain rather extraordinary means."

"What kind of extraordinary means?"

He waved the question away. "Let's not worry about that for now. Suffice it to say that on the rare occasion such a thing comes to pass, another Keeper—always a descendant of the original lesser angels—is appointed in their place. For eons, it has only been mildly worrisome. A new appointment is not often required, and there are always nineteen other Keepers to keep the world turning until the new one comes of age."

Griffin spoke softly from Helen's left. "But that was before."

Helen looked from him back to Galizur. "Before what?"

A sigh escaped Galizur's lips. "Before someone began murdering them."

Helen thought of her parents. Of the intruder who had killed them but had obviously been looking for her.

As if reading her mind, Galizur's eyes found hers. "You are one of the last Keepers, my dear, as are Darius and Griffin. The only three to have survived a string of mass executions that have taken place over the last few months."

The words hung in the room, winding their way around her like the smoke that had threatened to choke her in the hidden room of her burned home. She wanted someone to say something. To laugh aloud or even accuse her of being too young, as Darius had done.

But no one said a word. She allowed the silence to sit among them until she couldn't stand it any longer.

She stood up, pacing away from them. "That is . . . well, it's nonsense, that's all."

She expected Galizur to answer. To soothe her worries, as he had done since she arrived. But he didn't. Even Griffin remained silent. It was Darius who dared to speak the truth she couldn't deny.

"So you're just a normal girl, then?" He continued without

waiting for her answer. "It's normal for someone to come into your home in the dark of night, kill your parents, burn down your house? It's normal for you to make an escape and to follow directions on a piece of paper to find refuge?"

She relished the coldness in his voice. Only reason could help her now.

"And I suppose if you look back on your childhood everything else will seem normal as well. You had a childhood like any other? There were no strange games? No specialized lessons? Nothing to make you think you might have to escape one day or perhaps even fight to protect yourself?" His eyes dropped to the pendant visible atop her gown. When he spoke again, his voice was a notch softer— perhaps even kinder—than it had been before. "No inexplicable gifts?"

She swallowed against the lump that formed in her throat, thinking of her parents. Of fencing and chess. Of Find the Way Out and tea at Claridge's followed by strolls through the very same neighborhood she had traversed in her nightdress to find Darius and Griffin.

None of it—*none of it*—was an accident.

Darius's eyes burned into hers in the moment before she dropped her gaze.

"I thought so." His voice was missing the satisfaction she expected.

This time, she didn't let the silence settle for long before lifting her head to look at Galizur. She was grateful that her voice sounded stronger than she felt. "I'm listening."

He nodded.

"Over the past months, the Keepers, along with their families, have been executed, one by one. It was alarming enough in the beginning, for with the loss of each Keeper, Earth's future grew more and more uncertain. At first, the Dictata appointed replacements right away, but they, too, were killed, almost as quickly as they could be appointed. Now, new appointments have been suspended until the executioner can be found." Galizur gestured toward the Orb. "And as you can see, the demise of the Keepers has had a profound effect."

Helen's gaze slid to the massive, rotating globe. She was captivated by its beauty, yet its movement suddenly seemed laborious, even to her. She felt it struggling to stay alive. To keep turning.

"Assuming I believe you, what can we do?"

Darius's voice came from her right. "For now, stay alive."

"How do we do that? If what you say is true, I haven't even come fully into my . . . knowledge."

Helen was surprised to hear Anna's voice, soft but strong. "We'll help, Father and I. It's our task to oversee the Keepers. To ensure their safety and continuity. It has become harder, of course, but it's still our charge. One we'll die fulfilling, if necessary."

Darius flinched at her words but said nothing.

"There is one more thing," Griffin said.

"What is it?" Helen could not imagine anything stranger than what she had already heard.

"Those who hunt us are hunting something else as well."

"What?"

"Perhaps it will be easier to show you." Helen followed Galizur to the Orb. Stopping in front of it, he gestured to the floor beneath the Orb. "This is the gateway to the Akashic Records. And there is only one key."

Helen looked down, her eyes settling on a tiny pinprick of blue light emanating from the ground. She didn't know how she had missed it before. The light seemed to pulse with an energy that made the floor buzz beneath her feet.

"The Akashic Records are an accounting of everything that ever has happened or ever will happen in the history and future of mankind," Griffin explained, his voice ringing through into the cavernous room.

"I know what the Akashic Records are," Helen said softly. "But I thought they were a myth. A legend."

Galizur nodded. "It's standard protocol for things of this nature to be presented in such a way to the young Keepers."

She lowered her eyes to the blue light in the floor. "If they're as real as you say, how can they be accessed from here? And what does this have to do with the murders?"

Galizur tipped his head toward the light. "This is simply the gateway. The gateway to everything."

Anna approached, her eyes kind. "It's dangerous for mortals to have access to the records, Helen, which is why no one knows where the key is hidden."

"But that's not keeping someone from trying to find it," Darius added. His voice still held a trace of boredom, but she could hear the tension in it, as if it took effort to seem so apathetic.

Helen steadied her voice. "How do you know?"

Darius studied his fingernails, and she had the strangest sense that it took effort to compose himself in the moment before he met her eyes.

"Because they're killing us to find it."

The words echoed through the room, bouncing off the concrete walls of the underground bunker.

"Well, don't look at me," Helen finally said, glancing at the point of light glowing at the base of the Orb. "I don't have it."

"You don't know that," Darius said. "None of us knows, which is the point of the whole thing."

The blank look on Helen's face must have said everything, because Darius continued. "The Dictata always keeps the Keeper of the key a secret. It's safer that way."

Helen tried to make sense of all the disparate information that had been thrown at her. "So we have to find the key to keep it safe from whoever is killing us?"

"No." Griffin shook his head. "There will always be those who want the key. It doesn't matter who has it. In fact, it's better not to know."

"Then what are we supposed to do?"

"Eliminating the immediate threat is the most important thing," Griffin said.

And now Helen understood. "Find them before they find us."

"Want to jump?" Griffin asked his brother as they emerged from Galizur's some time later.

Darius shook his head. "Not with the girl. Not yet. Besides, the lamps will be turned off soon. We should be safe enough."

Griffin nodded. The exchange didn't make sense to Helen,

but she was too tired and overwhelmed to ask about it. She focused instead on keeping pace as they continued away from Galizur's building.

Dawn was beginning to lighten the sky in the distance, though overhead it was still a deep and mysterious blue. Helen was grateful the brothers didn't try to speak to her on the way back to the house. She couldn't have borne more conversation about angels, demons, and executions.

They moved swiftly through the streets of London, though Helen's exhaustion made it feel as if she were moving her body against a very strong current. She had to trot to keep up, all the while clutching the long wooden box Galizur had given her. But while Griffin sometimes looked at her with sympathy, Darius didn't spare so much as a glance. Still, she refused to give Darius the chance to feel smug by asking him to slow his pace.

Helen's instincts screamed as they skirted the streets with lamps in favor of those as black as pitch. Finally, in one particularly dark alley, she managed to gasp a question in spite of their pace.

"Why do we keep to the darkest streets? If we are in danger, wouldn't it be wiser to stay in the light?"

Darius, a few feet in front of them, snorted at her com-

ment. She ignored him, waiting for Griffin to answer instead.

He kept his eyes on the street in front of them, his eyes scanning the streets as he answered. "It's not safe to walk in the light right now."

She shook her head. "Isn't it safer than the dark where someone might sneak up on us?"

"No, it isn't," he said. "Light is another means of travel for us. And we're not the only ones who use it."

She didn't know what to make of the answer, but then she thought of Darius, appearing in the light of the lamp on the way to Galizur's. She scoffed inwardly at the idea taking shape in her mind. That Darius might have moved from one light to another wasn't possible. She wanted to tell Griffin so, to dismiss it as nonsense, but it was all she could do to keep up. She added it to the growing list of questions to ask later.

They came to the end of the alley. Darius stood, surveying the street in front of them. While it was far from brightly lit, the streetlamps cast their murky light across the road, making it seem infinitely brighter than the backstreet from which they'd just come.

Griffin stopped beside his brother. "I'll keep her with me."

Helen looked from Griffin to Darius and back again. "What do you mean? Where are we going?"

"Across the street," Darius said. "Now be a good girl and stay with Griffin, will you?"

She was so shocked by his patronizing tone that she didn't answer right away. By the time she'd gathered her fury, Griffin had a firm but gentle hold on her arm and Darius had already stepped into the street.

"Don't mind him." Griffin followed his brother with Helen in tow. "You'll get used to it."

"I highly doubt that," she said. "And for the record, I have crossed a street before. All by myself, too."

Griffin looked around, and she had the distinct impression that she was trying even his patience. "I'll explain everything later. For now, you're just going to have to trust me. The safety you once took for granted is gone. If you want to stay alive, you'll stay with us and do as we say."

The lack of mockery in his voice sobered her like none of Darius's snide commentary. This was someone who wanted to see her safe, and it seemed there were very few of those people left. She would have to trust him.

They crossed the road at an even quicker pace than the

one they had used in the alley. The brothers' eyes moved constantly, roaming the streets for danger as they headed toward the darkness on the other side of the street.

Stepping onto the cobblestone walk, Darius ducked into the shadows along the edge of a crumbling building as Griffin ushered Helen in the same direction.

They were only feet from the darkness when she heard the sound.

It reminded her of the time a bat had found its way into her room through the firebox. The poor creature had flown around her chamber, desperately seeking escape while she opened window after window, trying to coax it out-of-doors. She was not frightened, but later, she would remember the deep, slightly ominous sound of its wings beating the air.

It was this that made her stop, looking above her for the spread of something dark and in flight.

But Griffin was not looking upward. His gaze was pulled to the streetlamp closest to them.

A moment later, she understood why.

There was a man standing within the circle of its illumination. She did not immediately register that he seemed to appear out of nowhere. That she had not heard boot steps and

that neither Griffin nor Darius seemed to have suspected they were being followed.

She did, however, register the bloodred of his eyes, piercing the smoky light of the streetlamps.

The man stepped out of the light, his dark clothes making his pale face seem like an apparition floating above his body. A low growl sounded from his throat in the moment before he smiled, flashing teeth capped almost entirely in silver.

"I told you the light was dangerous." It was all Griffin had time to say in the moment before he shoved her back into the shadows. "Now, don't move until we say so."

NINE

She pressed her body against the crumbling building just as Darius stepped forward. An irrational satisfaction blanketed her fear. This stranger obviously intended her, and the brothers, harm. But there were two brothers and only one snarling . . . whatever it was.

Then she saw the other man stepping from the pool of light cast by another streetlight.

"I'm tired, brother, let's make this quick." Darius almost sounded bored, something that made Helen doubt her earlier faith in the brothers' ability to fend off the strange men now advancing. Perhaps Darius and Griffin were mad rather than competent.

"Fine with me," Griffin said. "I'll take this one. Did you bring your glaive?"

"No. You?"

Griffin shook his head with a sigh. "The sickle it is, then."

The silver-toothed fiend snarled as Griffin took a step forward. He pulled loose the strangely shaped object hanging from his belt. It opened with a clanging hum, and Helen saw that it *was* a kind of sickle, small enough to hold in the hand and shaped like a boomerang. But this was no boomerang. Forming a kind of open V, the light reflected off the honed blade on one side and caught the tips of metal teeth jutting from the other. It would rip a man apart.

"Keeper scum." The insult was hurled from the second man as he pulled a sickle from his belt.

His companion advanced on Griffin, his own weapon in hand. The two pairs circled each other as Darius replied, as casually as if they were having tea and talking about the weather.

"That's offensive coming from a wraith. I think I'm going to have to defend my honor."

There was a breathless pause before Darius raised his sickle against that of his opponent. The clang that followed was ear-splitting, and Helen, cowering in the shadows, looked around, expecting someone to emerge from one of the dingy flats and rail about the noise.

But no one came. As she watched the brothers, raising their

sickles, hooking those of the other men and making it difficult to free them and continue the battle, she had the feeling that their very existence was a dream. That she and the brothers and the two beings that fought them existed in another world—one that was separated by the finest of veils from the one in which she had lived all her life. That the sound of the battle in front of her was muffled and shielded from the sleeping world around her.

She clutched the long wooden box tighter as Griffin's sickle locked with that of the being that fought him. The other man growled, pulling on Griffin's sickle until Griffin was far too close to the man's body. Helen cringed, trying to watch the battle while she also planned her escape, should the brothers not make it out alive.

Find the Way Out was a game that died hard.

A moment later, Griffin seemed to loose his grip on the sickle. It brought him still closer to the other man, and for a split second, Helen thought Griffin was giving up. She realized his strategy when the fiend's grip loosened with their sudden proximity. Griffin, taking advantage of the momentary slack, drew his sickle down and away from the other man's in one effortless swing. Then, he brought it up in a graceful arc, slicing the razor edge of it across the fiend's belly.

She stifled a gasp, expecting the man to cry out. Or at least to bleed. But he did neither. He simply continued fighting even as Griffin, now with the upper hand, pummeled him with repeated kicks and slices of his sickle until the man's flesh was torn in places.

And still, Helen didn't see a drop of blood.

When she was finally able to tear her eyes away to Darius, she found much the same sight. Darius's opponent was on the ground, Darius bringing the sickle down again and again, slicing with one edge, ripping and tearing with the other. Yet even as the man on the ground seemed to give up, he, too, did not bleed.

Finally, Griffin's opponent toppled over, crashing to the ground like the man now under Darius's boot.

Darius spoke calmly. "I thought we were going to make it quick."

"You've had more experience than I have," Griffin said, his voice wounded.

Helen wanted to look away as they brought down their sickles. Now there would be blood, and they would have to leave these souls, however evil, in the middle of the walk to be pulled apart by the starving dogs that roamed the slums.

Yet, as the brothers brought down their weapons, she could

not look away. She watched in rapt attention as their blades swung through the smoky light, wincing as the blades crossed the necks of the men lying on the ground. She mentally prepared herself for the severing of their heads, but a moment later, their bodies disappeared in a rush of wind and a flash of hot blue light.

Helen stood motionless and stunned in the silence that followed. The world seemed to come back, little by little, until she could feel the wind lift her hair, smell the oil in the lamps lighting the street.

Griffin walked over to her, closing his sickle with a quiet clang, and hanging it back on his belt.

He wiped his brow. "Are you all right?"

She nodded, clutching the wooden box like a lifeline.

He reached for her arm. She was surprised to find his grip gentle.

"Come on," he said. "You've had a long night."

Darius did not speak on the way home. He walked in front of her and Griffin as he had before, only this time, she did not question their choice of the smallest, darkest streets.

When at last they walked through the back door of the house, Darius headed straight for the stairs.

"Get as much sleep as you can, Helen." He did not turn to her as he spoke. "Tomorrow we'll have to make decisions regarding your safety."

By the time she and Griffin reached the grand staircase, Darius had already disappeared into the halls above it.

"You shouldn't have followed us." Griffin's voice was soft as they climbed the stairs.

Had Darius made the same observation, she would have fired off a smart retort before she could stop herself. But there was no accusation or annoyance in Griffin's voice.

"I'm sorry, but I remembered something my mother said. Something about you and Darius taking me to Galizur. And then I remembered you and Darius saying you were going to see him." They reached the top of the stairs and headed toward the first hall. "I didn't want to wait here alone."

"Helen."

She did not realize Griffin had stopped walking until she followed his voice, finding it two feet behind her. She stepped back to where he stood.

"Yes?"

His eyes glistened in the dark. "I don't want to discourage your strong will—"

"But?" She could not help interrupting him, already sensing his desire to keep her in check.

"There's still a lot you don't understand. A lot that can bring you harm. If you want to survive, you must listen to us until you're capable of defending yourself."

She wanted to deny the kindness in his voice. But she could not. Instead of the heated reply for which she searched, she found, to her horror, the sting of tears. She looked away, not wanting him to see their shine in the light of the candles along the wall.

"Yes, well, perhaps I'm not concerned about remaining alive at the moment."

She expected him to protest, but he simply nodded in the periphery of her vision.

"What about retribution?" he asked. "Is that something that concerns you?"

She turned back to him, meeting his eyes. "That's of more interest to me, yes."

"Then you might like to consider staying alive to exact it."

He started walking once again, leaving her no choice but to follow. The halls were long and winding. She paid attention to the turns as they went—left, left, right—wanting a surer method of finding her way around than the instinct she'd used to find the staircase earlier that night. Finally, Griffin stopped at a door that looked like all the others.

"I'm two doors down on the right if you need anything, or you can ring the bell by your bed."

She nodded, stepping into the room. "Thank you."

He had already turned to leave when she found the courage to voice the question that had been nagging since the two men had appeared in the alley.

"What were those . . . things? On the street?"

Griffin turned, hesitating. She could feel him trying to find the right words. "They were wraiths."

"Wraiths?"

He nodded. "Lesser demons."

"*Lesser* demons?" She felt like an idiot repeating everything, but her brain was working as fast as it could, trying to process everything he was saying. "Is there such a thing?"

"Yes," Griffin said. "The Dictata heads up our side, the Alliance of Lesser Angels, and there is caste system within the ranks of the Legion, too."

"What is the Legion?"

He considered his words. "The Alliance is made up of the descendants of the original Lesser Angels, right?"

She nodded.

"Well, the Legion is made up of the *fallen* angels."

"Otherwise known as demons," she murmured, finally understanding.

"Exactly," he said. "There's a treaty that keeps order with the more powerful demons, but wraiths are just a nuisance. They don't have the intellectual capacity for real strategy, which is why Darius and I were able to defeat them so easily."

"It didn't look easy," she said.

His smile was small. "It comes with practice, and we have been taking care of ourselves for some time now."

She felt a pang of sadness—for him, and for herself, too—for all they had lost.

"Were they the ones responsible for . . ." She could hardly manage the words, though there had been no opportunity for grief since Galizur confirmed her parents' death. She forced herself to say aloud the thing that was true, whether or not she voiced it. "Did they kill my parents?"

Griffin shook his head, a lock of hair falling into his eyes. "They weren't knowledgeable enough for such a task. Whoever killed your parents—and ours—was much, much more dangerous."

He was already out the door when the next question came to mind.

"Griffin?"

He turned to meet her eyes. "Yes?"

"Why kill our families if it's us they want? If we're the ones who have the key?"

He shrugged. "Isn't it obvious?" She couldn't tell if it was sadness or anger that lit his eyes. "They have us right where they want us. On the run and unprotected."

TEN

Once alone in the bedchamber, Helen stripped off her clothes, leaving her chemise on as a nightdress. Her eyes, still gritty with smoke and soot, burned with exhaustion.

But she couldn't sleep.

Not yet.

She propped herself against the large wooden frame of the bed, the box from Galizur in her lap. Fingering its rough-hewn edges, she tried convincing herself that it would be better, wiser, to wait until tomorrow to look more closely at its contents. To read the letter that had been left for her by father.

It was a useless argument. Dawn was already lightening the world beyond the curtained windows, and there were some things that simply could not wait.

She pushed back the lid, watching the contents of the box become visible as the flat-paneled top slid to reveal them.

She first removed her grandmother's cameo. It twirled at the end of the chain, and she held it up for inspection, wondering if the key Galizur spoke of could be hidden inside the locket. She opened and closed it, turning it over in her hand and looking at it every which way. But no. It was simply a family heirloom, and she set it carefully on the bed.

She did not count the money or inspect it as she lifted it from the box, though in the back of her mind, she was grateful. Having money meant she wouldn't have to rely on Griffin and Darius forever. But right now, while she was still trying to grasp the losses of the past hours, the currency was a vulgar reminder.

Peering into the box, it seemed there was only the letter, but when she lifted the thick envelope from the box, she saw that there was something underneath it. She set the letter down, reaching back into the box. When she withdrew her hand, it held a photograph. She recognized it immediately. It had been taken on holiday at the country house. Father had surprised them with the photographer's visit, and she and mother had dressed in their summer best to sit with him on the lawn, as the photographer had disappeared beneath a curtain of velvet attached to his machine. The photograph had sat in the parlor ever since. Helen had not been aware that a duplicate had been made, but now, staring at her father's vivid smile, the light in her mother's eyes, visible even in the black-and-white tones of the photograph, Helen was glad for it. She set it next to the cameo and lifted the letter from the bed.

She could see a scrolled, silver opener on the writing table under the window but had no desire to leave the comfort of the mattress. Even now, her limbs were growing heavy. She slipped a finger under the flap of the envelope, hesitating for just a moment before breaking the familiar wax seal.

The letter was not long. Only one page. One page of Father's slim, slanted handwriting. But she bent her head to it. Then, she read.

My Dearest Helen,

By now you will have seen Galizur. If you are reading this, he has given you the box, and with it, all we dared set aside. I can hardly imagine how lost you must feel in a strange place with so few of your belongings, but given the small amount of space available, we thought currency the most useful inheritance. We always knew that if you had to flee, it would be with little time to gather your things.

Galizur and the remaining Keepers will have told you

much of what you need to know. I'm sure it has come as a surprise, but if you look to the past, you will find that you are more prepared for the challenges that lay ahead than you may believe. It is against the Dictata's edict to tell a Keeper of their place in the world order until the age of Enlightenment, but we all—every one of us—saw this coming. It is because of this that I increased the frequency and intensity of your lessons in recent months. You will need all of your resources to fight what is coming. Search your mind for every game, every lesson. The answers you need are there.

I will ask you for one final thing. It will be the hardest of all to ask.

You must not mourn your mother and me. We have lived long and full. It has been our honor and privilege to call you our daughter. More than that, it has been our joy to watch you grow into the strong young woman you are today and to love you as we do.

Time—and all the events held therein—plays out as it must. We cannot impose our will on it. The only true measure of strength is our ability to bear that which time demands. And you are nothing if not strong.

You must not look back. You must look only forward.
Look forward and make the world—and its Keepers—safe
once more.

The mantle passes to you. I know you will carry it
with grace and honor.
With love,
Father

Helen held the thick parchment between her fingers. For the moment, her father was there, sitting next to her, telling her in a firm voice that everything would be all right.

But soon his voice faded. Helen's eyelids grew heavy, and she put the cameo and the letter back in the box with the currency. She kept out only the photograph, holding it to her chest as she allowed her head to sink into the pillows. She willed herself to weep, for isn't that what any normal person would do? Wouldn't a normal girl weep for the loss of her parents? Her home? Everything she had ever known?

In the end, it didn't matter. It was now obvious that she was far from normal. The absent tears seemed only to prove the point. She clutched the photograph as she fell into sleep.

ELEVEN

Helen woke the next day, her mind and purpose clear. After putting the photograph on the bedside table, she took some of the currency from the box and replaced its lid. She slid it under the bed. It was a paltry hiding spot, but there was nothing to be done about it.

It was the only positive side effect of losing everything that mattered: There was nothing meaningful left to take. It made her feel reckless. But even as she reveled in its freedom, a voice warned at the back of her mind.

There is always something left to lose.

By the time she was dressed and ready to leave her room, it was after noon. She gave a moment's thought to postponing the day's mission until the next morning. It would be easier to sneak out of the house before the sun fully rose. But she quickly discounted the idea. Every second counted, and she would not be able to prepare herself for what was to come until her plans for the day were brought to fruition.

She opened the door carefully, glancing down the hallway before slipping from her room. Backtracking to the staircase was not difficult.

Left, right, right.

And then she was at the top of it.

It was not easy to remain unseen, standing at the top of the stairs as she was forced to do. If someone had been in the entry, she would have been caught. But the marble-floored foyer was empty, as quiet as a tomb. She ran lightly down the stairs, grateful for the well-maintained treads that didn't squeak.

She had her hand on the knob when she heard the clearing of a throat behind her.

"Going somewhere?"

Letting out a sigh, she turned to find Griffin leaning against the banister. He surveyed her with tired amusement.

She stood a little straighter. "As a matter of fact, I have an errand to run."

"An errand?"

"Yes. A *personal* errand."

He stood up, ambling toward her. "There's no such thing as a personal errand. Not anymore. Not for you."

Shock washed through her body and over her face. "Just because we're both in this . . . this unusual situation doesn't give you the right to act as my father."

He tipped his head, a weary smile playing at his lips. "I'm not trying to strong-arm you, Helen. Truly."

She nodded at the apology in his voice.

He continued. "It's for your own safety. You saw the wraiths in the street last night. They are the least of the threats against us."

She couldn't fight his reasoning, but it didn't change the necessity of her plans. "I do have an errand."

"And I'd be happy to accompany you."

There was something willful in his voice that she had not heard before. Something that made her wonder if Griffin was really as amenable as he seemed.

She smiled. "You don't know what it is yet. When you find out, you might change your mind."

"Care to fill me in on our destination?" Griffin asked.

Helen knew where they were going, and she led him around well-heeled women out for tea and young ladies out for a stroll with their chaperones.

"Well, if you must know, I need clothing."

He grasped her arm, pulling her to a stop. "We're going shopping?"

"Not exactly," she said. "We're going to the dressmaker. And if you're embarrassed to attend to such an errand, feel free to return to the house."

"I'm not embarrassed." He rubbed a hand across his chin, his forehead furrowed in thought. "But it isn't wise for you to frequent the shops you're accustomed to visiting."

"Why not?"

He took her arm, pulling her to the side of the crowd pushing past them on the street. "Because if whoever killed your parents plans to do a good job looking for you—and they do—they'll be watching the places you might go."

She couldn't help the disbelieving smile that rose to her lips. "You're telling me they know enough about me to know where I have my dresses made?"

"They know far more than that, Helen. We're only just beginning to put together the pieces, but whoever murdered your parents—and ours—is just a killer for hire. Someone very powerful is behind these murders. And they know more about you than you can imagine."

She shook her head. "What am I supposed to do, then? I

must have clothing, and it must be made quickly and to my specifications."

"And so it shall."

He placed her hand on his arm, turning in the direction from which they came. They passed the house and continued in the other direction.

"Griffin?" she asked as they walked.

"Mmmm?"

"Why do you and Darius remain in your family home? Doesn't staying there make it easier for the killer to find you?" The question had nagged at her since Galizur told her about the killings.

He answered without looking at her. "That's exactly the point."

"What do you mean?"

He looked toward the street before turning to look down at her. "Our parents were not killed at home as yours were. They were murdered on the streets. Like animals."

She looked down at her feet, pained by the suffering she heard in his voice. "How did you know it was related to the . . . executions?"

"The bastard left something. He always leaves something."

His words were cloaked in bitterness. "Darius and I have been waiting ever since. So that we might exact justice."

"I'm so sorry, Griffin." He flinched as she touched his arm.

They walked in silence a moment as Helen steeled herself to ask the next question.

"Who do you think is behind the killings?" It was difficult to say aloud. Her parents were dead.

She knew it was true, but saying it somehow made it harder to bear.

"I don't know," Griffin answered. They had reached a rougher part of town, and Griffin guided her around two laborers engaged in an altercation that involved pushing and foul language. "Galizur is still putting the pieces together. We'll see him again tonight after our people return from inspecting the remnants of the fire."

"The fire?" she murmured. "The one that burned down my home?"

He nodded. "So far, the killer has left something at every site. A clue, we think, though we're still trying to figure out what it means."

"What kind of clue?"

He hesitated before answering. "It will be too difficult to explain. I'll show you later this evening."

They crossed the street, minding the carriages rattling past, and Helen tried to imagine a killer heartless and morbid enough to leave a clue at the scene of his crimes. Finally, Griffin came to a stop in front of an aging storefront.

"Here we are."

She looked dubiously at the sign, so faded she could not even make out its lettering.

He laughed aloud. She turned to the sound of it, realizing that he had a wonderful laugh. Heartfelt but slightly self-conscious.

"I know it doesn't look like much," he said. "But like Galizur, Andrew works on behalf of the Dictata. He doesn't advertise his services. A place like this is less likely to draw the casual customer. Trust me, Andrew can make anything you need."

She hesitated at the mention of the man's name. She had only ever had female seamstresses. It would be strange to have a man pinning and measuring her. After a moment, though, she realized that a gentleman would serve her purposes quite nicely.

She nodded, reaching for the door. "All right, then."

He stayed her hand, stepping forward. "He doesn't know you. He won't answer unless he sees me."

Griffin stepped close to the glass door, covered in drap-

95

ery from the other side, and knocked. A sliver of the curtain was pulled back a moment later. Helen caught a glimpse of an eye in the seconds before she heard the locks disengaging. The door was pulled open in one fluid motion.

"Master Channing! What a pleasant surprise! Do come in." The man, small and lithe, stepped back, allowing them entry. "And is this . . . ?" He gestured toward her nervously.

"It is, indeed." Griffin waited for the man to lock the door, pulling the curtain back over the glass, before continuing. "Helen Cartwright, Andrew Lancaster. Andrew, Helen."

The man held out a hand. She reached out to grasp it, taken aback when he stooped to brush his lips across the top of her hand.

"I am sorry to hear of your parents. They were wonderful people."

She could not hide her surprise. "You knew them?"

"Distantly. They had a reputation for being kind and just."

Helen nodded, noting the warmth in the faded blue of his eyes. "How did you hear about their . . . about the fire? It only just happened last night."

"Word travels fast in our circle, Miss Cartwright. And, lately, we have become accustomed to bad news."

The silence, full of dark matter, sat between them.

Finally, Griffin broke the quiet. "Helen needs some things made quickly, Andrew. Can you help?"

He rubbed his hands together, already heading toward the back of the shop. "Of course, of course. Come. I'll get Lawrence."

Helen looked questioningly at Griffin, but he only held out a hand, indicating she should follow Mr. Lancaster. He was already well ahead of them, almost invisible in the dim recesses of the shop. Helen hurried forward, following the sound of his voice as it rang through the dimly lit rooms.

"We have company, Lawrence. Bring the tape and scissors, will you?"

The store was cluttered with rolls of fabric and pieces of parchment depicting various costumes. They lay atop tables and were pinned to the walls in odd places. When they reached the back of the store, Mr. Lancaster pulled out a chair from underneath a table, indicating that she should sit. When she did, he handed her a piece of parchment and a quill.

"Write down everything you need. Be specific now, or you never know what you'll end up with." His eyes twinkled with mischief.

Looking down at the paper, she began pondering how to word her request. Griffin, standing near her shoulder, cast a

shadow across the parchment, and she looked up, suddenly shy about her needs. Raising her eyebrows, she met his gaze.

"What?" He looked around like the answer to her gesture was in the cluttered room. "You want me to leave?"

"You don't have to *leave*. You could simply . . . move to the front of the store or farther to the back."

He sighed, running a hand through his tousled hair. "Very well."

He walked toward the front of the shop as Helen turned back to the table, bending her head to the parchment as she wrote. She had already given consideration the things she would need. With Griffin gone, she wrote in a flurry, citing the things that needed replacing and the special instructions for her new attire.

Finally, her hand cramping from all the writing, she slid the list to Mr. Lancaster.

He surveyed it with concentration before raising his eyes to hers. "My dear girl, are you quite sure?"

She nodded. "I know it seems strange, but it's necessary to be able to defend myself. And if there's one thing my father taught me, it's to depend only on myself, wherever possible."

Mr. Lancaster's eyes softened. "Your father sounds very wise." He leaned in, speaking in a low voice. "Though, if I may say, the Channing brothers are a safe place to put your money when the chips are down. If anyone can protect you, it will be them."

She smiled. "Thank you. But I'd just as soon be able to protect myself."

He nodded, seeming to find deeper meaning to her words. "Of course."

She stood. "May I ask how soon you'll be able to deliver the items?"

Mr. Lancaster looked around, the oil lamp on the table causing his bald head to shine. "Lawrence!" He lowered his voice to a mutter. "Where in God's name is he?"

A tall, stout man appeared a moment later as if conjured by Mr. Lancaster's voice.

"I was looking for the good scissors and the tape you left by the machine upstairs," he grumbled.

Mr. Lancaster looked at him. "Are the reinforcements available tonight?"

"I believe we can count on them."

Mr. Lancaster nodded with satisfaction, looking back to Helen. "We will make delivery tomorrow afternoon. I assume you're staying at the Channing house?"

"Yes, but, are you certain? How will you get it all done?"

Mother's seamstresses had taken at least a week for the first fitting of a dress.

Mr. Lancaster tipped his head. "Miss Cartwright, Lawrence and I have a number of . . . ah . . . resources we call on in times like these. Desperate times, aren't they?"

She nodded slowly. "I suppose they are."

He met her gaze. "You will have your things tomorrow."

She smiled. "Thank you."

He stood. "And now, we need to get you behind the screen and take some measurements."

He led her to the back of the shop and a large fabric-covered dressing screen. With both Lawrence and Mr. Lancaster measuring her every which way, there was no room for inhibitions. By the time she left the store an hour later, she felt as if she'd known both men forever. It was only as she and Griffin approached the door on their way out, Mr. Lancaster and Lawrence already beginning work in the back of the shop, that she realized they had not given her a bill. She had a feeling it was no accident. She slipped a thick stack of currency under a vase by the door, closing it behind her with a quiet click.

TWELVE

The sun was setting against an ominous gray sky as they made their way back to the house. They hurried through London in companionable silence, and Helen marveled that she could be so at ease with someone she hadn't known even the day before.

Darius was waiting in the library, sitting behind the desk and toying with something in his palm. The scar on his cheek made him appear menacing in the shadows of the coming night.

"Well, well," he said. "The prodigal brother returns."

Griffin seemed to stiffen as he walked farther into the room, sitting in a chair opposite his brother. Helen felt sparks trip through her veins until she could no longer hold her tongue.

"Yes, and he has a companion with him! Unless . . ." She looked around in mock confusion. "Unless she is invisible."

Darius leveled his gaze at her. "I don't find sarcasm amusing."

She took the seat next to Griffin. "You find directing it at others amusing."

He surveyed her coolly. She wondered how someone she hardly knew could bring out the very worst in her each and every time she was confronted with his presence.

A moment later, he slid something across the surface of the desk. Griffin picked it up.

"Another one," he said quietly.

"Another what?" Helen leaned forward to get a better look.

"Another key." He handed the object to her.

She looked at the object in her hand, something teasing the winds of her memory as she ran her fingers along the its edges.

"What is it?" Griffin asked her.

"I don't know." She turned the key over in her palm. "I feel as if I've seen this before."

"You have," Darius said. "It's similar to the ones that keep Galizur's compound secure. With one difference."

She looked up at him. "What difference?"

"It's blank. It hasn't been cut to fit anything."

"What do you mean?"

Griffin spoke from beside her. "It works like any traditional key, though it's more elaborate and difficult to copy. It has to be cut to match its lock before it can open anything. All of the ones we've found after the killings haven't been cut."

"You've found others?" she asked.

"One at each of the execution sites," Darius said.

Now she understood.

"This one was found at the house. My house." She was surprised to hear her voice emerge calm and steady.

"That's right," Darius confirmed.

"So they're really dead." She looked up at Griffin. She knew the answer, but she couldn't bear its confirmation to be delivered with Darius's characteristic lack of emotion. "My parents are really dead."

Griffin nodded. "I'm sorry, Helen."

She looked away, trying to bring forth the sorrow lurking like a prowler in the heaviness of her heart, but there were no tears. She had known all along, though she had nurtured a secret hope that her parents had somehow managed to escape the fire.

"What of their . . . remains?" She tried not to choke on the question.

"They're in care of the Dictata until you can see to the arrangements." Darius's voice was surprisingly kind. "There's no rush."

Helen nodded, taking a deep breath and forcing her mind from the past. She could only look forward now, if she wanted to find her parents' killer. She returned her attention to the strange key.

"What does it mean?" she asked. "Why would someone leave something like this after murdering each of the Keepers?"

Darius stood, pacing to the window. It took him a moment to begin speaking. "Three years ago, one of the most powerful of all the Alliance families, the Baranovas, was caught selling classified information to the Syndicate."

"The Syndicate?"

Helen had a flash of memory. She and Father were taking breakfast at the long mahogany dining table, the newspaper folded next to his plate as he explained the state of corporate affairs in England and the world. She saw the way his face tightened when he mentioned the Syndicate, his eyes growing dark, as he explained their role in the worldwide marketplace.

"It's never wise to have too much power in the hands of too few people, Helen."

"But the Syndicate is an industrial organization, isn't it?" she had asked. "A group of business leaders?"

"Four of them, to be precise," her father had said, "representing the most powerful companies in transportation, com-

munication, government, and finance. Four areas that give them complete and total control over the entire world of commerce."

She pushed the memory aside, as Griffin's voice brought her back to the present.

"Why would the Syndicate want information about the Alliance?"

Griffin answered. "We think they were trying to find out which Keeper held the key to the records. Andrei Baranova was in possession of a skill that gave him access to just such information."

"What kind of skill?" Helen asked.

"He was a key maker for the Dictata." Griffin plucked the key from Helen's palm, holding it up to the light. "This is one of his keys."

"Freshly cut and from the same machine as all the others," Darius added.

Helen shook her head. "How can you be sure?"

"There are only two machines in existence that can make such a key," he said. "One of them is with the Dictata, who now have the keys made outside the mortal world to insure such betrayal doesn't happen again."

"And the other one?" Helen asked.

"We assume it's still in the abandoned factory once run by the Baranovas," Griffin answered. "After their betrayal, everything was re-keyed by the Dictata using new machines. The old ones were never reclaimed. No one in the mortal world would have known what they were, and since they weren't used anyway . . ." He shrugged. "They were left to rust."

"What happened to them?" Helen asked. "To the Baranovas?"

"They committed suicide shortly after being banished from the Alliance." Darius's tone made it clear he harbored no sympathy for the traitors.

"Then who is murdering the Keepers and leaving the keys?"

Griffin looked at his brother as if for approval. Darius gave a small nod, and Griffin turned his eyes back to Helen.

"We can't be sure. But we might know where to start looking."

After much debate, the brothers finally allowed Helen to accompany them. Though "allowed" hardly seemed accurate since Helen had crossed her arms over her chest and flatly refused to remain at the house. Still, it was only after she threatened to follow them, with or without their approval, that they gave in.

They descended the front steps together. Helen stopped at the bottom, waiting for the brothers to provide directions, but neither of them moved.

"Aren't we going?" she asked them.

"We're going," Darius said with a smirk.

She made an effort to control her anger. She had a sneaking feeling his humor was at her expense. "Well, don't we need to walk, then?"

"Not necessarily." Darius crossed the sidewalk, holding the long, slender object he and Griffin called the glaive. "There are other ways to traverse the city. And you will be doing so with Griffin."

"Are we splitting up?"

"In a manner of speaking." Darius's voice was wry.

She looked at Griffin. "Would you care to fill me in?"

Griffin opened his mouth to explain just as Darius stepped into the light leaking from one of the streetlamps.

He grinned. "Have fun, brother."

And then he was gone.

"Darius? I . . . Where . . ." She looked back to Griffin. "Is he traveling the way the wraiths did last night?"

Griffin nodded, sheathing his own glaive in a loop at his belt. She still didn't understand how the object, nothing more

than a very long cane, could be a weapon, but there hadn't been time to ask.

Griffin stepped into the empty pool of light, holding out his hand. "You can travel with me. It will be safer than walking."

She looked at the proffered hand, her stomach knotting with anxiety. "Is this what you meant last night? About traveling with the light?"

His expression softened. "I know it seems strange, but scientifically, it makes perfect sense. And I don't want to risk leading you through the streets of London. Not after last night."

His words confirmed what she had already suspected: Her mother's fevered packing had been the beginning of the end. Every moment since had taken her further from the reality she had always known. And led her to the brothers and their strange isolation in the great house. To Galizur and the underground bunker holding the Orb that seemed to whisper her name. To a place where demons stepped from light on the street and one where she would consider stepping into that same light, knowing it would carry her through time and space.

Nothing would ever be the same again. Expecting it to be was the worst kind of denial.

She stepped toward Griffin, taking his hand. It was warm and dry. "If it's so dangerous, why did we walk back from Galizur's last night?"

"Traveling this way is dangerous, too. It's impossible to know what might be waiting on the other side. It's a risk, but one we have to take, given the appearance of the wraiths last night."

"Lovely," she said, gritting her teeth.

She felt the chuckle rumble through his chest as he wrapped his arms around her waist. He was surprisingly strong and smelled of mint and fresh linen.

"Don't worry. This is the safest means of travel for us at the moment. And the light, our bodies . . ." Something tingled in her stomach at his mention of the word, although there was no earthly reason for it. She sucked in her breath as he pulled her against his muscular chest. "It's all energy. We simply merge one with the other in order to harness that energy for travel."

"So anyone could do it, if they knew how?" she asked.

"Not exactly. The pendants allow us to tap into the ability, among others."

"It sounds confusing. And frightening," she added, trying not to think about his proximity.

"Trust me, Helen." His voice was a caress near her ear. It

took effort to hold her body still as a shiver rushed up her spine. "I know what I'm doing. Darius is excellent at jumping, and I learned from him."

She tried to slow her breathing. "Jumping?"

"Light jumping," he said. "That's what we call it, anyway." He pulled her more tightly against him. "Hold onto me. And don't worry; I've got you."

She reached down, grasping the arms that held her waist. "Will it hurt?"

He hesitated, as if surprised by the question. When he answered, there was tenderness in his voice. "I wouldn't let anything hurt you."

She thought he might need to say something to conjure the power to jump. That it might require some kind of magic. But a moment later, everything disappeared in a blinding flash. For a split second, she felt herself dissolving, breaking into a million tiny pieces of light. And then, all at once, she felt herself coming together again. Dark spots danced in front of her eyes as the flash faded. When her vision cleared, she was still wrapped in Griffin's arms, but now, they were standing under a streetlamp in the midst of what looked like a questionable neighborhood.

"It's about time." Darius stood, leaning against the stoop of a crumbling building.

"Give it a rest." Griffin stepped away from her. "I thought it might be a good idea to explain before I made her disappear into thin air."

"Well, I suppose chivalry is alive and well, then, isn't it?" Darius started across the street.

Griffin looked down into Helen's face. "Everything okay?"

She nodded. "I feel like I was taken apart and put back together slightly askew, but other than that, I think I'm fine."

He smiled. "You'll get used to it. And eventually we'll teach you how to do it yourself, so you won't have to depend on us to get you from place to place safely."

Helen wasn't certain she wanted to disappear into the light all alone, hoping she would show up at the right place a moment later. But she didn't get the chance to say it aloud. A second later, Griffin surprised her by taking her hand and leading her across the street after Darius.

THIRTEEN

They made for a massive building of deteriorating brick. Two nights ago, Helen would never have imagined that she would be an orphan, living in the home of two brothers she hardly knew, crossing a deserted street in the middle of the night, and feeling more secure in shadows than she did in the light.

Things had become very strange, indeed.

Griffin leaned down and whispered, "Stay close to me."

Helen nodded.

His eyes met hers. "I mean it, Helen."

"I know!" she whispered emphatically, wondering if he thought her a complete idiot.

She looked up, noting the darkness as they reached the other side of the street. There were four darkened streetlamps in front of the building. Their glass covers were broken.

Helen thought it no accident they weren't in working order.

The street may be in decline, but the lamps on the other side were working well enough.

She touched Griffin's arm to get his attention. He stopped, and she pointed upward, indicating the lamps. He followed her gaze before looking back at her, surprise in his eyes.

They were still standing there when Darius glanced at them, raising his eyebrows in question. Griffin pointed at the lamps, repeating the exercise with his brother until Darius nodded in understanding.

They continued forward. Helen didn't have to ask why they were moving to the side of the building rather than entering through the front. They could hardly announce their arrival by ringing the bell, especially if someone in residence was hoping to go unseen, as the broken streetlamps suggested.

They were just rounding the corner to an alley at the side of the building when she felt cool flesh brush her hands. She nearly screamed before she realized it was Griffin, trying to keep her close to him. She grabbed his hand gratefully, not caring that it would be considered unseemly in any other situation.

This was, after all, no ordinary situation.

They continued down the alley with Darius in the lead.

Helen's skirts swished against her legs until she was sure rats, and not the bedraggled fabric of her hemline, were bumping up against her. She heartily wished for her new attire, which was probably under construction this very moment inside Andrew Lancaster's little shop.

Finally, they stopped moving. Helen strained to peer over Griffin's shoulders, but it was no use. She couldn't see a thing. He must have sensed her frustration because, a moment later, he stepped back against the building, moving Helen to a position between his brother and him.

They stood before a large window. It began a few feet off the ground and reached all the way up the building, far above their heads. Even in the dark, Helen could see that many of the panes were broken.

"There are crates stacked in front of the window." Darius's voice was a whisper, his eyes shining black in the near darkness of the alley. "We can use them to get in."

Griffin nodded at his brother. "I'll go first. You help Helen up, and I'll get her on the other side."

"I'm right here," Helen whispered angrily. "And I'm sure I can manage getting through a window."

Even as she said it, she was grateful for their presence. The truth was, she might *not* make it through the window without assistance. Climbing and hoisting her body, encased in cumbersome skirts, over the threshold of the window wouldn't be easy, even with help. Without it, she'd likely be stranded in the alley with the rats.

Still, there was no reason to tell the brothers such a thing.

"Let us help you, Helen." Griffin humored her. "It will be easier and quicker."

He reached up without another word, grabbing onto the ledge with both hands and lifting himself up, as if it took no effort at all. His legs disappeared through the opening in seconds.

"Okay." Darius stepped closer, bending over and lacing his fingers together. "I'm going to lift, and you're going to grab onto that ledge and pull yourself over. Got it?"

She nodded, adrenaline coursing through her veins as she approached him. Wiping her sweaty hands on her skirt, she put her boot in the cup made by his hands.

"Wait," she said. "Where do I put my hands?"

"Haven't you ever snuck over a fence before?" He continued without waiting for her reply. "Put them on my shoulders until you get high enough to grab the ledge. Then, just let go and pull."

"Right," she muttered. "Let go and pull."

She placed her hands on his shoulders, but before she had time to properly prepare, she was lifted into the air, her leg wobbly in the uneven harness of his hand. She only had time to register the proximity of his face to her stomach in passing, for she was soon at eye level with the window ledge. She didn't want to let go of Darius's shoulders. They were so solid, so sure. And the ledge was at least two feet away. Two feet of empty space to cross before she reached the bottom of the window opening.

"Grab it!" Darius grunted under her.

Forcing herself to let go of him, she lunged for the ledge, grabbing tightly to the brick as Darius shoved her, none too gently, into the opening. For a split second, she thought she might tumble headfirst to the floor below, but she paused, her body teetering, as she gathered her balance. Then, she pushed up with her arms. It was harder than Griffin made it look, but she managed to pull her legs up until she was in a seated position, her legs dangling over the ledge and into the building.

Griffin's voice came softly from below. "Drop down. I'll catch you."

She peered into the darkness, trying to gauge the distance to the floor and Griffin's position beneath her. "Where are you?"

"Don't worry. I can see you. Just let go. I'll catch you."

He made it sound so easy. As if launching oneself into the dark with the hopes that someone might catch you was perfectly normal. But the truth was, she didn't have a choice. Darius was directing her from one side. Griffin, from the other. There was no place to go but down.

"Okay," she said. "I'm letting go."

In the end, it was just that simple. She let go of the ledge, her stomach dropping away in the moment before Griffin's arms closed around her waist.

"There." His voice was a whisper against the skin of her chest. "That wasn't so bad was it?"

Her body slid against his as he set her down. She knew from the heat on her cheeks that she was blushing, though she hoped Griffin wouldn't be able to see it in the darkness.

Darius spoke softly from above them. "Move aside."

Griffin pulled her against a stack of crates as Darius landed with a neat thump only a couple of feet away. The ease with which he made the jump made her feel foolish.

He took the lead, looking back at them only once. "We stay together unless otherwise agreed upon."

They nodded, following him into the shadows of the decaying building.

The machines were hulking beasts in the darkness. Some of them were covered in ghostly cloth, once white but now a dingy brown. Others were laid bare, their gears glinting like teeth in the little light that made its way through the windows. Knobs and controls littered the surfaces of the metal contraptions, small screens dark and empty of display.

Helen walked between the brothers, Darius in front, Griffin at her back. She felt safe between them. It surprised her, but she pushed the realization aside for later inspection as they made their way around the machines, treading carefully lest they should announce their presence. Finally, a dim yellow glow began to light their way, and they edged along a row of crates, staying out of the light.

When they came close enough to realize its source, Helen was surprised to see an old metal worktable, illuminated with a green-glassed lamp much like the ones that had lit her father's library. Parchment was scattered across the surface of the table. She could make out the faint outline of brushstrokes and realized the paper contained sketches, though the images on their creamy surface were impossible to decipher from where she stood.

A tinny clatter arose from above their heads, and they stepped farther back into the shadows. They followed the sound with their eyes, breathing a collective sigh of relief when a black cat slinked across the banister.

Helen didn't know how she'd missed the loft constructed high above the worktable, but she saw it now. Even from where they stood, she could see the upper level held at least one more room, separated from the rest of the building with frosted-glass windows.

Darius reached past her, touching his brother on the shoulder as he pointed to a ladder on their right. Griffin nodded in understanding before leaning very close to Helen, his breath in her ear.

"Stay here, Helen. In the darkness. We will—"

She began to protest, but he held a finger to her lips. The gesture shocked her, though she knew he was only trying to keep her quiet.

"We'll make too much noise, if we all go up the ladder. And it will take us too long to get down if we need to make a quick escape. If you stay here, in the shadows, you'll be safe until we come down." He looked into her eyes, his fingers still against her lips. "All right?"

She did not relish the thought of remaining alone on the ground floor of the old building, but she recognized the wisdom in his argument. She nodded.

Lowering his hand, he turned to Darius. The brothers moved forward without another word, keeping to places where the machines or the building itself cast shadows black enough to hide them, at least some of the time, even from her.

She watched the outline of their figures ascend the ladder. The moment they disappeared into the mysterious recesses above, Helen turned her attention to the worktable.

Adjusting her position, she tried to see the pieces of paper strewn across the desk. The lines and curves of the drawings made her intensely curious about their subject. She was trying to talk herself out of moving in for a closer look, even before she was aware that she was considering it.

No, she told herself, *you cannot go look. It's dangerous. And there is light there which makes it more so. Besides,* the little voice in her mind said, *Darius and Griffin will be back soon, and they won't be happy that you discounted their instructions.*

Except they didn't come back. Not right away. Helen waited, peering after them into the darkness beyond her head. They'd probably found something important, she rationalized, her impatience growing with each passing minute.

Finally, after looking around one last time, she cut the thread of indecision and stepped cautiously out of the shadows.

Nothing happened. No one descended. No one came after her.

She stepped forward slowly at first, gathering courage as she went until she closed in three long strides the remaining feet between her and the table. It took only moments to know they were in the right pace. The sketches were keys. Looping, whirling, scrolled keys very like the ones on Galizur and Anna's key ring. At first they all looked alike, but when she looked more closely, she could see the slight differences among them. Admiration swelled inside of her, despite their connection to the mystery at hand. How difficult it must be to craft something so fine. To design it and cut it just so and then do the same with a lock into which the key would fit perfectly.

She reached for one of the papers closest to her, wanting to inspect it more closely.

"Don't touch that." The man's voice, low and threatening, came from behind her.

She froze, her arm in midair, panic slamming into her all at once. She didn't know this voice, but she knew that it wasn't Griffin's and it wasn't Darius's.

"This is an unexpected bonus," the voice said. "That all three of you would appear at my door."

"We aren't here to make things easier for you." Helen spoke to the wall in front of the desk. She didn't know why she felt compelled to answer, but she used the time to let her eyes

rove around the worktable, seeking something with which to defend herself.

It was a futile hope. This was a surface used for drawing and planning, not the crafting of tools or keys. The desk held nothing but parchment, quills, and several ink pots.

"Turn around," the man commanded.

Helen swallowed, trying to compose her face into an expression that didn't betray the terror washing over her. She thought of Darius and Griffin, still upstairs, and hoped they might come down in time to help her. She didn't know if they had the power to overcome the one who had murdered their families, but at least there would be three of them. She turned slowly, not wanting to startle the man or cause him to act rashly in any way.

She expected to see his face, but when her back was at last against the worktable, she was staring only into darkness.

He spoke from the shadows in front of her. "I don't usually do the killing myself, on principle."

She heard the voice commanding another in her childhood chamber: *Burn it.*

She wondered if it was her imagination that the man suddenly sounded younger. That there was a hint of regret in his voice.

"You could let us go," she said softly. "No one would ever know."

"No." She could almost see him shaking his head in the slight movement from the shadows. "Though it's not that I *want* to destroy you. That's something you must understand."

And she could hear in his voice that he did want her to understand.

"Then what? Why?" She heard the plaintiveness in her own voice. The question. She was no longer simply stalling. This was the man who had ordered the murder of her parents. Whether or not he had done the killing himself hardly mattered.

She heard his hesitation in the pause that followed. As if he was searching for the right words to explain himself. "There's something I want. Something I need. I can only get it by ensuring that you're all destroyed."

"So you're killing us—having our families murdered—because of something you *want?*"

"It's not like that. You don't understand." There was frustration in his voice. "It's something I *must* have. It will make everything like it was. Besides, I already told you; I don't do the killing myself. That was part of our agreement."

"What agreement?"

"It doesn't matter." The man's voice deepened, anger sharpening its edges as he stepped toward her. Toward the light that would illuminate his face. "I don't have to explain myself to you. You've done me a service by coming here, and I will do you one by destroying you and your friends quickly."

She shook her head as he came into view, taller than she expected and as broad-shouldered as Darius. Hand already on the glaive at his belt, he emanated strength.

"No. Please . . ."

"Don't be afraid." His hair was black as a raven and nearly to his shoulders. "You'll be with your parents. It will be better for you in the other world. This one is good for little but suffering. Surely even you know this."

There was an undertone of desperation in his bitterness. As if he was trying to convince himself as much as her.

At last, he stepped fully into the light, appearing much younger than she expected. He was clad in tight trousers and a loose black shirt. When his eyes met hers, he stopped advancing.

"What . . . How . . ." He tipped his head, stepping closer to her, staring at her as if the answer to all of life's mysteries lay in her eyes.

And then, she saw the answer to one of her own mysteries in the sea-blue depth of his.

She knew this man.

She tried to find a way to say it. To explain to him the connection she was only just beginning to grasp. But nothing came.

All she could do was stare into the confusion and shock on his face.

That, and hear his words. Words that stole her breath.

"Your eyes . . . I've only seen color like that once before, but . . . it cannot be." Something fell from his hand with a clatter as he backed away, into the shadows, shaking his head. "It's you."

He turned and ran.

FOURTEEN

H elen?" Griffin made no effort to be quiet when he saw her on the ground. He sprinted down the ladder ahead of his brother, reaching her in seconds. "What happened? Are you all right?"

"I . . . It was . . ." Helen shook her head.

"What happened?" Darius looked around, sensing there was more to the scene than was currently obvious. "Was someone here?"

"It was him." She opened her hand, showing them they key that lay in her palm.

It was the key that made her sure. She'd rushed forward a moment after the man had disappeared, grabbing for the object that had clattered to the ground. In her palm, it struck the chord of recognition she had first felt when she saw the key found in the rubble of her home. This time, the bell rang louder.

She was transported to a day in which the sun shone on her tea party in the garden. She sat with her friend Wren at a small table, the dolls joining them in seats of their own. Wren had accepted the tea, shyly telling her that he had a gift for her as well.

Not something you can eat, like tea sandwiches, or something you can drink, he'd said. *Something shiny and pretty to look at.*

When he'd handed her the strange object, she had looked at it in wonder, much as she did now. It was not the same key, of course. But she understood now that it was from the same maker, and her imaginary friend had not been imaginary after all.

She heard her mother calling them in from the garden; *Helen! Raum! Come inside, children. It's getting cold!*

Raum, in the haze of childhood memory, had become Wren.

"Helen? Listen to me, Helen!" Griffin's hands were on her shoulders, and she realized with a start that he was speaking to her. Had been speaking to her for some time.

She blinked up at him. "Yes?"

He plucked they key from her hand and held it in front of her. "Where did you get this?"

"He left it for me." She looked into his eyes. "Raum left it for me."

127

"I don't understand." Griffin paced the floor of the library while Helen sat, still in shock, on the sofa. "How is it possible that you *know* him?"

"I don't." She looked down at her hands. "Not anymore."

"But you did." Darius spoke from a chair near the fire. It was odd, seeing him so still while Griffin moved with catlike energy across the library floor.

"Yes." She stared into the fire crackling in the firebox. "I didn't think . . . Well, I didn't think he was real. I played with him quite frequently when I was small. I don't even remember when he stopped visiting." She looked up at Griffin. "I mentioned him to my mother a couple of years ago. She told me that many creative people have imaginary friends. I remembered his name as Wren, and she never corrected me. He was the only friend I'd ever had."

"Raum Baranova is hardly a friend." Darius's voice was dry. "The key in your hand was probably meant to be left at the scene of our murder."

It took a moment for the words to sink in. When they did, she looked up at him in shock.

"Raum . . . Baranova?" She stood, pacing the room and struggling to breathe.

Griffin nodded. "Andrei Baranova's only child. He was just sixteen at the time of his parents' death. He hadn't even reached Enlightenment."

"Enlightenment?" Helen rose. Her throat threatened to close around her words, her mind connecting the things Griffin and Darius were saying with the things that had happened so far, the oddly familiar key, the blue-eyed boy from her garden. "Andrei Baranova's son was a Keeper."

Griffin nodded.

"It's him, isn't it?" she asked. "Raum's the one who's been leaving the keys."

"It appears so." Griffin's voice was quiet.

"Why didn't you tell me about him?" she demanded. "You obviously knew it was a possibility."

Griffin shrugged. "We weren't certain. Raum disappeared after his parents' suicide. The Alliance tried to find him. It was unheard of for them to turn their backs on a Keeper, even one who hadn't reached Enlightenment. But Raum just vanished. After a year passed, well . . . another Keeper had to be appointed in his place."

Helen fought against a newfound sympathy for the boy who had lost everything. She knew well that loss.

"But why would he want us dead when he was once one of us?"

"I think revenge is a safe bet," Darius said.

Helen couldn't hide her surprise. "Why would he take revenge on us? On our families? No one forced his parents to sell keys to the Syndicate! No one forced them to commit suicide!"

Darius spoke. "No one said it had to make sense, Helen."

She shook her head, pacing the floor. "There has to be some kind of explanation."

"Is there any explanation that could absolve him?" Griffin's voice was steely. "He murdered our parents."

"I already told you he doesn't do the killing." She regretted the words as soon as they were out of her mouth, but her regret was no match for Griffin's anger.

"That hardly matters." He looked down at her, his eyes bright with fury. "He ordered the executions. *He left one of his keys in my dead mother's hand.* The fact that he didn't take her life himself hardly makes him worthy of redemption."

She swallowed, wondering why it was so hard to speak. "I know. I'm simply saying there may be more to the situation than seems apparent."

"Actually," Darius surprised her by speaking calmly, "Helen has a point."

"Really?" Griffin's voice dripped with sarcasm. "Please

enlighten me, brother, because I can't seem to find it."

Helen flinched at the sound of his voice. She had only known the Channings for two days, but already it was difficult to reconcile Griffin as the furious, volatile person in front of her, while Darius sat in the chair, surveying the situation within the calm of his own mind.

"He said not doing the killing himself was 'part of our agreement,'" Darius reminded his brother, recalling the conversation in which Helen had told them everything, word for word, that Raum had said during their brief encounter.

"I understand that he's working for someone else." Griffin stopped pacing, dropping into a chair next to the sofa where Helen sat. "It doesn't matter. If he's the one who killed our parents—the one who plans to murder us—we have to stop him."

Darius nodded. "I agree. But don't you think it would be wise to use him first?"

Helen looked up at Darius. "What do you mean?"

"If we allow him, he might lead us to whoever is ordering the killings," he said. "That seems smarter than killing him now and never knowing who's behind the executions. If Raum is nothing more than a hired killer, disposing of him without getting to his employer would be foolish." Darius waved his hand absently in the air. "His employer would only hire some-one else once Raum is gone."

For a minute, Griffin said nothing. He heaved a tired sigh. "I suppose you're right."

"Besides," Darius said, "we have a new clue. We might as well use it."

"What clue?" Griffin looked sharply at his brother.

Darius pulled a long yellow envelope from his jacket. "This one."

He handed it over to Griffin. Opening the flap, he pulled a stack of folded papers from its interior. Helen checked her impatience as he flattened the papers across his knee, hold-ing them up to the light of the lamp. His brow furrowed in concentration as he read, shuffling through the papers with increasing speed until he finally lowered them.

He looked at his brother. "Where did you find this?"

Darius shrugged. "In the room at the top of the loft."

"You didn't say anything." Griffin's voice was heavy with accusation.

"Yes, well . . . It was right before the clatter from below." He looked at Helen, as if she had been responsible for the noise instead of Raum, who had dropped the key to the con-crete ground just before running.

"May I?" Helen held out a hand toward Griffin.

He passed them to her. "They're addresses."

Helen flipped through the parchment. Griffin was right. They were addresses.

Theirs.

Darius explained. "They contain the locations of every Keeper who has been murdered. Plus ours."

"We were next." All the anger seemed to go out of Griffin as he said it.

Darius nodded.

Helen read her address among the others, all of them reduced to numbers and street names. A rope seemed to wind its way around her heart until her chest felt so tight she wasn't sure she could go on breathing. She forced the air into her lungs. If she started mourning now, it might go on and on until it killed her as sure as if she had died with her parents.

She looked at Darius. "I don't understand how these addresses can help us find Raum's employer."

"They can't," he said. "But the parchment might."

Flipping through the papers on her lap, she scanned them for clues. A moment later, she raised her eyes, shaking her head.

"I don't see anything."

"That's because you're in the wrong light." Darius waved her over to his seat by the fire.

She stood, crossing the few feet between them with Griffin on her heels. Darius rose, taking the parchment from her hands and holding one of the pages up with the fire behind it. The parchment was fine and thick. Very much like Father's, Helen thought.

Even still, the fire highlighted the shadow of the watermark, faintly visible on the paper.

"What in God's name . . ." Griffin leaned in until his face was mere inches from the parchment. Helen wondered if he needed spectacles. "They're letters, I think."

He straightened, looking first to his brother and then to Helen.

She could make out the shape of them, but the detail was lost. Rather than moving closer, as Griffin had done, she leaned back, trying to see the letters hidden in the watermark as part of a bigger whole, relaxing her mind and hoping it would see what was there.

A moment later, it did.

"They're initials," she said, looking from Darius to Griffin. "I'm almost sure of it."

"I think you're right." Darius glanced at his brother. "And I think my brother's eyes are in need of assistance."

Griffin glared at him before turning to Helen. "Can you tell what they are?"

Helen held the note to the light of the fire once more, trying to see the image that was shadowed there. For a moment, she wondered if she had been wrong. The image suddenly looked very much like a set of triangles. But when she leaned back, looking again at the paper as a whole rather than focusing on the mysterious images hidden in the center, she saw it.

"It's a *V*, I think. And an *A*. There's a crest behind them." She shook her head as she tried to make out the image. "It appears to be an animal of some kind. A bull, perhaps?" She lowered the paper, turning to the brothers.

"VA . . ." Griffin muttered. He looked at Darius. "VA with a bull behind it. Does that mean anything to you?"

He shook his head. "But we've had a long night. Maybe it will come to us by morning."

"May I keep this for now?" Helen asked, indicating the envelope.

Darius nodded. "If you think it will help."

"It might." Her eyes itched from the strain of staring at the parchment. She resolved to think about it more tomorrow. "I'm so tired. But . . ."

"What is it?" Griffin asked.

"Do you think it's safe for us to sleep?" She was thinking about the envelope containing the Channings' address.

"If he'd wanted to kill us tonight," Darius said, "he could have done it two hours ago."

Helen heard the question implicit in his statement. It was the same one she'd been asking herself since Raum had fled the warehouse.

Why hadn't he killed her when he'd had the chance?

She was halfway up the stairs when Griffin caught up to her.

"I'm sorry if I was harsh in the library." His voice was low as they reached the top of the stairs. "When I saw you on the floor of the factory, I thought something had happened to you."

She heard how hard the words were for him to say, though she didn't know why that would be true. When she glanced over at him, she saw the same stray piece of hair falling into his eyes, a pained expression on his face that reminded her of a worried little boy.

"I understand," she said. "I was as shocked as you and Darius. I'm still shocked, actually."

They made their way through the darkened halls, and Helen marveled that they could seem familiar after so short a time.

She tried to recall what it felt like to traverse the hallways of her own home, but the memory was just out of reach.

"Did he . . ." Griffin paused as they came to her chamber door. "Did he hurt you?"

He faced her, turned away from the lamplight along the wall. His eyes shone green and gold in the darkness.

She shook her head. "I fell scrambling for the key. I didn't know what it was at first. I only heard the sound and saw something drop from his hand."

He seemed relieved, but when he spoke, it wasn't relief she heard in his voice but determination. "Tomorrow we'll spend the day working with the sickle. I hope you won't have to use it, but I don't like the idea of you being helpless if Raum comes after us."

For a moment, she bristled inwardly, but the protectiveness in his eyes soothed her ire. Besides, after seeing the brothers fight the wraiths in the street, she had to admit that she was not well equipped to face the threats that now seemed probable.

"All right." She smiled into his eyes. Something unnameable but dangerously close to affection stirred between them. Finally, she looked away, placing a hand on the doorknob to her room. "Good night, Griffin."

"Helen?" His voice stopped her as she was turning to close the door.

"Yes?"

"Why didn't he kill you?" Griffin's face was a mask of puzzlement. "Raum, I mean? Why didn't he kill you tonight when he had the chance?"

She wanted to hand him a reasonable answer, and she pondered the most obvious of the ones she could supply.

We were childhood friends.

He remembers me as I remember him.

The memory took him by surprise.

But none of it seemed to account for Raum's abrupt flight from the factory just as she was at her most vulnerable.

All she could do was meet Griffin's eyes and tell the truth. "I don't know."

It was a relief to be in the privacy of her chamber where she did not have to field the many questions that seemed to have no answers. It was as if she were standing on the deck of a ship in a roiling sea. Every time she thought she got her balance, something else came along and knocked her down again. She couldn't explain most of it to herself, let alone the brothers.

Her bed had been freshly made, a basin of hot water left on

the washstand. She surveyed the room with some suspicion, wondering again how things were attended in the Channing house. She had yet to see anyone other than Griffin and Darius.

She gave in to the mystery, washing her face and changing quickly, remaining in her chemise as she had the night before. The clock over the firebox chimed twice as she got into bed.

Her eyes burned with tiredness, but her mind would not stop turning over everything that had happened. She reached for the key on the bedside table. It had a dull sheen in the light of the fire, and she held it up, turning it over and inspecting it as if it held the answer to Raum's actions at the factory. She imagined it left in the charred rubble of the home in which she now slept. The home of the young men who had become her friends. The thought pained her, and she slipped the key back onto the table. She could not reconcile the loss she had suffered with the man who had let her go in the factory. There was anger, of course. Fury, really, that he had allowed—no, commanded—such horrific acts.

Yet there was something else, too. She wanted to call it gratitude for sparing her life, whatever the reason. But deep down, she knew it something far more complex.

FIFTEEN

They were finishing breakfast in the library when a knock sounded at the front door.

Both brothers jumped to their feet, toast almost sliding to the floor as they set their plates hurriedly on the tea table.

Griffin looked at Helen. "Stay here."

He did not wait for her response before following his brother out of the room, his hand on the sickle hanging at his side.

Helen waited in the silence of the library as she was told, though she did creep to the doorway, craning her ears for sounds from the entry.

She jumped back a moment later when she caught sight of Darius and Griffin making their way back down the hall.

"Don't try to pretend you weren't looking." Griffin entered the room first, four large brown packages wrapped with string piled high in his arms. "I saw you."

"I stayed in the room just as you ordered," she insisted.

"Your interpretation of instruction is frighteningly loose." Darius sat down, picking up his plate and continuing his breakfast.

She ignored the barb as Griffin set the packages on the small sofa where she had been eating.

"These are for you," he said.

She leaned down, inspecting her name, written in large scrolling script across the top.

"My clothing?" She tried not to sound excited. It was difficult to be the only girl around so much manliness.

"It looks that way." Griffin grinned, seeing through the charade of her nonchalance. "Why don't you change, and we can start training in the ballroom?"

She looked for him in the library some time later, the fabric of her strange new skirt brushing against her leg. After finding the library empty, she searched the remaining rooms on the ground floor until the only one left was the kitchen. She came upon him there, crouched at the back door and muttering something unintelligible to someone she couldn't see.

Approaching cautiously, she spoke softly so as not to startle him.

"Griffin?"

"Huh? What?" He turned, clearly startled despite her best efforts. "Oh, Helen! That was fast."

He shut the door quickly behind him.

She waved toward it. "Who is that you're speaking to?"

He feigned surprise. "That? No one. There's no one there."

She tilted her head, trying to place his strange demeanor. "But you were talking to someone."

He shook his head, leaning against the door as if that would prevent her from opening it.

She crossed to it in two long strides, reaching for the knob. "Don't be ridiculous. I heard you speaking to someone."

She tugged on the knob, trying to open it, but he wouldn't move.

"Griffin! Why are you acting so strange?" She continued without waiting for an answer. "I realize we don't know one another well, but surely you know me well enough to know that I'm not leaving until that door is opened and I see for myself who is on the other side."

He stared into her eyes for a second before stepping aside with a sigh. "Very well. Have a look at my small companion, then."

She held his gaze a moment longer, wondering at his choice of words, before pulling open the door.

No one was there. She was standing on the same small porch she had used to escape the house and follow Darius and Griffin that first night, but it was completely empty.

At least, that is what she thought before she heard the unmistakable meow at her feet.

She dropped her gaze, noting the black-and-white kitten lapping cream from a fine floral dish. Then, she understood.

She looked up at Griffin, leaning against the door frame, his face reddening slightly under her gaze.

He waved her off before she could speak. "It's nothing to make a fuss over. The poor thing was bedraggled when it first came to the door. Anyone in my position would offer it some cream."

A smile lifted the corners of her mouth. "You feed the cat? That's who you were talking to?"

"Well, technically, there is more than one of them. It didn't seem right to turn away Mouser's friends." He bent to pick up the kitten, now done with the saucer of milk. "Isn't that right, Mouser?"

"Mouser?" Helen said, trying to suppress her smile.

He held the ball of fluff against his body as if he had done it a thousand times before. "He needed a name." A note of defensiveness crept into his voice. "And he brought me a mouse the first night he appeared on the step, as if he wanted to trade it for some food."

"It's a fine name." Reaching carefully toward the kitten, she let it sniff her hand before touching it gently. "And for the record, I quite like people who take in strays." She met Griffin's eyes with a smile, and something powerful and warm rose in her as she stroked the animal's silky fur, her hand brushing Griffin's as he did the same.

"I suppose we should work in the ballroom before nightfall," he said, reluctantly putting the cat back on the ground. "You'll need good light to train with the sickle."

She had to suppress the urge to protest. She did not want to work with something so sharp and dangerous. Now, as they made their way through the kitchen, she wanted to apologize in advance for the fiasco that would surely be her training with the sickle.

"I'm not very good with anything physical . . ." she began as they turned down a hallway she had never seen.

He flashed her a grin as they walked. "I find that hard to believe."

She caught the innuendo in his voice and felt a blush creep to her cheeks. "You know what I mean."

His laughter was slightly less self-conscious than it had been even the day before. "Yes. But there's no need to worry. I've found the training sickles that Darius and I used when we were younger. They're made of wood."

She could not keep the breath from leaving her body in a rush of relief. She thought Griffin might laugh at her again, but instead, he touched her arm. She stopped beside him in the darkness of the hall.

"Helen." His voice was low, his words, a secret between them. "You don't have to be afraid while you're in my company. You know that, don't you?"

She nodded around the words stuck in her throat.

"Good." He started walking again. "But even so, it's best to be prepared for anything."

They traversed a long hallway. It was richly carpeted, polished bronze sconces gleaming every few feet.

Helen looked up at Griffin as they walked. "May I ask you something strange?"

He looked startled. "Of course."

She hesitated, slightly embarrassed at the question in her mind. "Is the house . . . enchanted?"

"Enchanted?"

"Yes. Everything is so perfectly maintained and attended, yet I haven't seen anyone but you and Darius. I thought perhaps it was . . . magic or something."

He chuckled, his gaze tender as he looked down at her. "We have a houseboy—an orphan, actually—who sees to things. He's quite skittish. We rarely see him ourselves, but I'm glad your needs are being attended with such efficiency."

She nodded, feeling foolish and naive. A moment later, they rounded a corner into an enormous, nearly empty room. Sunlight streamed in through windows that rose to the ceiling and dust motes hung in the air like a veil as Helen stepped onto the parquet floor.

"It's lovely." She turned in a circle, admiring the chandeliers overhead, the gilt-framed art on the walls.

"It hasn't been in use for some time." Griffin crossed to a small table against one wall. "I wasn't even old enough to attend the last ball that was held here."

Helen nodded, her mind touching on the experiences she always assumed would be hers before the murder of her family and the ruin of her home.

"I'll bet it was wonderful, though." She smiled at him as he came back toward her, holding something in his hands. "When it was all lit up, I mean."

He nodded. When their eyes met, his loss mirrored her own.

He held something out to her. Helen took it, closing her hand around the smooth wood of the V-shaped training sickle.

"It won't hurt you while you learn, but it will give you a feel for the advantages and challenges of such a strangely shaped weapon. I assume you've taken fencing?"

Helen couldn't hide her surprise. "How did you know?"

He shrugged. "It was part of the curriculum for most of us. All the usual studies plus Latin, religious history, intelligent defense, fencing."

"Intelligent defense?" She remembered Father's lessons on Latin and religious history and the more recent addition of fencing, but she didn't recall anything approximating intelligent defense.

"It might not have been presented as an actual lesson. Our parents were killed before we could study it outright. But when we were small, the lessons came in the form of games."

"What kind of games?" But Helen already knew what he would say.

"Games like Find the Way Out and What Would You Do

If . . ." He tipped his head. "You did play them, didn't you?"

She nodded, the pieces of the puzzle clicking together in her mind. "I didn't realize they were more than games until I escaped from the tunnel under my house the night of the fire. I emerged in front of Claridge's."

Griffin raised his eyebrows. "I take it you were familiar?"

"My father took me there for tea every week. We often walked the streets afterward. Right by this very house, I'm sure."

"It must have been difficult to prepare us without actually telling us anything. It cannot have been easy to teach children such things," he said. "As time passes, you'll discover a lot of things you didn't realize you knew."

She heard her mother's frantic voice the night of the fire. *You know more than you think, Helen.*

"Now, when you hold the sickle . . ." Griffin backed up, looking at her more closely, his eyes traveling to the hem of her skirts. "I do like your new clothing, Helen, but . . . well, your skirt seems shorter than normal."

She had wondered if Griffin would even notice the eccentricities of her attire.

Sighing, she reached down with her free hand, pulling the

fabric away from her legs so he could see the cut of the design. "It isn't a skirt. Not really."

His bewilderment turned to shock. "You're wearing trousers?"

"They're not trousers!" she protested. "It is a slightly shorter skirt sewn in the middle so I can move about more freely."

"Yes," Griffin agreed, laughing. "Pants! Like I said."

She slapped him playfully on the shoulder. "Gowns are made for strolling and sewing. I cannot hope to defend myself with all that fabric weighing on my legs. This can pass as a slightly short skirt while still allowing me some freedom of movement. Besides," she looked down at herself, feeling a twinge of pride, "I think I did quite well designing them on a moment's notice, and Andrew did brilliantly with creating them."

"All right." Griffin rubbed the stubble, faintly visible on his chin. "I see your point."

He backed up a few more feet, beginning to explain the use of the sickle. Helen listened intently, for though they were practicing with wood, she might well be holding the razor-sharp edge of a real sickle someday soon. And her life might depend on her ability to use it.

It was not very different from fencing in stance, Griffin explained. He reminded her to place her weight on her back foot when gauging the situation and to transfer it to her front when taking the offensive.

"It's trickier than fencing, though, because you don't have the length of the blade between you and your opponent." He demonstrated, moving closer to her. He held out the training sickle as if attacking her with its sharp edge. "You have to get close enough to do damage, but that places you near enough to be injured as well."

"How do I avoid that?" Helen asked, her mind already working to come up with a solution.

He smiled. "By keeping them too busy to go on the offensive or by knocking their own weapon out of their hand."

She nodded, storing the information for later as he stepped forward, tapping his sickle against hers. "The other thing you have to watch out for is the lock." He slipped the edge of his weapon into the hook of hers so that they were intertwined in the center of the V. "If someone gets a lock on you, it's tough to extricate yourself without injury. That's the bad news."

"What's the good news?" she asked, her sickle still intertwined with his.

"That you can do the same to them." He gave his sickle a

good yank, and the piece of wood in her hand clattered to the ballroom floor.

She bent to pick it up. "I think I'm beginning to understand," she said. "It's not a physical problem. Well, not really. It seems like it is, because we're moving around. But it's really more mathematical. More scientific."

He raised his eyebrows. "Scientific?"

She liked the way he looked into her eyes when she spoke. As if he truly wanted to hear what she had to say and was not just being courteous by asking.

"Yes. Probability, cause and effect, that kind of thing."

His brow wrinkled a little. "Go on."

She studied the sickle. "Using this as an example, if my opponent comes closer than two feet, the probability of his using greater strength to injure me is great. But if I can hook my sickle with his before that point or right as he reaches it, I have a better chance of disarming him altogether."

Griffin shook his head. "You wouldn't have the strength to disarm him."

"Strength isn't a requirement."

"I'm not sure I agree with that."

She raised her sickle. "I'll show you."

He lifted his arm, holding the wooden sickle in front of him, waiting to see what Helen would do. A split second later, she whipped her weapon around his, trapping it in the V.

"This is what I mean, Helen. Now you're trapped."

She could feel the pull of strength on his side of their battle. Their sickles were taut, and it took all of Helen's strength to hold her ground. She let a couple of seconds pass while Griffin became used to the idea of disarming her.

Then she released the tension in her arm just enough to cause him to stumble back. Before he could regain his balance, she tapped his sickle hard, sending it skidding across the parquet floor.

He nodded, his expression turned from one of surprise to admiration. "Nicely done."

She smiled, her cheeks warm. "Thank you."

He bent to pick up his sickle before once again facing her. "Again," he said.

They practiced for the remainder of the hour, Helen slowly becoming more adept with the wooden sickle. Her mind began to see practical solutions to her weaknesses. She was smaller than Griffin—smaller than most men. It allowed her to duck and dodge blows when there was no other way out.

If she was patient and didn't allow fear to overtake her, she could find an opportunity where luck and logic had a bigger part than strength and experience.

Of course, it would be different with a real sickle, but she was beginning to think that with a lot of thought, and a little luck, she might be able to defend herself if the need arose.

SIXTEEN

They walked toward the front of the house, making plans to meet later for dinner with Darius. Griffin had business to attend in the meantime and was halfway out the front door when Helen thought of something.

"Griffin?"

He looked back, the sun behind him lighting his hair gold. "Yes?"

"What about the sickle?" she asked. "Can I have one now? To defend myself if the need arises."

He paused, his eyes holding hers. Finally, he nodded. "I'll speak to Darius."

He closed the door quietly behind him. Helen stood at the bottom of the staircase, wondering if Griffin's hesitation was due to worry for her safety or fear of her incompetence with the sickle. She sighed. Perhaps it didn't matter.

She paced the foyer, running a hand along the gleaming

banister, the polished mahogany table. It was nearly impossible to reconcile a world where the unfamiliar house around her was the closest thing she had to home. A world where her own home, imposing and solid against the London sky, wasn't filled with light and laughter and fevered discussion almost every night.

There was a faint burning in her eyes, a distant exhaustion in her bones, but her nerves bristled at the thought of going to her room. Her mind would never allow her to rest.

Not until she saw it for herself.

She hesitated only a moment before unlocking the door. Then, she was out in the cool afternoon air, the wind whipping her hair, the clatter of the city all around her.

She walked first toward Claridge's, retracing her steps from the night she had escaped while trying not to remember the horrific moments that had required her to take them. Once she passed the hotel, it was not difficult to find the way home. Less than twenty minutes after she'd left the Channing house, she passed the apothecary on the street corner, followed by the sweet shop at the end of the block. It was all achingly familiar, and yet, it looked different through the lens of everything that had happened since she'd last walked these streets.

Her footsteps unintentionally slowed as Helen began to

wonder at the wisdom of her destination. She knew what had happened. How it had ended.

Didn't she?

Or maybe it was not enough to be told that her parents were dead. That her home had burned to the ground with her mother and father inside it. Maybe she had to see for herself, however horrifying the discovery. She continued slowly down the walk, steeling her resolve.

The smell drifted to her first. It was only the faintest of memories from her time inside the chamber walls, a more acrid undertone to the ever-present residual smoke from London's streetlamps. The odor became stronger as she made her way down the street.

She felt the altered landscape ahead of her before she saw it, as if the very air around the house had changed through the disintegration of the wood, paint, and furnishings that had once occupied it.

Despite her state of preparedness, Helen sucked in her breath when the house finally came into view. Her mind rejected the image. The blackened shell of stone and brick. The windows staring like vacant eyes as she approached.

This was not her home. It couldn't be.

Not the richly carpeted floors where she had learned to

crawl and walk or the dining room in which she and Father, eyes glinting playfully behind his spectacles, had debated all manner of politics. This desolate landscape could not have been home to the lush garden where she had taken tea with Wren—*Raum*—when she was a child. Not the place her mother had knelt, a wide-brimmed hat shielding her delicate skin from the sun, to clip the extravagant roses from their stems.

Yet it was. She knew it was. She recognized the shape of it, like the daguerreotypes of her mother as a girl in which Helen could more sense the familiar lines of her mother's face than see the resemblance.

She approached the house cautiously, resisting the urge to cover her nose and mouth against the stench. Resisting the meandering of her mind that wanted to know what it was.

Finally, she came to a stop in front of the iron gate, which stood slightly askew on its hinges. Staring up at the soot-stained facade of the house, Helen found it almost possible to believe the fire had been minor. Aside from the blackened brick surrounding the window frames and empty doorway, the front of the house was intact. It was only when she allowed her eyes to drift that she saw the extent of the damage.

The library, once sheltered by brick along one side of the

house, was now exposed to the world. She could only dimly make out the shelves behind a pile of rubble that appeared to be the fallen second story. Father's many books—books from which she had taken lessons—were likely nothing but ash. It was somehow obscene that passersby should glance up to see the rooms that had sheltered her since she was born. She felt suddenly vulnerable, as if she were standing outside in only her corset.

Smoke rose from the rubble, a bitter fog that muted the edges of the destruction. She hardly registered the creaking of the gate as she pushed it open. Stepping through it was instinctual. She had to see for herself. Too much was left undone, the night of the fire nothing but a hazy imprint of memory. It had all happened too fast. She needed to reconcile the things she remembered with the things that had actually happened while she hid in the walls of her chamber. While she escaped through the tunnels under the house.

Like a coward, an angry voice whispered in her head. She did her best to ignore it. Making her way up the walk, she lifted her chin to get a view of the roof. It had fallen on one side, leaving a gaping hole open to the sky. Through it, Helen could make out blackened plaster, the looking glass still on the wall of her mother's chamber.

She continued up the walk, surprised to see the steps lead-ing to the front of the house still intact. Someone should stop her, tell her it wasn't safe.

No one did.

The people passing on the walk below seemed very far away, the noises of the street and its occupants from another world entirely. She stopped at the threshold of the house, remembering the carved wooden door that had once stood in its frame. There was no sign of it. No burned remains at her feet. It was as if it had disappeared into thin air or had never existed at all.

She stepped into the darkness beyond, testing her weight on the floorboards as she made her way through the front hall. The staircase, once grand and curving on two sides to meet in the center, was now impassable. Helen assumed the pile of smoking wood directly in front of her represented some of it, but there was no way to be sure. In any case, there would be no last look at her childhood chamber. No scavenging for salvageable mementos. Not on the upper floors at least.

Continuing down the hall, she turned into the parlor. She knew it for the parlor because of its location, but it was so charred and damaged she would not have recognized it oth-erwise. The floor was a murky river of soot, strange objects bobbing in the water that must have been used to squelch the flames. On the exterior wall, black with smoke, trees and vines outside were visible through intermittent holes in the plaster and lath.

There was nothing recognizable in this place. The furniture was all gone, as surely as if a contingent of movers had come and carted everything away. They hadn't, of course. The fire had done that all by itself.

She was weighing the wisdom of making her way to the kitchen when a floorboard creaked behind her. The sound stopped her in her tracks. For a moment, she was too paralyzed by fear to do anything but stand, perfectly still, in the middle of the room, hoping she was mistaken. When it came again, she spun around, backing instinctively toward the wall.

For a moment, she was in another room from another time. A crowded party in which she was at least a foot shorter than everyone else in attendance. People in gowns, holding glasses and laughing too loudly. Her father's voice in her ear.

"Suppose you spotted someone right now, Helen. Someone to whom you'd like to remain invisible. What is the first thing you must do?"

She had answered without hesitation. Her voice was small and soft in the haze of memory. "Go unnoticed."

She saw her father's solemn eyes gazing into hers. "And why is that?"

"Because my chances of escape are smaller if someone sees me first," she had said.

"That's right, my girl." Her father had nodded, a sad smile playing at his mouth. "That's right."

His voice was clear as a bell in her mind, and she stepped backward into the shadows, testing each step as she went to make sure the floorboards would not creak before putting the full force of her weight on them.

When the figure shadowed the doorway to the parlor, she forced her breath slow and steady. Her eyes found the exits in under five seconds.

The wall behind her, unstable enough that a good push might get her through.

The glassless panes at the front of the house which she could reach in four long strides.

And the doorway in which the tall, shadowy figure now stood.

Obviously, a last resort.

She didn't know if she could be seen, but before she could weigh the wisdom in making a run for it rather than staying and hoping she hadn't been spotted, the figure spoke.

"I imagine you've already found the exits." The voice was familiar and male. "You've all been well trained."

Raum.

She meant to stay hidden. To give herself as much time as possible to work out an escape plan. But the words angered her, and she stepped out of the shadows without thinking, her mind a haze of red-hot fury.

"*We* were well trained." She spat the words at him. "You were one of us once."

He took a step into the room, casting an eerie shadow in the dim light leaking in from outside. When he spoke, the anger in his voice mirrored her own.

"It has been a very long time since I was one of you."

She shook her head. "Not long enough to justify your betrayal."

"You're in no position to judge me." He almost roared the words, and she felt the first threads of fear wind their way through her stomach. "You don't know anything about my life."

"In no position to judge?" She was incredulous. "I'm in every position to judge. You murdered my family. You would have murdered me, too, if I hadn't escaped."

He seemed to flinch in the moment before he covered it

with an impassive expression. "I told you, I don't do the killing."

"Oh, yes. I remember. You only *order* the killings." Her fingers itched for a weapon. A sword or even a sickle. "That makes it all right, then, doesn't it?"

He looked at the floor before meeting her eyes. His hair shone like polished ebony even in the half-light. "I didn't know it was you."

"How could you not know? Your murders have hardly been random. You've been killing the Keepers, one by one."

She flinched as he stomped toward her. Stepping back, she gauged her chances for escape. She was too close to the wall to get enough momentum to break through it. The window was still a possibility, but Raum looked fit and fast. He was much taller than she, his legs far longer. It was a gamble.

And then he was right in front of her, his hand on her arm in a grip that made no mistake of the fact that she was out-matched in strength.

"I wasn't given the names of the Keepers," he said defensively. "I only had the family names. Cartwright and an address. And in any case, I didn't remember your given name. I only remembered a serious girl with soft hands who had me to tea in a garden overflowing with roses. It was your eyes . . . those violet eyes that made me sure it was you."

His voice had become softer and so heavy with sadness that Helen had to rally her anger around an unwelcome feeling of kinship with the man who had ordered the killing of her parents. Of her.

"I don't care what you did and didn't remember. You murdered my mother and father. You murdered the other Keepers and their families." She hesitated, swallowing and lifting her chin. "And now I suppose you'll murder me, too."

She had no intention of giving up without a fight, but she needed to buy herself time. Time to extricate herself from his grip and plan an escape.

But Raum didn't move for a weapon. He didn't move at all. He simply stared down, his eyes licking like fire toward hers. The seconds stretched between them, nothing but the sounds of their breath in the room, his iron grip burning around her arm.

Finally, he let go. Stepping back, he dropped his hands to his sides.

"Perhaps you'll entertain the idea that this isn't the first or last time you'll be wrong," he said quietly.

He made his way toward the door.

"What's that supposed to mean?" she called after him.

He didn't answer. He simply kept walking, availing himself

of the escape she was already recriminating herself for not trying to make.

Just before he disappeared into the hall, he turned. "Your friends took something from my worktable. Now you have everything you need."

"What do you mean?"

"I've let you live. For now." His words dropped like a stone in her belly. "The answer is in plain sight. I can't give you anything more."

And then he was gone.

SEVENTEEN

She sat on the stone steps leading to the house for some time after Raum left. At first, instinct screamed at her to give chase. To follow him. To kill him as he'd killed her parents.

Or ordered them killed, as he was so fond of saying.

But she had been trained too well. Reason quickly took over. By the time she'd shaken off her shock and emerged from the house, Raum was long gone. Besides, she had no weapon.

She contemplated his appearance with a mixture of anger and curiosity. How dare he return to this, the scene of one of his horrific crimes?

On the other hand, why had he left her alive yet again?

Twilight was upon the city when she finally gave up. She made her way down the walk, closing the iron gate behind her with a squeak. The lamps along the street had already been lit, smoke rising from their flames in a sooty smudge.

Dark gray clouds moved swiftly overhead. They blocked out the sun completely, and Helen couldn't help wondering if it was a sign of the end. If the atmosphere itself knew that the Orb—and the world it represented—was dying. She crossed her arms against the cold, rubbing her arms and worrying about what Darius and Griffin would say about her long absence.

The thought of Griffin brought a welcome flush of warmth to her chilled body. He was not as daring or certain of himself as Darius, but he had a quiet confidence that soothed her. Despite Darius's easy strength, it was Griffin who made her feel safe.

That was no small thing, at the moment.

She was stopped at a street corner, waiting for a line of carriages to pass, when she saw the paper.

The newsboy stood on the corner, heckling passersby to purchase a copy. And although it was just an ordinary paper for an ordinary day, something caught her eye as she passed.

She doubled back, digging in her bag for a coin to give the boy in exchange for the paper.

"Thank you, miss," he said, handing her a copy.

She nodded, already moving away, her eyes on the article splayed across the front page.

Syndicate Now Owns 92% of Business and Industry!, the headline screamed.

Yet this was not what got her attention. It was the grainy photograph accompanying the article. She brought the paper closer to her face, trying to get a better look at it in the waning light. Her attention was pulled from the paper by a hard jolt to her left shoulder.

"Watch yourself!" An old laborer turned, glaring at her as he made his way down the street.

She stepped aside, oddly shaken. A few moments later, leaning against the brick of a milliner not far from the Channing house, she tried again. Now, without the distraction of jostling passersby, she could make out the image of a gentleman emerging from a strange kind of horseless carriage. The details of the man's face were lost in the blurry photograph, but there was something on the side of the carriage. Something familiar.

She tipped the paper toward the light from the nearest streetlamp. When the image at last came into focus, it was Raum's voice she heard.

. . . *the answer is in plain sight.*

And though she could not remember the last time she

had run, she tucked the paper under her arm and made her way through the streets of London as fast as her feet would carry her.

Dimly aware that she was making a clatter, Helen closed the door with a bang and ran down the hall. She found the brothers in the library, their mouths hanging open in astonishment as she burst through the door.

"What the hell—" Darius started.

Helen held up a hand, trying to catch her breath while simultaneously heaving the words. "I know . . . what . . . the initials are on the . . . paper."

Griffin shook his head. "What initials?"

She crossed the room, thrusting the paper at him. "The ones on the parchment. From Raum's."

He studied her for a moment, trying to find the answer in her eyes.

"Look!" she cried.

He lowered his gaze to the paper. She could see his eyes move across it, and she stepped forward, pointing to the image.

"Not the article," she said. "The picture."

He tipped the paper toward the lamplight while Darius looked on, his usual expression of practiced boredom slipping in the face of his curiosity.

It seemed like forever before Griffin looked up, a horrific understanding dawning in his eyes as he met Helen's gaze.

"Victor Alsorta?" It was all he said.

Helen nodded, trying to ignore the burning in her lungs. "It's the same, isn't it? The insignia on the carriage?"

Griffin passed the paper to Darius. "Have a look."

Darius looked at it for less than a minute before he smacked the paper down on the desk. Jumping to his feet, he paced the library.

"Why would Victor Alsorta order the execution of the Keepers?" he muttered. "And how would he even know who we are? There must be some other explanation."

Helen knew she should tell Darius and Griffin about her run-in with Raum. About his veiled hint that they could find the pieces to the puzzle if only they looked carefully.

Yet, when she opened her mouth to speak, the words wouldn't come. Her face flushed when she remembered Raum's proximity in the scorched parlor. His breath on her face. His hand on her arm.

It was not attraction that brought the heat to her face.

Of that much she was certain. It was shame. Shame that she stood passively by, having a civil conversation with the man responsible for her parents' death. Shame that she had not found a way—any way—to kill him when she had the chance.

She could not tell the brothers now. It would only anger them further when they all needed to be levelheaded. She would wait. Raum might appear again, and next time, she would be ready.

Her mind whispered that she was rationalizing. Making excuses to avoid doing the thing she knew she should. But it was no matter. A moment later, Griffin spoke, and she had all the excuse she needed to let go of her thoughts of Raum and their strange meeting.

"It does seem improbable, but it's the closest we've come to a real clue," Griffin said to Darius. "Whoever is behind the killings has successfully murdered seventeen of us despite the fact that we were well hidden by the Alliance and with no small power ourselves. That would require tremendous influence. The kind of influence held by someone like Victor Alsorta. It seems we should at least explore the possibility that he's involved."

Helen nodded. "I agree. The initials are the same. The logo

behind it is blurry, but it could be the same as well. It would be foolhardy not to consider a connection."

Darius rubbed the stubble at his chin. "All right. We'll go see Galizur tonight. If anyone has information on Alsorta, it will be Galizur."

Griffin looked at Helen. "Nicely done, Helen. We were becoming worried about you, but it seems your time away from the house was well spent." There was a subtle question in the statement.

Raum's face flashed before her eyes, a silent recrimination for the lie of omission she was about to tell. "I went to the house. I . . . I had to see it for myself."

"The house?" Darius looked over at her from his position near the window. "Your house?"

She nodded.

"You should have told me that you wanted to go." Griffin's voice was soft. "I would have gone with you."

She turned away from the concern in his eyes, busying herself by rubbing a smudge from the otherwise gleaming desk. "It was impulsive. And you were already gone."

"Still," he said. "I don't like the thought of you walking the streets alone. It's too dangerous."

"Thank you. Truly. I'll keep it in mind." She didn't want to

imagine what Griffin would say if he knew the danger she had really been in, to say nothing of the fact that she had let Raum walk away without even a protest. "I think I'll lie down before we go to Galizur's."

She made her way from the room without another word. Griffin looked wounded by her dismissal, but she didn't wish to invite company. There was too much swirling through her mind. Too much guilt and confusion. She could not bear the pressure of trying to put a name to it all. Not even for Griffin.

Back in her chamber atop the comfortable mattress that had become her bed, Helen's eyes itched with exhaustion. She knew she needed sleep. That whatever was to come would require her attention and vigilance. But her mind would not stop turning over everything that had happened.

She had come face-to-face with the undeniable truth.

The house was all but gone. Her parents were never coming back.

She reached out for the photograph on the bedside table. The paper was glossy and thick in her hand, the edges beginning to curl. She stared into her mother's eyes, trying to see the things to come in their depths. Could her parents have known, even on that warm summer day, that they would come to this eventuality? That they would perish at the hands of a murderer? That Helen would be all alone in the world and unable, even, to shed a tear for any of it?

When all was said and done, it was the last that caused her the most anguish. She knew terrible things happened in the world. Deep down, she even knew her parents must have seen this as a possibility.

But her own inability to grieve properly was something she could not understand, least of all forgive. Good people grieved when bad things happened, didn't they? They felt loss and sadness in a way that was transparent to others.

And while it was true that her insides felt hollowed out, that there was a dull and ceaseless ache where her heart lay in her chest, there was no real pain in the wake of everything she'd lost. Her soul was as cold as the air that bit through London in winter, her grief a shadow to the vengeance that itself had dimmed since the appearance of Raum.

Raum. The thought of him brought her anger back to the surface. It was Raum's fault her parents were gone. His fault Helen must feel not only their loss, but the loss of her very self. The loss of everything she'd thought herself to be, back when she believed she was kind and compassionate and, if not physically strong, at least brave and willing to defend the things she loved.

She held her building rage close. Nurtured it like the lone spark necessary to light a fire.

And all the while she told herself it was because of what Raum had done that she was forced to see herself not as she once imagined herself to be, but as she really was.

EIGHTEEN

Some time later, Helen sat up in bed, wondering how long she'd been asleep. Her rest had been fitful. She could only hope it would be enough to see her through the coming hours.

The space beyond the curtains was dark, but Griffin had not come to retrieve her for the trip to Galizur's. She dressed quickly, adding a buttoned waistcoat to her snug top, too fitted to be truly appropriate, though that was hardly the point. It was ease of movement she was after and fabric that wouldn't catch, should she find herself scaling another fence. The waistcoat was for warmth alone. Masculine and many buttoned, it was reminiscent of a military coat and would only add to the oddity of her attire. Even still, it was quite cold, and she could not afford to be preoccupied by physical discomfort on the trip to and from Galizur's.

Heading for the door, Helen grabbed her gloves off the mantle. Crafted of supple ivory leather, they covered her knuckles while leaving her fingers bare.

All the easier to hold a sickle. Or better yet, a glaive.

Of course, there was no guarantee Darius would see fit to arm her with either, but she would have to insist. It was the unexpected nature of her meeting with Raum that had thrown her off guard. If she had been prepared—if she had been armed—she would not have let him leave the rubble of her home alive.

It was this she told herself as she made her way through the darkened hallways toward the staircase. The rest, however short, had done her good. She felt in control for the first time since the fire.

The house was quiet, the ticking of the grandfather clock in the foyer the only sound as she descended the stairs. She began to worry that Darius and Griffin had left her behind, but a moment later, she heard their voices coming from the library. She continued to the back of the house. The voices rose in agitation as she approached the doorway, and she stopped just outside, catching bits and pieces of the conversation.

"... however you justify it," Darius finished. "It's unwise to form an attachment."

"What about your attachment to Anna?" Griffin's voice was challenging. "Is that unwise as well?"

"That is not the . . . and you know it." She could hear the steel in Darius's words.

"It is. And just because you're my older brother, doesn't mean you can tell me what to do in my personal life."

Helen took a step back toward the wall, trying to process what was being said. Were they talking about her?

"Your mistakes are yours to make," Darius said quietly. "I'm simply trying to save you the pain of making them."

"Your reference to my affection for her as 'a mistake' only proves how little you know. Now, kindly stay out of my affairs, will you?" Griffin asked, but Helen knew it wasn't really a question. She had never heard him take a stand with his brother in such a way. The fact that it might be due to her made her exceedingly uncomfortable, and her cheeks burned even in the shadows of the hall.

She turned around, walking carefully back toward the staircase before turning yet again. This time, she announced her arrival.

"Griffin? Darius?" she called, heading back to the door of the library.

"In the library." She wondered if it was her imagination that Darius's voice was curt.

Retracing her steps, she plastered a look of calm on her face and tried to forget the conversation she had overheard minutes before. It didn't quite work. When she met Griffin's eyes, she could only hold his gaze for a second before her eyes flitted away from his.

"What time is it?" she asked. "How long did I sleep?"

"Nearly three hours." Griffin rose from the sofa. "It was obviously needed. Do you feel better?"

She nodded. "Much. Though I was worried you might have left for Galizur's without me." Without meaning to, she cast a look in Darius's direction.

He laughed aloud. "I suppose you're not far off to think I'm the one who would suggest leaving you behind, though probably not for the reasons you imagine."

"Please." she said, already annoyed. "Enlighten me."

He stepped around the desk, grabbing a waistcoat off the chair as he made his way toward her. "It's simply a matter of safety. Yours and ours. You're not ready to face the wraiths and

demons that hunt us, and your untrained presence is a distraction." His eyes swept to his brother's face. "To some of us more than others."

Helen saw Griffin's cheeks flush in the moment before he turned away. She hated being used as a pawn in the game of one-upmanship Darius insisted on playing. And she hated being used against Griffin most of all.

Lifting her chin, she tried to sound nonchalant. "Perhaps I wouldn't be such a distraction if you gave me a weapon to defend myself."

Darius's laughter was a bark into the room. "On the contrary. It would be even more of a distraction to have you wielding a weapon for which you have had no training. More so because we would be in close proximity. One slip and we'd be the ones dead."

Her chest tightened with anger, a sensation she was growing accustomed to around Darius. "Yes, but—"

She did not have time to lodge her protest before Darius, one hand raised against her words, stopped her.

"Griffin has already argued your case, Helen. I won't arm you. Not now. And that's the end of that." He was already heading for the door, his next words directed at no one in particular. "Shall we?"

With Darius well ahead of her, Helen was still seething when Griffin pulled her under the light of the streetlamp.

"I don't understand why he gets to make all the decisions," she ranted.

"He doesn't," Griffin said. "Sometimes it's simply more effective to ease him into an idea."

The touch of his hand on hers was oddly intimate. Her tirade was immediately forgotten, though she hardly remembered the moment when Griffin had held her close the first time they went to Galizur's. Now, as Griffin's fingers grazed her waist, his arms pulling her tightly against him until she felt the strength of his body against her back, a tingling started in her belly, rising upward until her cheeks grew hot.

She spoke to cover her nervousness. "I think I should learn to jump on my own soon, don't you?"

"And deprive myself of the opportunity to be near you?" His voice was husky in her ear, his breath tickling the tender skin of her neck. "That seems foolish on my part, but if you'd like to learn, I'll teach you."

She nodded, her voice stuck in her throat.

"Very well," he said. "But not tonight. Tonight you'll stay with me."

There was something possessive and bold in his voice. Something she hadn't heard there before. But she didn't have time to put a name to it. A moment later, he pulled her more tightly against his body and she felt the odd displacement she'd felt before. Her physical being breaking itself down, disappearing like smoke into the London air.

And then she was back under the streetlight in front of Galizur's, Griffin's arms still around her.

"You can let go now." Helen followed Darius's sarcasm to the step where he stood, waiting for their arrival.

Griffin did, stepping away, and Helen was surprised to find she missed the warmth of his body next to hers.

They made their way toward Darius, following him to the door. Anna answered his knock a short time later and, after a short and hurried greeting, they trailed her through the darkened halls as they had done before. Helen was already used to the silence. The journey to the parlor seemed like a passage to another world, the quiet only adding to the feeling that they were leaving one world behind and entering another, as if the labyrinthine halls were a place of transition and speaking would break their spell.

Finally, Anna closed the last door behind them, turning to

lock it with one of the keys from the oddly ornate ring. She turned to them with a smile.

"Father is in the laboratory. He's a bit frustrated with the progress on one of his newest inventions." She looked at Darius. "Perhaps you'd like to take Griffin down while Helen and I prepare tea?"

Darius nodded, his eyes soft, and Helen marveled that he could look so different by virtue of the fact that he was gazing upon Anna. His affection for her changed his features completely. Or rather, he seemed to come more fully into them, as if his everyday countenance, the one that was angry and smug and sarcastic, was a mask he only let drop in the company of Anna.

"Will you be all right?" Griffin asked, turning to Helen.

She smiled. "Of course."

He gave a small nod of his head. As Helen watched him descend the stairs after his brother, she couldn't help wondering at the look in his eyes. She appreciated his protection, of course, but she was not sure if she wanted to be looked at in the way Darius looked at Anna. As if she were fragile. A thing to hold gingerly, as one holds a delicate rose, careful not to bump its silken petals lest they should spill to the floor.

"Well!" Anna's voice interrupted her thoughts. "I daresay you'll know how I feel soon!"

Helen's cheeks grew warm. "I don't know what you mean."

"Of course, you don't." Anna grinned, and Helen caught the first glimpse of something clever and sly in it. She linked her arm with Helen's. "Come. We can talk all about it while we get the tea."

Other than her parents, Helen had had little company over the years. She was only now beginning to sense how very alone she had been. Anna's offer of friendship was a lifeline, and though Helen was unused to being touched by strangers, she allowed herself to be pulled from the room, unable to stop the smile that sprang to her face as Anna told her of the difficulties she had suffered due to Darius's over-protective nature.

"He's simply maddening!" she said, letting go of Helen's arm to cross the kitchen. She made her way to the kettle, steaming angrily atop the stove. "The way he behaves, you would think I'm about to fall over dead any moment."

"Why does he worry so?" Helen asked.

Anna sighed. "My heart has a small irregularity," she said. "It gets bored beating to the same rhythm day after day, you see."

Helen shook her head. "I don't understand."

"Well," Anna hesitated, reaching into one of the upper cabinets for a tin of tea before continuing. "It skips a beat now and then, and sometimes it speeds up so that I'm short of breath."

"Does it hurt?" Helen asked, moving toward the counter where Anna spooned tea into the cups.

Anna stopped for a moment, looking into the distance as if the answer to Helen's question lie against the faded paper on the far wall.

"Not exactly." She laughed a little, turning her gaze to Helen. "It rather feels like I've been running too fast. I can feel it beating in my chest, and then my face feels very hot as if I'm coloring from embarrassment. But no." She shook her head. "It doesn't hurt."

"Is it . . ." Helen paused, searching her mind for an appropriate word. "Is it dangerous?"

Anna turned to Helen, placing a hand gently on Helen's arm. "You're wondering if I'll die from it."

It was not a question, and Helen was surprised at the ache that formed in her own heart at the idea of something happening to Anna. Yet, Anna deserved the same truth she seemed to give to everyone else.

Helen nodded. "I suppose so."

Anna's smile was kind. "You needn't worry. The doctors are still learning about my condition, but I've had it since I was born and have managed just fine." She poured the steaming water into the waiting teacups and turned back to place the kettle on the stove. When she spoke again, it was under her breath. "Darius has to understand that I have obligations equal to my love for him."

Helen tried to hide her surprise at the boldness of the confession.

"He worries that something will happen to you?" Helen asked. "Because of your heart?"

"Among other things. And I understand it. I do." Anna set a saucer of sugar and a small dish of lemon on a silver tray. "But my family has been in service to the Dictata for centuries. They've suffered an assortment of hardships, yet they've all done their duty, as I will do mine."

Helen assisted her in placing the cups on the tray. "And what is it, exactly, that you and your father do? That your ancestors have done for the Dictata?"

"We're an intermediary of sorts," she said. "We interface with the Dictata on behalf of the Keepers, giving you a representative in those matters that concern you. And we provide you with assistance to fight those who hunt you."

Helen shook her head. "I don't understand. I thought the executions were recent."

"These ones are." Anna's voice was solemn.

"What do you mean?"

"The Keepers have been hunted on and off throughout history. This threat is new, and in truth, the closest someone has ever come to extinguishing your kind. But you have always been in danger." Anna lifted the silver tray from the counter. "Get the door for me, will you?"

Helen held open the door. "May I help?"

"It's quite all right. I'm used to bringing tea to Father while he works."

Helen followed Anna through the parlor to the staircase, marveling at the steadiness of the other girl's hands. The cups, bowl, plate, and spoons made not a clink as she began descending the stairs with Helen at her heels.

"I don't understand." Helen picked up the thread of their conversation as they reached the bottom of the staircase. "Other than the Syndicate, who would want to harm us?"

"Who wouldn't?" Anna said softly. Their footsteps echoed across the stone walls of the tunnel as they made their way toward the faint blue light of the Orb in the distance. "One of you has always held the key to the records. To the past, pres-

ent, and future. There have always been those with enough power—or simply ambition—to attempt a coup."

"Then why the alarm this time?" Helen asked.

She saw the worry in Anna's soft brown eyes. "Because no one has ever some so close to rendering the Keepers extinct."

NINETEEN

They entered the large open room Helen remembered from two nights before. The Orb spun laboriously through the air, the blue sea of the Atlantic rippling as it turned past. Darius and Griffin were observing Galizur as he worked with various instruments and tools atop a long work-table. Oddly, a row of melons were lined neatly along one edge.

Galizur turned at the sound of their footsteps. "Ah! There you are. You're just in time for the demonstration."

"What demonstration?" Helen asked as Anna busied herself pouring tea.

"I've been working on a solution to the size of the glaive." Galizur's eyes dropped to the stafflike weapons hanging from the brothers' belts. He held out a hand. "May I?"

Darius turned his gaze to Griffin, who sighed and reached

for his glaive. With a brief glare at his brother, he handed it over to Galizur.

Galizur turned it over in his hand. "It will have to be retro-fitted." He set it on his worktable, reaching for a short, slim rod sitting on its surface. "Try this one."

It was significantly shorter than the glaive Griffin had handed to Galizur.

"I'm not sure how this will help me defend myself," Griffin said, taking it.

"Will it to open with your mind," Galizur said, "the same way you will the glaive's blades to engage."

Griffin stared at it a moment more before holding it away from his body. His face went very still, the pendant glowing at his shirt collar. A second later, the rod in his hand elongated until it became the same size as the glaive Griffin had brought with him from the house. Griffin's eyes lit up in wonder as he lifted it, inspecting its tip, pointed and sharp.

Darius took the glaive from his brother, running his hand along its shaft before turning to Galizur. "How did you do it?"

A smile touched the older man's lips. "I created interlocking pieces to the outer skin and mechanized it so your power would cause it to open, just as your power now causes the glaive's inner blades to deploy."

"What about the inner blades?" Darius asked.

Galizur reached for a melon on the table behind him. He set it on the floor, taking the new glaive from Darius's hands and lifting a hand in warning.

"Stand back."

They were taking their second step back when Galizur plunged the tip of the glaive into the melon. A second later, it burst into pieces, juicy orange shrapnel hitting the walls and floor.

Griffin tore his eyes from the spectacle, looking at Galizur with reverence. "Incredible! It activates the inner blades on its own?"

"It's pressure sensitive," Galizur explained. "Once embedded in the flesh of your enemy, the blades will engage on their own."

"Wait a minute." Helen was still staring at the melon, now dripping down the wall. "Do you mean to say that this is what will happen to someone if you use the glaive against them? They will be . . . torn apart?" She turned her eyes on Griffin.

His expression, once full of awe, softened. "It must seem barbaric, but short of total destruction of the body, the glaive is the only thing that can kill those of the Alliance or the Legion."

"What about the wraiths on the street last night? You killed them without it."

Galizur raised his eyebrows at the mention of the wraiths.

"They're not dead. We wore them down with the sickle. They were sent back where they came from, but they could appear again at any time."

"And they'll keep coming back until they're dispatched for good with the glaive," Darius added. "Don't waste time feeling sorry for them. They would do the same to you in a heartbeat." He turned away, walking toward the Orb. "You would do well to remember that, Princess."

Delivered as it was with Darius's sarcasm, the term was not one of endearment. Anger unfurled inside her, and she advanced on him, coming to a stop only once she was in his path. She put her fingertips on his chest.

He looked down at her hand, a mixture of surprise and growing fury clouding his eyes. But she couldn't stop. Not now. She had too much in front of her.

"I may not be familiar with a sickle and a glaive. I may not have been forced to defend myself until now. But I'm not as sheltered or weak as you would like to assume." She glared up at him. "I'm no princess. And maybe *you* should try to come up with a wittier insult, if that's how you want to play."

The room had grown quiet. Too quiet. Somewhere beyond Darius's shoulders, Griffin stood with Anna and Galizur, but they might as well not have been there at all. Darius stared at her, his eyes darkening gradually. She wanted to look away, but she knew doing so would mean defeat.

It took only a moment for a laugh to burst from Darius's throat. Unlike Griffin's soft, knowing chuckle, Darius's laughter was loud and admiring.

"Good," he finally said. "There's some spirit in you, after all. You're going to need it."

He stepped around her, taking a cup of tea from Anna's outstretched hand. His fingers lingered on Anna's a few seconds longer than necessary.

Anna handed the rest of them tea, and Galizur lowered himself to a chair in front of a large black box.

"I understand we have some research to do," he said.

Helen nodded. "We found—well, Griffin and Darius found it, actually—a piece of parchment at the Baranova's old key factory. The paper had an unusual logo with the initials VA. I think it refers to Victor Alsorta."

"So the boys tell me." Galizur met her eyes. "They also tell me you are acquainted with Baranova's son, Raum."

Helen flushed, thinking of Raum's proximity to her in the

ruins of her childhood home. But of course, that was not to what Galizur was referring.

"I don't know if acquainted is the right word." She tried to keep her voice level. "I knew him as a child."

"And you didn't remember this before last night?"

She shook her head. "I thought I had imagined him. That is, I had a vague recollection of playing with him in the garden. My mother always told me he was imaginary. It wasn't difficult to believe. She said it was a common phenomenon in only children. I think I was only four or five when he stopped coming around."

Galizur sighed, leaning back in his chair. "It's understandable that your parents would seek to distance you—and themselves—from the Baranovas even before their betrayal. Their alliances outside the Dictata were . . . questionable for some years before it was proven that they'd provided the Syndicate with keys to our most sacred locations and treasures. Your parents were not the only ones among the Alliance who thought it wise to cut ties with the family."

"So Raum and his family were isolated before his parents were actually caught and tried as traitors?" Griffin spoke from the sofa.

"That would be an accurate assessment," Galizur confirmed.

"Which means he's probably bitter. And angry," Darius said.

A harsh laugh escaped Helen's lips. "I should think that would be obvious."

She was surprised when Darius shot her an annoyed glance without the cutting comment that would usually accompany it. She busied herself squeezing more lemon into her tea, oddly uncomfortable in the conversation. Her fury toward Raum was dulled by a traitorous sympathy.

She didn't like it. Not one bit.

Galizur straightened in his chair. "Yes, well, it's apparent that there is some kind of connection between Raum and Victor Alsorta. Let's see what we can find."

He reached toward the black box, turning a couple of the knobs that marched along the bottom until a hum emerged from within the box's interior. A moment later, there was a visible shimmer on the surface just before a vaguely familiar, multifaceted object made up of interlocking circles took shape on the screen before them.

Incredulous, she leaned toward the machine. "What is it?"

"It's a simple delivery system for data," Galizur said. "The Dictata put information in, and this device keeps track of it so that I may call upon it later. A visual library, if you will."

Helen's eyes were drawn to the symbol on the screen. It

twisted and turned, morphing into a figure eight, a long, inter-locking strand, a hexagon, a multifaceted cube, and finally, a doorway.

"And what is that?" she asked.

"It's the Flower of Life," Galizur explained.

"It's . . . It's beautiful." She said it because it was true and because the symbol both moved and frightened her in a way that she could not explain. "I think I've seen it before."

"You probably have. It's a geometrical figure said to hold within it all of the mysteries of mankind. It's also the symbol of the Alliance. Of our connectivity to the mortal world we are tasked to protect," Galizur said, leaning forward to place his hands over a rectangle covered with alphabetized buttons. The Flower disappeared as Galizur's hands flew across the keys. "Let me see what we know about the Syndicate."

Helen was transfixed as a series of letters and numbers spilled across the screen, too fast for her to properly register any of it.

"Here we are." Galizur, oblivious to her awe, leaned back in his chair. He lifted some spectacles from his pocket and placed them on his face. "Victor Alsorta. Head of the Syndicate, a partnership between four of the world's most powerful busi-ness owners."

Galizur pushed a button, and the grainy image of an older

man, gray at the temples, emerged on the screen. It was the same man Helen had seen in the newspaper. Even through the screen, Helen could sense his royal bearing, feel the intensity in his gaze. As if he were, even now, looking at her from some far-off place. She would not have been surprised if his eyes were an icy blue, though she could not make out their color on the screen.

"Born in Romania, Victor is fifty-four years old and has no living family. At least, that's what we're led to believe," Galizur added.

"What do you mean by that?" Darius asked.

"All the information I was able to find on Victor was from secondhand sources. Press releases, company biographies, news articles. That kind of thing."

Helen turned to Galizur. "Where does your . . . information usually come from?"

"Typically we can find birth records, death records, marriage certificates. Sources of a more official nature," he said. "But Victor Alsorta may as well be a ghost. The only facts we can find could easily have been manipulated. And were it not for his association with the Syndicate and the volumes that have been written on them across the world, there would likely be far less."

Helen could see from the pained expression on Galizur's face that he was unused to such a lack of results. She stared at the image on the screen, contemplating what little they knew about Victor Alsorta and how they might use it to further their quest for information.

"What of his involvement with the Syndicate?" she asked Galizur. "Could that have something to do with the executions and Raum?"

"We do know something about the other members of the Syndicate." Galizur tapped away at the buttons, the image of Victor replaced by one of a younger man, his hair as black as ebony. "This is Clarence Thurston, head of a multinational technology corporation holding more than two hundred patents on the most advanced technological developments of our time."

"Wasn't he involved in a treason scandal a while back?" Griffin asked. "Accused of selling our enemies technology that was developed exclusively for use by Britain's military?"

Galizur nodded. "That he was."

Helen wanted to ask about the scandal. About what kind of power would allow a man to commit treason and walk free rather than go to prison. But Galizur had already moved on.

The image of a strong-faced woman appeared on the screen.

She looked to be the age of Helen's own mother, though the steel in her eyes hinted at none of the warmth that had been in Eleanor Cartwright's.

"Margaret Latimor," Galizur intoned. "She heads up the Finance Council as well as the largest bank in the world, Western United." He pushed a few more buttons. "Lastly, we have William Reinmann, Speaker for the Symposium on Multinational Security that meets once a year. He owns a consulting firm that specializes in advising political figures on damage control."

Helen tore her eyes away from the screen, looking at Galizur. "Damage control?"

But it was Griffin who answered. "Scandal, personal and professional. People like this cheat and steal and lie. When they get caught, they need someone to come in and tell them how to behave. How to manipulate the public so it doesn't ruin their careers."

Galizur nodded. "Griffin is right. And because of Mr. Reinmann's vocation of choice and his position with the Symposium, it's believed that he's owed more favors from politicians the world over than any other person in the world."

"Which makes him one of the most powerful people alive," Griffin added.

"Quite right," Galizur said. "But perhaps the most important thing of all, aside from Mr. Alsorta's astonishing lack of recorded history, has to do, not with these people individually, but with the Syndicate itself."

"And what would that be?" Helen's mind was already turning over the possibilities.

"Apparently, there's turmoil within its ranks," Galizur said. "The others want Victor out, and the rumor is that they plan to force him out at the Summit in three days time."

Griffin leaned forward in his chair. "A power grab?"

"From the looks of it." Galizur nodded. "And it makes sense given the recent acceleration of the murders."

Helen turned to look at him. "What acceleration?"

"The executions have been happening with greater frequency of late," Galizur explained. "In the beginning, we were losing one Keeper every few weeks, but the past couple of months we have sometimes lost more than one a week."

"As if whoever is responsible is in a hurry," Helen murmured.

"How does the hierarchy within the Syndicate work, Father?" Anna asked. "Couldn't they simply vote Victor out of his leadership position?"

"I don't know the inner workings and politics of the Syndicate," Galizur said. "But one thing is certain."

Helen stopped pacing, finishing Galizur's thought. "Whoever controls the past, present, and future, controls everything."

Galizur nodded. "If Victor can gain access to the records before the Summit, it won't matter what the others plan to do with him. All it would take is one change and ultimate power would be his. By changing the past, he could render the Syndicate helpless, erase the Alliance entirely, even eliminate each of you from the face of the Earth simply by preventing your birth. The changes he could make are limitless."

"More than enough of an incentive to murder the Keepers in search of the key," Griffin added. "Alsorta would be able to alter the course of not only the future—but history itself. All of which would keep him in control not only of the Syndicate, but of everything imaginable."

The words echoed in Helen's mind. There was another person who had everything to gain by altering the course of history.

Raum.

His alliance with Victor was beginning to crystallize. She

pushed it aside for the time being, unprepared for the train of thought.

"Now what?" she asked. "Supposing this is all true, what do we do about it?"

"We kill the bastard," Darius asserted.

Galizur's voice, when at last he spoke, was low. "It would be a crime against humanity. The Dictata would not stand for it."

Darius stood, pulling his hand from Anna's and pacing the room in long, angry strides. "I don't care about the Dictata, at the moment," he said. "Where were they when our parents were murdered? When we were orphaned by our task to keep the world in balance? A task *they* assigned us?"

"Mother and Father wouldn't want this," Griffin said quietly.

"Are you afraid, little brother?" Darius's voice took on an ugly edge.

Griffin stood, his own face flush with anger. Helen was surprised to see that he was just as tall as Darius. That the differences in their height—their strength—had been an illusion cast by Griffin's willingness to allow his brother to take the lead in all things.

Suddenly, Helen saw it for what it was. Not weakness, but strength. Griffin had given his brother the lead willingly. Not out of fear or uncertainty. Out of love.

But now, they were standing toe-to-toe.

"It's not the Dictata I fear, Darius. It's the shame of our parents, wherever they may be. The soiling of their legacy." He shook his head. "I won't do it."

The silence seethed between them, the air growing thicker and heavier before Darius turned to the concrete wall. Helen was horrified when, a moment later, he reached out and punched it with all his might. Anna rushed to his side, taking his hand in hers.

"Darius." Her voice was gentle but firm. "Don't."

Helen wondered if Galizur would admonish Darius for his outburst, but he simply cleared his throat and began speaking.

"Though I understand your desire for vengeance, Darius, your brother is right. It would dishonor the memory of your parents and all those killed."

"Can't the Dictata send someone after him?" Helen asked. "Isn't there some type of enforcement within their ranks?"

Galizur nodded. "There are . . . resources that are used to maintain peace when necessary. But deploying them takes time. There are processes which must be adhered to and I'm afraid none of it would be done before the Summit."

"Then, what?" Darius still faced the wall, but Helen could hear the anguish in his voice. "What can we do? Alsorta can't simply get away with it. Nor can that traitor, Raum Baranova."

A shiver ran down Helen's spine at the mention of Raum.

The answer came not from Galizur, but from Griffin. "We'll bring them in. Alsorta first, before the Summit, and then Raum."

A sarcastic laugh escaped Darius's throat as he turned to face them. "And let the police take care of them?" He answered his own question before anyone else could. "A man like Alsorta would be free in an hour."

Alsorta, but not Raum, Helen thought. He would be left to rot.

"Not the police." Griffin said. "The Dictata."

A surprised silence descended on the room. Helen had no idea how the Dictata worked, but Griffin's idea was the closest they'd come to something that made sense. She turned to Galizur.

"Would the Dictata accept the task of meting out punishment to someone like Victor? Someone who is neither one of them nor one of us?"

"Well, it is a bit irregular. The Dictata normally keep order only within their own ranks. The mortals consigned themselves to their own law long ago." Galizur rubbed at his jaw. "However, the murder of a Keeper is a capital crime by the

Dictata's laws. Though Victor is a mortal, I would think the Dictata would have to see him punished were he brought to them."

"Victor Alsorta is a powerful man." Anna spoke from beside Darius. "Bringing him in would be dangerous. Might we speak to the Dictata first, Father, to insure their willingness to see justice done?"

Helen felt a rush of respect for her new friend. Even with Darius's safety at risk, Anna did not seek to shield them from harm. She knew what must be done and was willing to make her own sacrifices. She sought only to make the sacrifice measured. It was all any of them could do.

"Very good, Anna. Most wise." Helen heard the note of pride in Galizur's voice. He continued. "Better not to risk anyone's safety in the interest of bringing Victor to justice at the hands of the Dictata until we know for certain that justice will be done."

Galizur tapped the buttons a few more times until Victor's face appeared once again on the screen. Helen could not take her eyes off the man. Though he looked like any gentleman on the outside, Victor Alsorta was anything but ordinary. He was the key. The key to her parents' death and the strange mission Raum had committed to support, despite his apparent misgivings.

"I'll wait twenty-four hours." Darius's steely voice broke into the silence. "No more. Every minute that passes takes us closer to the Summit. And the closer to the Summit we get, the more at risk we become. If we're right, Victor will only increase his attempts to locate the key—and eliminate every one of us."

But Raum won't kill us. Not now. Helen didn't say the words aloud. She didn't even know how they could feel so true. It was more than the fact that Raum had twice let her go. That he had even given her a clue—however cryptic—to the identity of the man who had commissioned their death.

It was something in his eyes when he'd looked at her in the ruins of her home. Something that spoke of their forgotten history. Of a bond they shared across time and all reason.

As if reading her mind, Griffin glanced her way before speaking. "Raum has had our address for some time. He knows who we are. What we look like, even. Yet he hasn't come for us."

"That's no reason to be careless," Darius snapped. He met Galizur's gaze and Helen felt her blood run cold. "Twenty-four hours. Then I'm going after them—with or without the Dictata's approval."

TWENTY

"Let's jump," Darius said, making his way down Galizur's front steps. "I'm not up for a wraith attack."

Helen gathered her courage before speaking.

"I'd like to do it on my own, this time." She aimed the words at his back, trying to project her voice so that it wouldn't betray the fear coursing through her veins.

Darius turned. "You'd like to try what?" He narrowed his eyes. "Jumping?"

She nodded.

"Yes, but . . . Well, you've never done it before," Griffin interjected.

Helen rolled her eyes with a smile. "That's rather obvious. But I think I can."

"Jumping is complicated," Griffin said. "Complicated and dangerous."

Helen folded her arms across her chest. "You can do it and you're not that much older than I am. You must have learned somewhat recently."

He stood up a little straighter. "I learned earlier than most, actually. Circumstances called for me to learn many things before the age of Enlightenment."

"Right." Darius's laughter split the night air. He clapped his brother on the shoulder. "You've been jumping for all of nine months, brother."

She raised her eyebrows in Griffin's direction, trying to stifle a triumphant smile. "If you can do it, I can do it."

"She's right." Darius stepped under the light before Griffin could answer. "Teach her. I'll see you both at the house."

A moment later, he was gone.

Griffin turned to her, grumbling. "I didn't mind jumping with you. And it's much safer than trying to teach you under such circumstances."

She realized suddenly why Griffin hadn't wanted her to jump alone. He was concerned for her safety, just as he said. But there was something more and she suddenly understood what it was.

"I'm only trying to pull my own weight. I don't want to be

a liability." She reached out, smiling. "And I would imagine I'll still be required to maintain close contact with you while I learn. At least in the beginning."

He looked at their joined hands before turning his eyes to hers, a slow smile spreading across his own lips. "It would be, ahem, wise to maintain physical contact while learning, that is true."

Pulling her under the lamplight, Helen didn't think it her imagination that he stood closer than necessary while explaining.

"The most important thing about jumping," he said, "is knowing you can do it. Not thinking or hoping you can do it, but knowing you can. You were born with the ability, as we all were, and would have learned soon in any case."

"Right." She nodded, mumbling to herself. "I can do this. I was born to do it."

"It helps if you close your eyes, but don't do that yet. Just listen," he instructed. "You have to see the light as the energy source it is and then, imagine yourself breaking down into the tiny pieces of matter that you are."

She scrunched up her face, trying to see herself as billions of tiny dots that could be broken apart and put back together

at will. It didn't work. Questions flooded her mind, drowning out the understanding that seemed to float just beyond her grasp.

"But what if my body doesn't put itself back together right?" she asked, looking up at Griffin.

"It will," he answered. "It knows the form it's supposed to take."

"But how?"

"It just does. Now," he continued, "after that you'll—"

"What if the pieces of . . . of me get lost along the way?" she interrupted. "What if they're not all there when it's time to put it all back together?"

He sighed, favoring her with an indulgent smile. "It is a legitimate question, but you don't have to worry. All of you travels together, whether walking the streets of London or channeling yourself through space via light energy."

"But I'm not in tiny pieces when I walk the streets of London," she said. "If I were, some of them could easily be delayed while waiting for a carriage to pass or lost when I stop to look in a shop window."

He sighed, squeezing her hand. "You're just going to have to trust me. I had the very same fears when I learned to jump, but here I am. Simply follow my instructions, hold tight to my hand, and we'll be back in front of the house before you know it."

She nodded. "All right."

"Now," he said. "Close your eyes."

Everything went black as she did.

"Breathe in and out. Nice and easy." She did as he instructed, his voice a velvet whisper. "Your body is made of millions of pieces. Most of them are invisible to us, but they're there. They know where they belong and can assemble and disassemble themselves at will. I'm going to count to three. When I do, I want you to see your physical form breaking free of its bodily confines. See it disappearing into the light and traveling, as if in a very fast tunnel, to the streetlight outside the house. It will do the rest all by itself." He paused, his voice leaving a cold spot in the darkness of her mind. "Are you ready?"

She nodded.

He must have had his eyes open, because a second later he began counting.

"One . . ."

Helen imagined her body, as whole and real as it was to her every day of her life, preparing to disassemble.

"Two . . ." Griffin squeezed her hand, and she saw the light

stretching far beyond this streetlamp. Tunnels and tunnels of light connecting every part of London to the other. Then, one tunnel connecting the light under this lamp to the one in front of the Channing house.

"Three."

Something tugged at her stomach, pulling her as if she were attached to a string. There was a split second of weightlessness. A moment in which it was if she had no body at all. She only had time to wonder if she was dead. If this is what being dead felt like. And another moment to think it wasn't bad, to feel so light and so free.

And then Griffin's voice was low in her ear.

"You can open your eyes now."

She was inexplicably afraid. As if she might open her eyes to find the world changed, when reason told her there was only one of two possibilities.

Either she had failed and they were still standing in front of Galizur's.

Or she hadn't and they were home.

She opened her eyes, willing them to make sense of what they were seeing and feeling a rush of relief when she realized that they were, in fact, near the Channing house. Not right in front of it as she'd imagined, but only four streetlamps down.

"Well done." Griffin's voice came from her right. "And quite close for your first try."

She looked up at him. "Did I . . . miss?"

He laughed aloud and she found herself smiling. "It was a near miss. We all do it in the beginning and some of us by a lot more. I was two blocks over my first time."

She felt a rush of pride. "Really?"

He nodded. His eyes grew serious as he looked down at her, and she saw something else in their depths. "Really."

She felt suddenly shy. "Thank you for teaching me."

He stepped out of the light and, still holding her hand, pulled her along with him toward the house. "It was nothing. You're a good student. Although . . ."

She glanced up at him as they walked. "Yes?"

He smiled down at her. "I must confess I will miss your . . . proximity when jumping together."

"Well," she said, answering his smile with one of her own. "There's always sickle training in the ballroom."

"That there is."

And this time when he laughed, something more urgent than friendship slid through her veins.

Weariness settled over Helen's shoulders almost as soon as she shut the door to her chamber. Whether from the visit to Galizur's, everything they'd learned while there, or the jumping, she was thoroughly exhausted.

She bent over to unlace her boots, grateful for Andrew's craftsmanship. The leather was as supple as a rose petal. Her feet had not hurt a bit.

Undressing was easier without the accoutrements of a gown and voluminous petticoat. She couldn't help but feel proud as she unlaced her newly designed corset, laced in the front. She could not fathom why they weren't all designed in such a fashion. It made no sense to be imprisoned by such a garment until such a time as someone else could free you. Her design was unlaced and strewn on the floor in less than a minute, along with the buttoned blouse and split skirt.

She breathed a great sigh of relief, stretching her naked body toward the ceiling before approaching the bureau and pulling a nightdress from its second drawer. The fabric was thinner than the material of Helen's childhood gowns, but that could not be helped. She had only specified color and content, not weight. Clearly, Andrew and his team of seamstresses had thought her old enough for a mature nightdress. Even still, she felt self-conscious when she turned to the mirror to unpin her hair. The nightdress was quite see-through in the firelight, though she supposed it didn't matter when she was alone in her chamber.

She ran her fingers through her unbound hair, her eyes growing heavy as she approached the bed. Tomorrow, they would have their instructions from the Dictata. She didn't want to contemplate Darius's actions should they be ordered not to seize Victor Alsorta. Helen was certain Darius would go after him anyway.

And Griffin would surely follow, out of loyalty.

Pulling back the coverlet, she slid into the cool sheets and pulled the blankets over her as she thought of him. She saw his kind eyes, gazing down at her with something too like affection to be called anything else. His grin, suddenly rakish, as they'd walked the rest of the way home after jumping from Galizur's. Did he feel the same flush of heat when she looked at him that she was growing accustomed to when his eyes looked into hers?

She shook her head against the notion. It was too late and too complicated a matter to consider. It only led her to further questions. Questions about the future. About her own ability to fully love someone when she could not even mourn her parents properly.

Clearly, she was deficient in her ability to form meaningful attachments to others.

Turning over in bed, she reached for the photograph on the night table. What she saw stopped her cold, and she sat up in bed, reaching for it. It wasn't the image that had changed. Her parents still stared back at her from another time and place as a younger, rounder-faced Helen did the same.

But now it was not lying loose atop the table, but safely ensconced inside a silver frame.

She reached for it hesitantly, as if it harbored a mysterious brand of magic. Once it was in her hand, she studied the elaborately fashioned silver, encrusted with tiny pearls in the corners. It was not a frame she had ever seen. Surely, not one belonging to her. There was only one explanation; someone had stolen into her room and placed the photograph inside it.

She thought back to the last time she had looked at the picture, holding it in her hands. She had not even looked at the night table before her afternoon rest. Which meant that someone could have placed the photograph there while she was out this afternoon.

She thought of the orphan boy who cared for the house. Could he have placed it there? No, she was quite sure he wouldn't do so without permission. Besides, the frame was fine. Too fine to be in the hands of an orphan.

It had to be Griffin.

Throwing back the covers, she stepped onto the cool carpet, the framed photograph still in her hand. She did not think through the social implications of making her way from her chamber to Griffin's room. He had said she could come if she needed anything, and if their current circumstances didn't place them outside the social norms, she didn't know what would.

She stopped at the second door on the right, surprised to find it half open, dim yellow light leaking from its frame. Glancing first left and then right down the hall, she found it as empty as always. But she knew there was no guarantee it would stay that way, and she finally leaned toward the door, speaking Griffin's name softly through the crack, not wanting to wake Darius should his room be nearby.

A few moments later, there was still no answer. She heard a slight shuffle from within and found herself reaching for the door, pushing it slowly open.

Stepping into the room, her eyes scanned it for signs of

Griffin. The layout was much like her own chamber. She took in the large four-poster bed, the blankets askew, as if it had not been made since the night before. The firebox was in the same position as hers, though this room only contained one wardrobe instead of two, and the bureau was significantly smaller.

But all of this was forgotten when she finally caught sight of Griffin, shirtless and with his head bent over a bowl of steaming water. His muscled back rippled as he reached blindly for a towel on the washstand. She felt something inside her shake loose and expand, spreading like a hot wind through her veins as he stood, his broad shoulders and back fully revealed in the glow of the fire.

She could hardly swallow as she tried to make sense of the image etched onto his skin. It was not the marking itself. It was a combination of everything. The warmth of the room. His bare skin. His proximity to her and the sudden realization that she could step toward him and be against him in seconds.

She was trying to force the thought from her mind when he turned toward her.

"Helen?" She wondered if he would be angry that she had been presumptuous enough to enter his room without permission, but there was only concern in his eyes as he crossed the room to her. "Is everything all right?"

"Yes, I . . ." The words came out in a croak, and she cleared her throat before continuing. "I simply wanted to ask you . . ." The words in her mind disappeared like vapor. It was distracting having him stand so close, his skin stretched taut over the muscles of his chest and arms.

"Yes?" he prompted. "You wanted to ask me what?"

Her cheeks grew hot, and she looked away, trying to get ahold of herself.

"I shouldn't have come. It can wait until morning." She turned to leave, wanting nothing more than to get away from the over-warm room where she could no longer think clearly. "I'm sorry to have disturbed you."

"Helen." She felt his hand close over hers, pulling her back toward him. His eyes dropped the length of her body, and she realized she was still in the thin nightdress. And standing right in front of the fire. When he spoke again, his voice was low. "You're not disturbing me."

His eyes locked on hers, an ocean of silence moving between them. She had an almost uncontrollable desire to reach up, entwining her fingers in the hair at the back of his neck. To run her palms against the hard expanse of his bare chest.

Instead, she thrust the silver picture frame, now gripped so tightly in her hand that her fingers hurt, between them.

"Did you do this?"

He dropped his eyes to the frame, nodding slowly.

Looking down at it, emotion welled inside her like a wave. When she spoke, her voice was softer than she intended. "Why?"

He shrugged. "Our parents were murdered while traveling back to London from our country house. We, at least, still have our home and everything in it. It's true that it's a cold comfort compared to the loss of our parents, but it is something to remember the way things were." He hesitated, meeting her eyes before continuing. "You've lost so much. I wanted you to have something solid to hold on to. To remind you of a time when you were still together with your family."

He shrugged, seeming embarrassed as he looked away, avoiding her eyes.

"Griffin." She reached up without thinking and placed a hand on his cheek. He turned to look at her. "Thank you."

She was immobilized, his skin warm against her palm in the moment before she raised up on tiptoe and kissed his cheek. Then, she hurried back to her room before she could do something even more foolish.

TWENTY-ONE

They were finishing a late breakfast when the bell rang at the front of the house. Griffin rose to answer it, taking a last sip of tea before heading for the hall.

Helen sat in silence with Darius, occupying herself by adding marmalade to her toast and trying to squelch the feeling that he knew all about her midnight foray into his brother's room. She could not help but think his gaze too knowing, though she told herself she was only being paranoid.

"It's from Galizur," Griffin announced, returning to the library with an envelope in his outstretched hand.

"Are you certain?" Darius rose, snatching it from Griffin. "It's only been a few hours."

Griffin sighed. "I'm sure. It was dropped off by Wills, that little urchin Galizur uses for errands."

Darius tore open the envelope, pulling a stiff piece of

parchment from its interior. Griffin and Helen watched him, hoping for a clue to the envelope's contents based on Darius's expression.

"What does it say?" Helen finally asked.

"The Dictata has agreed to see justice served in the matter of Victor Alsorta and Raum Baranova." Darius continued in a distracted voice without raising his eyes. "It says the knowing murder of a Keeper is a capital offense that supersedes mortal law. Further, Raum is, technically, one of us and therefore still under the authority of the Dictata."

Darius lowered the paper. He made his way to the window and stood, gazing at the garden beyond.

"What happens now?" Helen asked.

She was surprised when Griffin answered. "Now we go after them."

The words fell like lead on her heart. She tried to stifle her alarm by focusing on practical matters.

"There is one thing I don't understand," Helen began. "How, exactly, will it be possible to bring Alsorta to the Dictata for justice? I cannot imagine he'll simply come when asked."

"He'll bow to the sickle like any other," Darius promised. "If it's enough to strike fear in the soulless wraiths and demons, it will be enough for Alsorta."

Helen thought of the sickle. Of its jagged teeth and razor-sharp edge. It was not hard to believe that even a man like Alsorta would succumb to fear when faced with such a weapon.

"All right, then," she said. "How will we know where to find them?"

"*We* won't find them anywhere," Griffin said, his voice tight. "Darius and I will go while you stay with Galizur and Anna."

Without thinking, Helen rose from her chair. "I'm not staying there while you risk your lives." She shook her head. "It's out of the question. This is my fight, too!"

Griffin stepped toward her, his back to his brother as he lowered his voice to a level only she could hear. "Don't be rash, Helen. It will be dangerous."

She put her hands on her hips, glowering at him. "Perhaps it wouldn't be if I were armed."

His eyes bore into hers. "You're not going."

"Try and stop me." She lifted her chin. "I'll follow you if I have to. I can only hope I remember how to jump and don't end up somewhere even more dangerous." This last bit she added just to make a point. She *would* be going, with or without their blessing. "Now, how will we know where to find Victor Alsorta?"

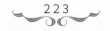

Darius's voice sounded from the window. "Galizur's note says he is working up schematics on Alsorta's home outside London. It appears that's where he's staying at present."

Griffin nodded slowly. "So we'll get the plans from Galizur and move on Alsorta tonight."

Helen heard the worry in his voice and wished she hadn't been the one to put it there, but there was no helping it. She had not mourned her parents properly. Had not even had time to see to their remains. This was, at least, something she could do.

And she would, despite the fear that coursed through her, even now.

"There's one thing we'll have to see to before going to Galizur's," Darius added.

Griffin turned to him. "What is that?"

"Helen is right," Darius said. "If she's to accompany us, she must be armed."

Helen didn't bother trying to hide her surprise.

"And if she's to be armed," Darius continued. "She'll have to prove herself capable of wielding a sickle, at the very minimum. Come, Helen. Let's retire to the ballroom, shall we?"

"I'll spar with her!" Helen heard Griffin's desperation and knew he was trying to protect her.

Darius shook his head, a knowing smile turning up the corners of his mouth.

"I think not. That would be no proof at all. Helen must prove her ability to stand with us." He leveled his gaze at his brother. "And she must prove it to someone whose personal affection will not force him to be gentle."

They made their way from the library to the ballroom in silence. Once there, Darius removed his sickle from his belt. She felt a morbid sense of satisfaction at the knowledge that Darius meant for them to spar with a real weapon instead of the training sickle she had used with Griffin.

Good. She would be forced to prove herself for real, as was only fair.

But when Darius ordered Griffin to give his sickle to Helen, Griffin refused, shaking his head.

"This is ridiculous," he said, crossing his arms over his chest and glaring at his brother. "I won't stand for it. Helen doesn't have to prove anything. To you or to anyone else."

Helen could no longer deny that there was a warm place in her heart for Griffin. Now it opened further, settling into all the emptiest places until it felt as if it had been part of her forever.

She stepped toward him, placing a hand on his arm and looking into his eyes. "Yes, I do. I have to prove it to you and Darius—and I must prove it to myself as well."

He looked away, as if by doing so he could avoid the truth in her eyes.

"Now, please, Griffin." She squeezed his arm until he met her gaze. "Give me your sickle."

It took almost a full minute for him to move, but when he did, it was to reach for the sickle swinging from his belt. His eyes did not leave hers as he handed it to her.

"It will be heavier than the training sickle," he said. "And unwieldy at first because of the sharp edge on one end and the jagged edge on the other."

She nodded, swallowing hard as she looked at the object in her palm. A smooth piece of curved metal, it didn't resemble a sickle at all. "How do I get it to open?"

"You will it open," he said, "as you willed yourself to travel in the light."

She had no sooner absorbed his instructions that the sickle sprung open with a clang. It clattered to the floor as Helen dropped it in surprise.

"We're off to a winning start." Darius said from behind her, his voice full of sarcasm.

She bent to pick up the sickle, careful not to graze either of the sharp ends. She turned to Darius.

"You might at least try to be supportive," she said.

Darius's expression grew serious. "The wraiths that hunt us will not be *supportive*," he sneered. "Victor Alsorta will not be supportive. Even your beloved Raum will not be supportive. Not when it comes to this battle."

In her peripheral vision, she saw Griffin tense at the mention of Raum. Willing herself to think of nothing but Darius and the test at hand, she forced her eyes to focus on him.

"You're right," she said. "Better that you should be as obnoxious as possible. That way, being killed at the hands of Victor Alsorta will be only a minor inconvenience by comparison."

Darius laughed aloud. "You're funny when you're terrified."

"I'm not as terrified as you might think. And certainly not of you or being hurt." She was surprised to find that it was true. That there were worse things than being ridiculed or even injured. "I've already lost everything. My only fear now is not being allowed to seek the vengeance that is mine."

She didn't expect his silence. His lack of witty retort. His eyes shone with something she could not define.

"Let's get on with it," he finally said, already moving toward

her with his own sickle drawn. "And don't think I'm going to go easy on you just because you're untrained."

"I wouldn't dream of it." She had to force herself not to take a step back as he approached. It was instinct to shy away from someone with a weapon. Especially when you knew that you were outmatched.

She breathed deeply as he came closer, seeing her father in one of their last fencing practices. Hearing his voice.

"Take a moment at the start of any match, Helen, to weigh your opponent's strengths and weaknesses. Take into consideration their height and weight, the speed with which they move, injuries that might be used to your advantage. Any seconds lost will be more than worthwhile in strategy gained."

"Yes, Father." She saw herself, as if watching the scene unfold in a dream, standing in trousers and holding a foil.

"What do you see?" he had asked, circling her.

"You are taller than me. And heavier."

He had nodded. "Continue."

"But also slower, I think." She hesitated, not wanting to offend him. "And the foil in your hand seems too loosely gripped, as if you have an injury and cannot keep hold of it very well."

He nodded. "Good, good. I wounded myself on the prun-

ing shears this morning. It makes holding the foil more difficult than usual. You can use that to your advantage."

She had nodded. "Yes, Father."

And then she was back in the ballroom at the Channing house, watching Darius circle her as her mind made furious notes. It registered in seconds the ready stance he maintained at all times. Ready, yes. But also stiff. Inflexible. Her agility would be a challenge for him to overcome. His lack of it, one of her only advantages. There was not much else to hold onto except perhaps her smaller size—something that could be both a disadvantage and an advantage depending on the circumstances.

"Ready?" Darius asked, looking into her eyes as they circled one another for the second or third time.

She nodded.

He lunged for her, lightning fast, tapping her sickle. She was so fearful of the jagged edges that she pulled her arm back, dropping her own weapon. It skidded to the floor with a clang.

"Pick it up." Darius stepped back, allowing her time. "I'm afraid my brother was too soft in his one training session with you. Rule number one," he intoned. "Fear will get you killed."

She bent forward, picking the sickle up and placing it firmly

in her hand before turning back to Darius. "Fear will get me killed," she repeated.

Darius stepped toward her, tapping her sickle once again. This time she was ready. She twisted her weapon away from his, pulling her arm back out of his reach.

He smiled wordlessly, lunging forward on one leg. This time, he tapped her sickle harder. The force of it vibrated all the way down her arm, though she managed to keep hold of it. Instinctually, she loosened her grip, recognizing the too-tight hold as another potential pitfall. When Darius hit her yet again, her arm moved a little with the contact, allowing for some give that prevented the impact from rattling her bones.

He nodded his approval, moving two steps closer. Helen forced herself not to retreat. Doing so always led to defeat, no matter the battle. This she had learned from her father.

This time, Darius surprised her by lunging forward in four quick bursts, twisting and turning, tapping her sickle with his along the edges, from the bottom, and finally in the "V" made by the meeting of the sharp and jagged edges. For a moment, their weapons locked, but when Darius let up the pressure, Helen stumbled back a couple of steps.

She should have known better. It was the same tactic she had used on Griffin.

She got her balance and waited for him to come at her again.

"Rule number two," Darius said. "Being on the defensive will get you killed. You must take the offensive if you hope to win any battle."

She knew this. She knew it from her father, though she had never mastered it. Being in possession of a weapon—or even the facsimile of a weapon as with the foil—made her nervous. She was not a creature of battle. She was a creature of observation.

But that would have to change.

She stepped toward him swiftly, ordering her mind to work instinctually so that her body would move the way she knew it could. The way it had been trained to do. She simply needed her fear out of the way.

She lunged for Darius, tapping his sickle with her own wherever she could, forcing notice of the jagged parts of the weapon from her mind. They didn't matter. What mattered was the whole.

And getting it out of Darius's hand.

It was not that easy. She parried with him for a couple of minutes, bending backward during one close call in which Darius's sickle came so close to her abdomen that it ripped a

clean tear in her blouse. Finally, he came at her in a series of quick steps and lightning-fast movements that left her no time to think. No time to be on the offensive. It was all she could do to react. To block his blows with her weapon when possible, the sharp edges of his sickle biting against her own until he got close enough to swipe the razor edge of his weapon against her forearm. She felt the sting of it all the way up her shoulder but didn't dare look down.

Darius took two steps back, his body suddenly still, his sickle retracting with a soft clink. His expression was neither remorseful nor concerned.

Griffin advanced on his brother, grabbing his shirt front and shoving him against the plush upholstered walls of the ballroom.

"I told you she had nothing to prove. But you did, didn't you, brother? You had to prove that you were stronger than an untrained female. One who hasn't even reached the age of Enlightenment." Helen heard Griffin's breath coming fast and hard. Saw the uncontrolled rage on his face.

Darius grinned. "Actually, I simply wanted to see if she had what it takes to be one of us. Proving I was stronger was just a bonus."

Griffin lifted his brother from the wall before shoving him back again, hard enough to make Darius's teeth rattle. "Maybe you and I will spar," he said through clenched teeth. "See if you can manage fighting someone of your own size and experience."

Darius chuckled. "Relax, brother. It was necessary to see if she would bleed for us, as we may bleed for her. And look." His eyes moved to Helen even as his body remained imprisoned by Griffin's hands. "She will."

Griffin's eyes didn't leave his brother's face. "If you're not very, very careful, you will be the one to bleed."

Darius didn't answer. The silence between them was so ominous that it shook Helen into action. She stepped toward the brothers.

"Griffin, stop it. Darius is right. He had to know. You both did." She shook her head, looking down at the blood leaking down her arm. "Now you do. And so do I."

Griffin's eyes followed hers to the rivulets of blood dripping onto the floor. He let his brother go, stepping toward Helen as Darius brushed at the wrinkles in his shirt. When he looked up to meet Helen's eyes, he smiled.

"Not bad," he said. "You're still holding your sickle."

Helen looked at her hand, hanging at her side, and was surprised to find that he was right. The sickle was still in her palm despite the injury she'd sustained.

Looking up to meet Darius's gaze, she had the sudden urge to say thank you. For the first time since she had been spirited into the walls of her chamber, she believed that maybe, just maybe, she had the strength to do what must be done.

But the words didn't come, and she allowed Griffin to take her gently by the elbow. He led her from the room, one step closer to whatever the night would bring.

TWENTY-TWO

Hold still. This may hurt a bit."

Griffin knelt before her on the floor of her chamber. He had settled her on the dressing table chair and left the room, returning with a bowl of warm water and what looked to be bandages tucked under his arm.

He reached for her hand, turning it over to expose the soft flesh on the underside of her forearm. Her skin tingled at the touch of his warm fingers. She tried telling herself it was only her injury and the shock of it, but when his eyes met hers, she knew there was no lying to herself.

Not anymore.

Even with her bleeding arm in his hand, there was no denying the feeling rising from her stomach all the way through her body and into her cheeks until she felt sure her face was aflame with it. She had never been with a man in such close proximity and with as much intimacy as with Griffin these past days. And yet she knew the sensation for the desire it was, as if it had been a part of her since the beginning of time and had only been lying in wait for Griffin's touch.

He bent his head to her arm, slowly unraveling the strips of cloth he had tied there to staunch the bleeding while he went in search of supplies. His fingers were gentle against her skin. They soothed the ragged edges of her pain, even when the cloth stuck and had to be pulled loose. When her arm was at last free of the cloth, he positioned her arm over the bowl.

"Can you lean forward a bit?" he asked.

She did, and he reached down with his free hand, pulling a dripping cloth from the bowl.

"This will hurt less than rubbing, I think." Holding the cloth over the gash in her arm, he squeezed, letting the water spill over the cut.

She jumped a little.

He looked into her eyes. "Does it hurt?"

She shook her head. "Not really. I think I simply thought it would."

He nodded, repeating the action until her arm was clean. The wound still dripped blood, but at a much slower pace than it had before. He rested her arm across his knee as he unraveled the clean bandages.

"I don't want to soil your trousers," she protested.

"Nonsense." He shook his head. "They can be cleaned. And we're almost done."

Lifting her arm with the utmost care, he began coiling the bandage around it. She tried not to flinch when the first layer of cloth came to rest against the cut. She could see how careful he was being, how much he didn't want to hurt her, and she sat quietly as he wrapped her arm until there was no trace of blood.

Setting the unused bandages aside, he looked up at her.

"There. I think that should do it," he said. "How does it feel?"

She looked down at the arm. "Good, I think. Well, as good as can be expected."

Lifting the basin of water, he rose from the floor. His face was tight, his expression so closed she had no idea what he was thinking. He placed the bowl of water on the washstand against the wall, rinsing his own hands in the basin that was always full in her chamber.

The sight of his strong back and broad shoulders hunched over the washstand caused an unexpected tide of tenderness

to rise within her. There was blood on his shirtsleeve. He looked suddenly weary and in need of care himself.

She stood, crossing the room with no real idea of her intentions. When she came within two feet of his back, he grew very still, as if he heard her approach and was afraid to scare her away. For a moment, she was frozen with indecision. There was a line between them now. She could almost see it pulsing in the air. Once it was crossed, nothing would ever be the same again.

She stepped forward, placing a hand carefully on his back.

"Thank you." She hesitated before continuing. "I'm . . . I'm sorry for all the trouble."

He turned slowly until he was facing her, his body only inches from her own.

"You're no trouble, Helen." His voice was deep and low.

Her eyes dropped to the front of his chest. She had not noticed the blood there before, but now she saw that it was not just on his sleeve, but on his shirt front as well. A small triangle of smooth flesh was visible near his collarbone. She could see a smudge of her blood on his skin.

She didn't even think about reaching forward.

"I've bled on you," she said as her fingers grazed the fabric of his shirt. "It will stain."

He lowered his eyes to her fingers, and she thought she heard him suck in his breath as she began undoing the buttons.

Reaching down, he covered her hands with his, stilling them. "It's not necessary."

She shook off his hands, continuing the task of unbuttoning his shirt. "Don't be silly. You've played nursemaid to me. Let me help you now, Griffin. It's the least I can do."

She did not say what she now knew; that she didn't want to stop. That she relished the feel of his chest under her hand and could not have stopped if she tried.

He nodded, saying no more as she finished the last button.

"Turn," she said softly.

He turned toward the basin, offering her his back, and she slid the linen from his shoulders. His muscled back was revealed a little at a time, the tattoo she had seen in his chamber becoming visible bit by bit until she held the shirt in her hands.

The image was breathtaking. It was the same symbol she had seen on Galizur's strange screen, though this one was elaborately rendered in deep blues, greens, and purples. Her fingers moved unbidden toward it. Griffin's body stiffened as she traced the circles that overlapped across the sinew of his back.

"It's . . . It's breathtaking," she whispered. "It's the Flower of Life, isn't it?"

He nodded without speaking.

"How long have you had it?" she asked, her fingers continuing their journey across his skin, pausing atop places where the circles seemed to form smaller, abstract flowers. The image on Galizur's screen had been cold, scientific. But somehow on Griffin's back the symbol was transformed into something strong and beautiful. His skin was warm as she tracked the design down the length of his spine, her fingertips working their way outward to the place where the circles disappeared beneath the waistband of his trousers.

He cleared his throat. "Since the death of my parents. Darius and I did it to remind us."

Her fingers stopped moving at the base of his spine, still resting against his skin. "Remind you of what?"

Turning, he caught her fingers in his hand as if her touch was painful. "That we are still and always will be connected to our parents. To one another. To the other Keepers and to the people of this world we all inhabit."

"It's a lovely reminder. And true." She reached beyond him for the wet cloth and began rubbing gently at the blood on his skin.

"Do you mind?" he asked suddenly.

"Mind what?"

"Being one of the Keepers."

She thought about the question. She had lost everything because of her role, unbeknownst as it had been, in the Alliance. And yet her parents had trained her for the position, had obviously wanted her to assume it. To shun it would be to dishonor them, to say nothing of her attachment to Griffin and Anna and even, in some strange way, to Darius.

"No," she finally said. "Not if it means I'm connected to my parents. And to you."

He caught her gaze and all at once, she was lost in the green-gold sea of his eyes. He shook his head suddenly as if angry.

"What is it?"

"I should never have let Darius challenge you. I know how much it means to you to be armed. I thought he would engage in a little harmless sparring and you would have your weapon. I had no idea he would take it as far as he did."

She gave him a small smile. "I meant what I said in the ballroom, Griffin. You had to know you could count on me, and while I certainly proved myself an unskilled fighter, at least I know I'm not a coward."

Surprise touched his face. "A coward? Why would you say such a thing? Why would you even think it?"

She looked away. "I've never stood up for anything. Not really."

"You've never had cause to until now," he said.

But I have, she thought. *I had both cause and opportunity when I was alone with Raum.*

"Yes, because I've been nothing but a coddled child," she said instead, her words full of bitterness.

"You've suffered more than most." His voice was gentle. "We all have. Throughout history, most of the Keepers have lived sheltered childhoods before taking their place among the others and living in obscurity until the task was passed on to another generation. You haven't even reached Enlightenment, and look at all you've suffered."

"It doesn't count," she said stubbornly. "Not really. Not until I actually do something. And today, for the first time, I felt like I might be able to do just that. Like I might be able to make a difference instead of standing by while everyone else makes sacrifices."

"Helen." Something in his voice made her look into his eyes. "I wish you could see what I see."

"And what is that?" she whispered.

He took the cloth from her hand, placing it on the wash-stand, his eyes never leaving hers. "Someone who is brave and intelligent and true."

"Yes?" Her breath caught in her throat.

"Yes." His hands traced the fine bones of her cheek. They were so close she could feel the warmth of his breath on her face. "And beautiful."

"You . . . You think I'm beautiful?" She had never thought of herself as beautiful before. Had never even thought to wonder about it. Now she felt the heat rise within her at the knowl-edge that Griffin thought so.

His eyes darkened as he looked down at her. "The most beautiful thing I've ever seen."

She could find nothing to say as his hand slid from her face to the curve of her neck, his fingers sliding into the waves that had come loose during her fight with Darius. The distance between them closed further, filling up with their bodies as they moved together. When he lowered his face to hers, she leaned up and met him halfway.

At first, his lips lingered gently on hers. She wasn't sure what to do. What came next. But it didn't matter. Even this was enough, and she stood as still as she could, not wanting the moment to end. Wanting his mouth on hers forever. Then the passion between them erupted, and all at once, his mouth opened on hers and she fell into the warmth of his kiss.

The floor dropped out from beneath her feet, sending her spinning into a black abyss where there was only Griffin. Only him and his mouth and their bodies molded together. She lost all track of time as his kiss transported her to a place where there was no death, no loss, no Raum. It was not until Griffin's lips left hers that she realized she had pressed herself shamelessly against him. But even this realization was a whisper through the desire that was still thrumming through her veins.

They didn't move. His fingers were still entwined in her hair, his breath coming fast and heavy as he looked down at her, his eyes dark with desire.

"This will complicate things," he said.

"Yes." She nodded. "Darius won't be pleased."

"Whether or not Darius is pleased doesn't matter." Griffin's voice took on a hard edge, and for a moment, he almost sounded like his brother. "He has what he needs. He always has. Now . . ." he began.

"Yes?" she prompted.

"I need you," he said.

TWENTY-THREE

They met in the library to go over the schematics delivered by Galizur's messenger boy.

"All right?" Darius asked, glancing distractedly at her arm.

"Right as rain." She did not tell him that the gash throbbed every time she so much as moved a muscle.

He nodded in reply, his eyes shifting to Griffin, standing at her side. An imperceptible shift occurred behind the armor of Darius's face. An appraising, as if he could sense that something had changed between Helen and Griffin in the two hours since the exercise in the ballroom.

Griffin's mouth was set in a thin line. She had only seen the expression on his face a couple of times, but she already knew what it meant. Griffin was prepared to battle his brother, whatever the cost.

A moment later, Darius turned his attention to a large roll of paper sitting atop the desk.

"These are the plans for Victor Alsorta's manor house outside the city. We need to go over them until we know every inch of the grounds and every way in and out of the house. That's where you come in, brother."

Helen looked up in question.

"Griffin is something of an expert at reading drawings like this. Architectural, engineering . . ." He shrugged. "My brother can read them all."

Griffin said nothing as Darius unrolled the paper, spreading it across the surface of the desk and using odd objects to hold down its curling corners. Helen and Griffin leaned in, taking in the obvious markings of the house and its grounds.

"The first thing we need is a way in and a way out. A couple of backups on both ends wouldn't hurt, either." Darius placed a fingertip on a circular marking on the paper. From the looks of it, the area was some distance from the grounds. Darius continued. "There is a tunnel entrance just inside the gates connecting the house to the sewage tunnels of London. If we enter the tunnels here—"

"Excuse me," Helen interrupted. "Did you say sewage tunnels?"

Darius grinned. "That I did, Princess."

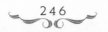

Helen took a deep breath. "Why can't we jump?"

"Because according to the schematics of the surrounding roads and grounds, there aren't any streetlights near the house. And even if there were, I'm not sure we could find a way over the fence."

"Fine," she sighed, trying not to envision the tunnels in her mind. It would do no good to think about them now. "The tunnels it is."

Darius nodded. "It's about five miles to this exit point. If we hurry and don't encounter any trouble along the way—"

"What sort of trouble would we encounter?" It had never occurred to Helen that they might encounter trouble even before arriving at Victor's estate.

There was no hiding the exasperation in Darius's eyes when he answered. "Wraiths, demons, rats, thieves. Anything of that sort."

Helen nodded, trying not to panic. "Right."

Darius's gaze lingered on hers for a moment before he continued, as if he wanted to make sure she wasn't going to interrupt him again. "Barring any trouble, we should be able to make the trip on foot in about two hours."

"And then what?" Helen asked.

"We come up here." Griffin tapped the circle and began tracing a line from it toward the house. "Then we make our way up the path to the house. It should be dark and easy to manage without being seen."

"What about guards?" Darius asked. "Does the schematic show where they're posted?"

"Here, here, and here." Griffin tapped three sets of Xs on the map. One was at the gate, one at the front of the house, and one at the rear.

Darius narrowed his eyes. "Seems a little light for a man of Alsorta's position."

"These are just the ones we know about," Griffin said. "There are almost certainly others inside."

"What about the guards at the gate?" Helen asked. "They look to be close to our entrance point."

"Not as close as they look on paper," Griffin said. "But, yes. We'll have to be quiet and careful when we make our ascent from the tunnels until we get our bearings."

Helen's mind was working in pictures. She could see the grounds, the tree-lined drive depicted in the plans spread out on top of the desk. She envisioned the imposing stone house in the distance, though she had no real idea what it would look like once they got there. It didn't matter. Her mind simply needed a placeholder for everything so it could do the work of calculating their options.

"All right," Helen said. "So we make it out of the tunnels without being seen. Then what? We sneak our way up the pathway and into the house?"

"That's right." Griffin agreed. "There's a dark side to the house here." He tapped the grounds to the right of the house, and Helen could see a thick patch of diagonal lines drawn in close to the building. "The trees come almost all the way up to the house and there's only one small light near the front. If we use the wooded area to skirt the more open grounds, waiting to move in closer until we get around to this side, we should be able to find a way in from there."

"Should?" Darius raised his eyebrows at his brother.

Griffin shrugged with a smile. "It's the best we can do."

Darius dropped his eyes, scanning the center of the schematic. "How will we know where he is once we're in the house?"

"We won't," Griffin said simply. "He could be anywhere. And as you can see, it's a rather large house. But Galizur has confirmed that he's in residence. The rest is up to us."

The room grew silent as they stared at the plans spread out in front of them.

"When do we leave?" Helen finally asked.

"Nine o'clock," Darius said. "It will be fully dark by then

and easier to slip into the tunnels unnoticed. Until then, it would be wise to rest and prepare. It will be a long night."

She said good-bye to Griffin with a chaste kiss at the door to her chamber, and though they did not linger as they had before, Helen felt herself dissolving once again into his embrace. This time, it was she who pulled away. It would be too easy to lose herself in the feel of his mouth on hers. The press of his body against her own.

And now was not the time for distraction.

They agreed to meet in the hall just before nine o'clock, and Helen closed the door resolutely behind her. She was halfway into the room when she heard a voice from the shadows in the corner.

"That was touching."

"Oh, my goodness!" She nearly jumped out of her skin.

"I hope you'll forgive my unconventional entrance." The voice was masculine, with a tinge of wry humor. "I didn't think my presence would be welcome through the front door."

She peered into the shadows, the smudge of darkness in the wing chair finally clarifying.

"Raum?"

He rose, stepping toward her. "The one and only."

She took a step back, too many thoughts and possibilities running through her mind. She gave only passing consideration to screaming or running for help. Raum would be gone by the time Darius or Griffin arrived. And besides, he had helped her, in a manner of speaking, discover the identity of Victor Alsorta. Or had opened her eyes to it, at least.

"Your 'unconventional' entrance hardly excuses you." She continued into the room, stopping at the small sofa in front of the firebox to remove her boots. "I think it's safe to say you aren't welcome through any door—or window—in the Channing house."

"It's not surprising." He stopped near the bed. "I don't seem to be welcome anywhere anymore. Even those few places that once offered me solace."

His sarcasm was steeped in sadness. Helen looked at him, trying to see beyond the rough exterior. "What do you mean?"

He laughed a little. "Let's just say that my employer has not been pleased with my work of late."

"Alsorta?"

He waved away the question. "It doesn't matter. I was alone long before I came to know Alsorta. I'm no stranger to isolation."

His words were not a ploy for sympathy. There was not

martyrdom in them. They were instead cavalier, and for one fleeting moment she understood all that keeping her alive had cost him.

She took a deep breath, pushing aside the sympathy that threatened to bubble to the surface.

"What are you doing here, Raum?"

"I heard you figured out Alsorta's part in the killing of your parents."

His mention of her parents' death caused her to feel their loss anew. She swallowed against it. "How do you know that?"

He wandered to her dressing table, lifting from its surface a jar of face powder and holding it up to the light for inspection as if it were a foreign object. "I hear many things."

His knowledge of their discovery made her blood run cold. "Because of Alsorta?"

He laughed, setting the powder back on the dressing table. "Hardly. Alsorta only knows what money can buy. There's greater knowledge which cannot be had for any price."

She tried to decipher the cryptic words as Raum picked up a vial of her perfume, squeezing the bulb and spraying it into the air. He closed his eyes. "This smells like you."

She blushed, crossing her arms over her bosom as if to

defend herself from the words. "How do you know what I smell like?"

He opened his eyes slowly, as if reluctant to return from a pleasant dream. "I don't know. I simply do."

The statement sat between them in the moment before Helen gathered her wits enough to speak yet again.

"You should leave. I've let you stay too long already, and for no good cause. I should call Darius and Griffin right now. You deserve whatever is coming to you for what you've done to our families."

His expression darkened. He turned to the window. "I'm sorry, Helen. I already told you; I didn't know it was you. Didn't even know you were one of them."

She stalked toward him, stopping a few feet away. She relished the anger sparked by his words. She wanted—needed— to feel something. Anger was better than nothing at all, and certainly better than the sorrow that threatened to overtake her if she thought too long and hard about all she had lost.

"The fact that you would even say such a thing only validates how despicable you really are." She practically spat the words at him.

It took him a few seconds to answer. "You think I'm despicable?"

"What would you call it? You've murdered people—families, children—for your own personal gain."

His shoulders stiffened. "Not just for my gain. And not the way you think. It isn't as if I was paid."

She shook her head. "I don't understand."

"I told you; I need something." He didn't turn as he spoke. "Something Alsorta promised me."

And all at once, Helen knew. She saw Raum as a little boy, handing her the key in the garden. She heard Galizur, speaking in the depths of the laboratory, the Terrenious Orb turning its movements laborious and slow.

Have you heard of the Lost Keeper?

When the Dictata got wind of it, the Baranovas were banished from the Alliance. Andrei Baranova and his wife both committed suicide a short time later.

She stepped closer to Raum, still facing the wall. "You want access to the records."

Raum turned to meet her eyes. And now, she saw the anguish there laid bare. "Alsorta promised that if I found the key and brought it to him, he would allow me into the records so that I could change the past."

"You want to bring your parents back." She heard the wonder in her own voice. "But that's . . . That's mad."

His face flushed with anger. "Spoken as someone who was not orphaned at the age of sixteen."

She stomped toward him, stopping only when she came within inches of his body. "Spoken as someone who was orphaned days ago. By *you*."

"You don't understand."

"Yes," she said. "I do. I understand that you sought to ease your own pain, whatever it took. Even murder. Even bringing that pain upon others."

She saw his throat move, as if swallowing her words was painful. "It's not that simple."

"It *is,* Raum." She looked into his eyes. "It is."

"What would you have done?" He said suddenly. "What would you do now? If there were a way to bring your parents back—to right my wrong—would you do it? Would you lie to do it? Would you kill to do it?"

He seemed to look into her very soul in the moment before she turned away, making her way to the firebox, his questions ringing in her mind. She didn't want to think about the answers. Didn't want to imagine herself in Raum's shoes. Most of all, she did not want to find reason for the sympathy she had felt for him almost all along.

"I'd like you to leave now," she said quietly.

At first, she thought he had left. That he had gone through the window the way he came without another word. But then she felt the touch of his hands on her shoulders. She didn't flinch. As if his touching her were the most natural thing in the world.

"I'm sorry, Helen. I . . ." She heard him suck in his breath behind her as if drawing strength from the air in the room. "Now I have more than one reason to wish I could go back."

The admission sent a wave of regret crashing through her body.

"Will I ever see you again?"

He didn't answer right away. She wondered if she had gone too far. If she had pushed the limits of their strange acquaintance beyond that which even Raum could abide. But then he spoke, his voice soft.

"If you need me, I'll be there."

She turned in time to see him sitting in the window frame, his legs dangling out-of-doors as he prepared to lower himself to the ground.

"And Helen?" He looked back at her.

She swallowed, steadying her voice. "Yes?"

"Watch out for the dogs."

TWENTY-FOUR

It was just after five o'clock, and the afternoon was as gray as ever. Helen didn't know how much light was required to jump, but it did not seem advisable to attempt it in the dim glow of the table lamp. Especially since she'd only jumped on her own once before and that was with Griffin's help.

She had less than four hours to see to her errand. Four hours until Griffin would expect her in the hallway outside her chamber.

She hoped it would be enough.

The trip to Galizur's was a necessary precaution. She had watched the streets after Raum's departure, committing to memory all that Griffin had told her about jumping and hoping for the best.

By the time the lamps were finally lit, darkness was already hovering, waiting for its turn to take over London. Helen waited until the streets were clear before lifting her foot over the windowsill. She would not have attempted it had she not seen it used recently for the very same purpose. She may not be as quick on her feet as Raum, but if he could do it, so could she.

That the window faced the home next door rather than the street was not surprising. Raum had obviously chosen the entrance—and exit—point for its discreet location. Helen was grateful for it as she straddled the windowsill, throwing both her legs over before she had a chance to change her mind. She sat there a moment with her legs hanging out the window, trying to calm the unruly gallop of her heart. Then, she gripped the ledge with both hands and dared a look down.

It only took a moment to spot Raum's method. An elaborate stone molding, at least six inches thick, seemed to run the length of the building just below the sill. She thought back, imagining the front of the building as if she were still standing in front of it the first night of her arrival. She could see it, as clearly as if it were before her now. And yes, above the front door, an ornate peak crafted of stone or marble.

If she shuffled along the molding to the front, she could hold onto the top of the peak, sliding down to the point where she could safely let go and land on her feet.

Or this is what she hoped, at least.

It made her nervous to attempt such a feat where any pass-erby could look up and see her there, hanging like a common thief. But Raum had managed it and so would she.

Sliding carefully off the windowsill, she moved slowly until her feet came to rest on something solid. For one terrifying moment, she hung by her elbows, bent at an almost-painful angle behind her as she attempted to gauge exactly how solid the placement of her feet was. Finally, her hesitation left her by force. Her arms began to shake, and she let go, pressing herself back against the cold stone of the house as she forced her breathing steady. The sooner she got to the front, the sooner she could get back on solid ground.

Shuffling along the length of the building, she stopped for a minute when she reached the corner. The molding was wider here, a scrolled cornice set into the right angle of the building. It gave her a place to catch her breath, and she lifted her head, looking toward the front door and trying to gauge its distance. Thankfully, it was growing smaller.

When she at last reached the decorative molding that topped the massive doorway, she spent only a few seconds looking it over and plotting strategy. The ground was about eight feet below. Not as near as she'd hoped, but it would have to do.

Grasping the top of the molding, she dropped her belly flat against one side of the peak before letting go. The slide, which was faster than she'd expected, took her by surprise, and she let out a small cry as she tried to slow her progress enough to give herself time to prepare for impact.

The ground came upon her too fast. She hit it hard, almost stumbling down the stairs before she placed a hand against the stone facade of the house to regain her balance.

It had all been clumsier and louder than she'd planned. She half expected Darius or Griffin to open the door and inquire about the noise. No one came, and a moment later, she brushed herself off and made her way down the steps to the street below.

The light they usually used for jumping was there, but she walked past it, looking for one less obvious. She had no idea how the brothers spent their time when they weren't fighting wraiths and seeking justice, but with so much time before their rendezvous, it was entirely possible one or both of them would leave the house, to say nothing of the passersby that still walked the street. Observing the people walking to and fro, she understood why Darius and Griffin preferred jumping so late. It was far more uncommon to see people about at midnight than it was at five o' clock in the evening.

She continued down the street until she came to an alley. It stretched, dark and mysterious, to the street one block over. She couldn't make out any light within it, but she noted a streetlamp at the end. Thanks to the many times she and Father had strolled after tea and her uncanny knack for remembering things, she could see the streets surrounding the Channing house as clearly as if she were looking at a map. She saw where they intersected, ended, and where they ran past popular theaters and attractions. She saw it all and knew with certainty that the street at the other end of the alley was less populated than the one on which the Channing house stood.

Of course, it was still early. There was every possibility of pedestrians, even on the more deserted streets of London, but it was better than trying to jump where Darius or Griffin could see her should they decide to leave the house. And with no light in the alley itself, the odds of a wraith appearing were slim.

She stepped into the blackness. Almost instantly, everything in front of her disappeared. Glancing back at the street behind her, she was relieved to see light leaking from it. But here, in the alley, the darkness was total.

She took a step forward, willing her eyes to adjust to the total lack of light. A few steps in, she was surprised to find that they did. It was still dark, but now she could make out piles of rubbish along the walls of the building sheltering the alley. Her boots crunched on rock and the odd bit of trash as she made her way deeper into the alley. The sound of her own footsteps only highlighted her isolation, her vulnerability. She forced herself to continue even when she heard the rustling of small creatures nearby and saw their bodies creep and scuttle across the road. That they were likely simple rats was little consolation.

She was halfway to the other side when she noticed a weak yellow glow leaking from beyond a stack of wooden crates. Halting her forward motion, she listened, trying to place the source of the light and the possibility of others. But the alley remained quiet, and she continued, stepping more hesitantly when she came to the crates, wanting to be sure no one lurked in the light. She stopped at the edge, peering beyond the crates stacked halfway to the roof of the adjacent building.

It was some kind of lamp built into the wall, its flame licking around a broken, smoky glass cover. Obviously meant to illuminate the door set into the brick of the building, Helen couldn't imagine why anyone would choose to frequent a place where one had to gain entrance through such a desolate alley. She wasn't even tempted to use it to jump. The light was too weak, the location too dangerous, and she continued past it, almost screaming when a rustling near her feet revealed a bundle of rags much larger than a rat. The movement was followed by a slurred mutter and a groan. A vagrant, sleeping off too much drink.

She continued down the alley, anxious to put the light behind her. She was still some distance from the streetlamp that was her destination when she heard the strange but unmistakable rustling of air.

She froze, the breath catching in her lungs as fear coursed through her body. Instinct told her to run. To run and not look back no matter what.

But she couldn't.

She had to know, and she turned her head ever so slowly, gazing back at the broken lamp. The wraith was there, standing in the frail light, his fist closed around something Helen was sure was a sickle. She could see the silver shine of his teeth as he came toward her, his steps reverberating through the alley in a way her own had not.

She had nothing. No defense of any kind. The promised weapon that was a result of her exercise with Darius had not yet come. Helen had assumed it would be given to her before they made the trip to Victor Alsorta's. Which did her absolutely no good now.

Alone and unarmed, she was left with only one recourse.

Simply forcing her eyes from her pursuer took strength of will, as if not looking at him would make his presence more immediate, his pace quicker. But she did it. She pulled her eyes from his face and ran. Her footsteps beat against the ground as she flew toward the light at the end of the alley. It took effort not to look back. Not to check the progress of the thing giving her chase.

And he *was* giving her chase. She could hear his footfalls as he raced toward her. Her only hope was to reach the light before him with enough time to conjure herself into the light to Galizur's.

Would the wraith follow her there? Could he, given that he didn't know her destination?

The questions were fleeting, touching upon her mind like a leaf in the wind. In the inevitability of her actions, the answers didn't matter.

She was almost to the end of the alley. Could see the light from the streetlamp growing brighter and brighter with every step. She had a moment, one small sliver of hope when she thought she would make it. Then her foot caught a piece of rubbish and she went down, thrown to the pavement with the full weight of her body.

She lay there, sprawled across the pavement, half in and half out of the alley as the wraith came closer. Her mind was roaring both with the shock of her fall and the fear of her swiftly approaching pursuer, now at the end of the alley and looking down at her with a mixture of pleasure and disdain.

Afraid to take her eyes off him even for a moment, she scanned as much of the surrounding area as she could, looking for anything that would give her hope of escape. She found only one possibility. It was neither clever nor assured, but her mind could find no reason why it shouldn't work.

Griffin had not said standing was a requirement for jumping.

She took a deep breath, recalling everything Griffin had told her about traveling through the light. Then she pushed herself forward across the dirty ground, scrambling on her hands and knees toward the light, until she was close enough to throw herself into it.

The wraith was already moving when she closed her eyes,

imagining all the little pieces of her body and soul traveling through the energy of the light and landing under the streetlamp in front of Galizur's.

For a split second everything went quiet, and she wondered if she was already dead.

TWENTY-FIVE

"Y ou're a quick learner, to travel here so quickly under such conditions." Anna, her eyes worried, handed Helen a cup of tea. "Are you certain you're all right?"

Helen nodded. Her knees were scraped and she was fairly certain her heart was still beating too fast for its own good, but she was otherwise fine.

She had been surprised to find herself under the streetlamp in front of Galizur's, despite the fact that it had been her intended destination. When she realized she had made it, she raced up the stairs, banging with no thought to discretion. Anna had opened the door only moments later, as if she'd been expecting Helen all along.

Now, in the comfort of the parlor with a cup of hot tea by her side, Helen raised her gaze to Anna's. "How did you get to the door so quickly? I'd only knocked a moment before."

Anna smiled. "We have monitors in the laboratory. They project images of all the exterior entrances."

"There are other entrances?" She and the Channings had only ever come through the front.

Anna simply smiled, taking a sip of her tea without speaking.

Helen raised her eyebrows. "I see. You're not allowed to tell me."

Anna reached over and took her hands. "Our secrets are kept on your behalf, Helen. You must know this." She removed her hands and placed her teacup back on the tray. "Now, Father told me you and the Channings are making your way to Victor Alsorta's tonight. Your reason for being here—alone, no less—must be important."

Helen nodded. "We went over the schematics for the Alsorta estate today. They seem very thorough, but I believe they may have left something out."

Anna shook her head. "What is it?"

"Dogs," Helen said. "I think Victor has guard dogs."

Anna sat back in her chair, a look of concentration passing over her face. "Well, the plans do focus on the layout of the house and grounds, with the addition of the more obvious guards. I can see where dogs might be omitted from mention." She met Helen's eyes. "How did you find this out?"

Helen rose, walking to the firebox as if to warm her hands. In truth, she simply wanted to escape Anna's piercing gaze. She stared at the fire as she spoke.

"I'd rather not say."

There was a pause behind her as Anna considered her words. "All right," she finally said. "I take it you don't wish to tell Darius and Griffin about your source, either?"

Helen turned. "Not if it can be helped."

Anna sighed. "So be it. What can we do for you?"

"How are you with a knife?"

Helen turned to Galizur as he spoke, trying not to show her alarm. They had found him down in the laboratory, tinkering with his many tools and inventions. He had not seemed surprised to see Helen. She was beginning to wonder if he knew more than he was letting on.

"I don't like them," she said in answer. "I've never liked them."

Galizur's forehead was wrinkled as if she were speaking another language. "But you fence?"

She shook her head. "Not really. That is, Father was trying to teach me, but I'm afraid I've never been good at the more . . . physical aspects of my schooling. We've only ever sparred with a foil."

He rubbed the wiry hair at his chin. "Archery?" he asked hopefully.

She tipped her head, recalling her lessons with Father in the fields surrounding the country house. He'd told her all about Artemis, Goddess of the Hunt, and her golden bow and arrow. Helen was instantly smitten, seeing in the deity all the things she would never be.

"Moderately better." She paused. "But I wouldn't like to kill a dog, even one of Victor Alsorta's guard dogs."

Galizur laughed. "I'm not expecting you to kill it, my dear girl! How uncivilized! No." He shook his head, rising from the chair and making his way to one of the worktables against the wall. "Now, where in God's names did I put it . . . ?"

Helen's thoughts turned to Anna as he searched. She had left them to go upstairs after delivering Helen to her father. Helen couldn't help wondering what her new friend would think if she knew about her encounters with Raum. Would Anna consider her a traitor? Would she, in her devotion to Darius—to all the Keepers—think Helen disloyal for conversing with the man who had ordered their execution? And would it make any difference if she knew that Raum's motivation lay in the hope of saving his parents? Of turning back time so that they might choose a different course?

Helen still wasn't sure if it made a difference. The empty part of her, the part left barren by the loss of her parents, said no. Motivation didn't matter. The ends did not justify the means.

Raum's words echoed through her mind; *if there were a way to bring your parents back—to right my wrong—would you do it?*

The matter of right seemed less certain in such a context. It was a crime that her parents had been taken from her as they had. A crime that they had been murdered because of Helen's position as a Keeper. Would it, then, be wrong to bring them back? To use the records to restore that which was wrongfully destroyed?

She thought of Griffin. Of the anguish on his face as he'd talked about his parents, murdered on the street, a cold, metal key left in the palm of his dead mother's hand.

And there were others. Other families murdered so that Alsorta could gain access to the records. Other Keepers destroyed for one man's greed.

Would Helen bring them all back? Would it be enough to restore her sense of justice, or would there be an endless stream of wrongs to be righted?

She again saw her father's words, written in a letter she was destined to read only after he was dead.

Time—and all the events held therein—plays out as it must. We cannot impose our will on it.

Her father had thought her honorable. Had thought her strong enough to bear the demands of time and fate.

Which meant the answer to Raum's question was obvious. Her parents wouldn't want her to abuse the records in such a way. Not for them, not for anyone. Even in her anguish, she knew it was true.

Galizur's voice broke into her thoughts. "Ah! Here we are."

He made his way back across the room, holding a small pouch tied with string. Sitting next to her, he placed the pouch on top of the table and began untying the laces.

"They've not been field-tested. Not properly anyway." He opened the flaps of the pouch, exposing what looked to be five minuscule darts. "But they work here in the laboratory and I think they might just do the job."

"Darts?"

He pulled one from the pouch, avoiding the pointed end. "Not simply darts. Tranquilizer darts of my own design." He held one up to the light, giving Helen a better look as he touched the end. "Hidden in this part, here, is a small motor which allows the dart to move through the air with the power and force you would find in a much larger arrow expended by a typical bow."

"I don't understand," Helen said. "How will this help us with the dogs?"

He looked away from the miniature weapon, meeting her eyes as if surprised by the question. "Why, you will throw it at them, of course. As long as you hit your mark, it should take the animal down in less than five seconds."

"And it won't hurt them," she said softly.

"Not a bit." He pointed to the sharp tip of the dart. "The ends are covered in a sleep-inducing toxin. It's under a protective coating that dissolves only once the dart is deployed."

"You mean the darts will put the dogs to sleep?"

Galizur's forehead wrinkled as he considered the question. "It's a bit more than your average slumber, to be sure, but the point is small and should do no long-term harm to the animal." He hesitated. "Although, there is one important thing you must remember."

"What is it?"

He met her eyes with his own. "Don't leave any of the darts on Alsorta's premises. Once the dogs are down, retrieve the darts and return them to the pouch. Just be careful not to touch the ends once the dart has been released or you will experience firsthand symptoms of the chemical at its end."

"What symptoms?" She was equal parts fearful and fascinated.

Galizur held the dart close to his face, studying it with something like pride. "Oh, temporary paralysis at first. Then a deep sleep lasting approximately an hour depending on body weight."

"Temporary paralysis?" Her voice came out in a squeak.

He lowered the dart to the pouch. "You do want to capture Alsorta?"

She didn't even have to think about it. "I do. Of course, I do."

He nodded. "Well, then. You'll have to get around the dogs—if your source is, in fact, correct about them."

Helen's nod was reluctant. "But what if I can't hit the mark? My experience with anything requiring aim is minimal, and I have not exactly demonstrated a talent for it."

"Not to worry. I've built something into the model that I think will help." He stood. "Come. I'll show you."

She followed him to one of the other worktables. He set the pouch down, reaching for a pair of cloth mittens hanging from a hook. Then he turned the lever on a small iron box. Flames leaped from inside, and Helen jumped back.

"Goodness!" she said. "What on Earth is it?"

He lifted a pair of long-handled tongs from the table. "My work often requires the heating of metal and other compounds," he said, pushing the tongs into the fire. "Besides, I've found that it keeps the room toasty."

The tongs emerged a moment later with an orange-hot piece of metal in their grasp. Galizur placed it on the table atop a piece of silver fabric. Helen expected it to catch fire, but it didn't. Galizur set the tongs down and reached over with his gloved hands to wrap the piece of molten metal inside the cloth.

Picking it up as if it were nothing, he made his way across the room to a large muslin bag propped up in the corner. Helen watched, fascinated, as Galizur pushed the tiny bundle of fabric, still holding the hot metal, inside the bag. He turned and made his way back to Helen.

"It's just a bag of straw, but with the hot metal inside, I can show you how the darts work." He picked one of the darts up from the table, aimed at least two feet to the left of the muslin bag, and released the dart.

Instantly, Helen heard a tiny whir from within the dart. She watched with shock as the dart accelerated through the air—presumably due to the motor mentioned by Galizur— and hit the bag about a foot from the opening where Galizur had placed the hot metal.

She was still staring at it when Galizur spoke. "There. You see? Nothing to it."

"But you . . . How did you . . .Your aim . . ." She could not seem to formulate the question.

Galizur chuckled. "It was terrible, of course."

She turned to him. "How does it work?"

"I've been experimenting for years with a heat-seeking compound. Something that would be drawn to heat—like a moth to a flame." He smiled. "It seems I finally got it right."

She crossed to the bag, placing a hand near the spot where the dart still stuck out of the muslin. It was warm.

She turned back to Galizur. "Do you mean to say the dart will find its own target?"

"If that target has a heat signature—as all living animals do—then yes. It will find its target with one caveat." He paused. "If you are too close to the object and your aim is even more terrible than mine, the dart might not have time to make its way to the target. But as long as you aim somewhat close and with enough time for the dart to do its work, even someone with relatively poor aim should be able to find his— or her—mark."

She closed the remaining feet between them, holding out a hand. "May I?"

He smiled, reaching for another dart. "But, of course."

She spent the next thirty minutes practicing on the hay-stuffed bag in the corner. Even with her initial, shaky aim and a target that she could only assume was cooling, the dart found its mark every time. Galizur stood by, removing the darts after each throw so that Helen could use them again. Finally, he took all five darts back to the worktable and used a slim brush to paint their tips with an acrid concoction from inside a tiny pot. Once they were dry, he placed them carefully inside the pouch and handed them to her with solemn eyes.

"Thank you," she said with a smile. "I hope I won't have to use them. Hitting an inanimate object in the corner seems a bit easier than a moving target."

"Indeed." He nodded before crossing the room to a row of locked metal cabinets. He took a ring of keys from his pocket and bent to one of the drawers. The keys jingled against the metal, and she had to listen attentively to make out his next words. "There is one other thing I think you should have."

She walked toward him. "What is it?"

When he turned, his palm was closed around something she could not see. He came closer, holding out his hand. In it lay a bundle of cloth. She met his eyes.

"Is it for me?"

He nodded, pushing his hand closer toward her until she reached with hesitant fingers toward the fabric-encased object.

Lifting it from his palm, she was surprised at the weight of the hidden item. It felt cumbersome. Heavy in the way only something of great importance can be. She slowly peeled the fabric away from the center. When the object at last lay bare, she knew instantly what it was.

"Oh!" She could not keep the gasp from escaping her mouth. "It's lovely!"

"It was your grandmother's," Galizur said softly. "I asked the Scouts to search the remains of your house for one owned by your parents, but they weren't able to find anything. I thought this might be the next best thing."

Although closed, she knew it was a sickle. Its shell was crafted entirely of opal, and it glimmered with an iridescent shine that gave it a pink cast one moment, green the next, when she tipped her hand.

Galizur spoke. "It's very, very old, but I've kept it in perfect working condition. If you close your hand around it, the blade will engage with no more than a thought as long as you wear your pendant."

She transferred the cloth to her left hand, reaching for the sickle with her right. As soon as her palm closed around it,

the sickle opened, the blades glimmering menacingly from either side. When she looked down, the pendant emitted a soft blue glow at her throat.

"It's lovely." Her own voice was breathless with the power and beauty of it. "Are you certain it's all right for me to have it?"

Galizur smiled. "As the last surviving member of the Cartwright family, it is yours more than any other. Your blood tie to it will make it even stronger in your possession."

She looked up at him. "How do I close it?"

"The same way you open it." His voice was matter-of-fact. "Will it closed."

She looked down at it, telling it to close with her mind. It did.

"Thank you, Galizur." She smiled at him. "This means so much to me."

He nodded, his expression grave. "Do be careful, Helen. We cannot afford to lose a single one of you. More than that," he added, "I should hate to see it so."

Her heart swelled with emotion, but there was no time and no words so she didn't speak. She simply rose on her tiptoes, kissed his cheek, and turned to go.

TWENTY-SIX

She approached the journey back to the Channing house with trepidation. Jumping once hardly made her an expert, and she had no desire for another confrontation with a wraith. The sun had long since set, and although she could not be certain of the time, she knew it must be close to nine o'clock. She could not afford to be delayed.

Her fears were unfounded. She traveled from Galizur's streetlamp to one a block away from the Channings' without incident, appearing next to a young couple walking along the street. They looked over at her in surprise, and Helen stepped onto the walk, continuing down the road as if she had been there all along. Doubtless, they would tell themselves they simply hadn't noticed her there before.

Helen was almost to the house when she realized her mistake. In her eagerness to escape unnoticed, she had not planned a way back in. Approaching the forbidding stone facade, she gazed up at the point from which she'd dropped earlier in the evening. It was far too high to climb back up. In fact, the thought of having made the jump down from such a height caused her to question her sanity.

She stood in the shadows a moment, pondering her options. She didn't have a key, and knocking was hardly an option. Darius and Griffin would answer, of course, but then she would have to explain why she'd gone to Galizur's.

And if she had to explain why she'd gone, she'd have to explain how she knew about the dogs.

Taking in the many ground-floor windows, she wondered at the possibility that any of them would be open. She knew it was unlikely, but acknowledging her lack of other options, she began circling the house, eyeing the windows for one that might give her an opportunity to slip inside unnoticed.

She had made her way around the house without success and was preparing to investigate the back when she noticed a sliver of golden light shining along the door frame to the kitchen. Ascending the steps, she realized that the door was open a crack. She looked down, noting the nearly empty dish of cream that sat on the stoop.

She pushed open the door, relieved that it didn't creak on its hinges, and shut it quietly behind her. Making her way through the kitchen, she headed down the hall toward the glow of light cast on the floor from inside the library.

At first, she thought the room empty. A recently stoked fire crackled in the firebox, but there was otherwise no sign of life. Then she heard a soft hum from behind and, turning to follow the sound, found Griffin asleep on the sofa with a black-and-white ball of fur on his chest.

Lowering herself carefully next to him, she could not keep the smile from rising to her lips. After days of seeing Griffin's face taut with worry, it was startling to see him in repose, his expression one of utter serenity as he slept with the kitten on his chest. She reached out to stroke the soft space between the animal's ears.

"So you're the intruder, then," she said softly.

Griffin's eyes opened at the sound of her voice. For a moment, he was caught in the haze of sleep, his face still at peace. Then, a furrow appeared between his eyebrows.

"Is everything all right?" he asked. "What's happening?"

Helen smiled, reaching over on impulse to brush a stray lock of hair from his forehead. "Nothing. It's nearly nine o'clock. How long have you been sleeping?"

"I have no idea." He yawned, noting the kitten on his chest. "How did he . . ."

"I found the back door open a crack. Someone must have left it unlatched. He's a clever little thing, isn't he?"

She leaned in to drop a kiss on the kitten's soft head, reaching to move him from Griffin's chest. He reached for her hand, stopping her.

"And what about me?" he asked, his eyes burning into hers.

"What about you?"

"Am I not clever enough for a kiss?" His voice was gruff.

She favored him with a shy smile. "You're more than clever enough, Griffin Channing."

Leaning toward him, she lowered her mouth to his. His lips were warm and soft on hers. Heat moved between them, rising through her body in the moment before the cat meowed softly in protest.

Laughter rumbled through Griffin's body. She felt the vibration of it in her own.

"Well, well."

The words, spoken from the doorway, startled her. She sat up quickly, the kitten jumping to the floor and disappearing around the corner of the sofa in one fluid motion.

Darius strode into the room. "I found a sickle for you, Helen." He held out a hand. "It's old, but it will do the job should you require it."

Panic clutched at Helen's throat. She had not thought to explain her grandmother's sickle to Darius and Griffin.

"Well?" Darius was impatient now. "Take it."

"I . . . uh . . . I don't need it," she said, frantically searching her mind for a plausible explanation for the weapon now in her possession.

Darius took a deep breath. "You want a sickle, you don't want a sickle. Which is it?"

"Galizur sent one over." She lifted the opalescent weapon from her bag. "This one."

"Galizur?" Griffin shook his head next to her, the lazy sleep gone from his face as if it had never been there at all.

Helen nodded. "It came with a note that said he had a feeling I might need it." The lie rolled smoothly off her tongue. She did not have time to question its source. "It was my grandmother's."

Darius's eyes dropped to the weapon in her hand. "May I?"

She handed it to him carefully, her heart in her throat.

He studied the exterior for a moment before it clanged open. There was awe on his eyes. "This was your grandmother's?"

"According to Galizur," she said.

Darius raised his eyebrows, whistling. "Your grandmother must have been quite a woman."

Helen's eyes dropped back to the weapon. "Why is that?"

"That is no ordinary sickle," Griffin said. "It's old. Much older than any I've ever seen."

She shrugged. "So?"

"It was crafted in the traditional way, by the ancient ones. It will be more powerful than a newer one. It must have been in your family for centuries," Darius said. He met her eyes, handing the sickle back to her as gingerly as she'd given it to him. "You're lucky to have it."

There was new respect in his voice. She did not care that it came through her association with her grandmother's weapon. She would take Darius's regard where she could.

"Thank you." It was all she could think of to say.

Darius nodded. His face was grim as he turned his attention to her and Griffin.

"I hope you're both well rested," he said. "It's time."

They entered the tunnels a couple of blocks from the house. The street was empty when Griffin bent to lift a large wooden disk from the road.

"I'll go first," he said. "Helen, you follow me down and Darius will come last, pulling the cover back over the entrance."

Staring into the darkness below, she couldn't find her voice to answer.

"Helen." Griffin's voice commanded her attention. She met his eyes. "It will be all right. I'll be at the bottom when you get there."

She could only nod as he began descending. She could not see beyond the mouth of the opening, but from the way Griffin lowered himself into the darkness, she gathered there was a ladder of some kind built into the wall of the tunnel entrance. A few minutes later, a clear blue light trickled from the inky depths of the tunnel.

Griffin's voice was soft. "You can come down now."

She swallowed hard, jumping as a hand closed around one of her own. When she turned, she was surprised to see Darius looking at her with something that wasn't sarcasm or annoyance.

"It will be fine. We've walked these tunnels many times."

She nodded, and he moved with her to the opening, holding onto both of her hands as she lowered one foot into the tunnel. She felt surprisingly secure. Darius's hands were like iron, unmoving on her own. Despite their earlier disagree-ments, she somehow knew he would not let her go.

Feeling around with the toe of her boot, she was begin-ning to despair of ever finding the first rung when her foot hit something hard. She moved her leg back in that direction until her foot felt the object again. Once her first foot was firmly in place, she took a deep breath, placing her other one next to it.

Darius held onto her hands as she stepped down three more rungs. Finally, her face was level with the ground. Unless she planned on pulling Darius in after her, she would have to let go.

"See you at the bottom, Princess." There was uncommon warmth in Darius's voice as he let go of her hands one at a time, giving her a chance to grab hold of the pavement as she took another step.

The world above disappeared from view. She was in a black abyss. Even the blue light from below was absent now, her eyes trained on the walls of the tunnel as she descended. The rungs were slippery underfoot. Twice, she lost purchase, her boots sliding from the rung until she was forced to grasp the ones above her even more tightly, her heart beating ferociously while she steadied herself for the continuing climb.

For a while, it seemed that the descent would go on and

on. There was no time, only the expanding blackness. She felt sure that if she were to emerge on the road once again, she would find that the darkness had filled up every corner of the world she had once known.

Then, from a few feet below, came Griffin's voice.

"You're almost there, Helen. I can see you."

Locked in the effort of her downward climb, she hadn't noticed that the light was visible again. It shone white against the wall in front of her, illuminating the mud and rocks that lay between the tunnels and the streets of London above. The light became stronger as she took three more steps down.

"I've got you." The light bounced around the walls as she felt Griffin's hands close around her waist. "You're only two steps from the bottom."

She took the last steps, practically fainting with relief when she felt the ground beneath her boots. A dank, putrid smell assaulted her and she fought a gag.

"It's awful, isn't it?" Griffin stood only inches away, his face oddly distorted in the light from his pendant bouncing off the walls of the tunnel. "Don't worry. You'll get used to it."

"Lovely." She barely managed to choke out the words.

Griffin aimed the light upward, calling to Darius.

"She's on the ground, Darius. Come on down."

Darius's descent seemed to take only seconds. Helen wondered if her own climb into the tunnel had been as ponderous and lengthy as it had seemed or if it was only a product of her fear. As Darius, still six feet up, jumped gracefully to the ground without so much as a bead of sweat on his brow, she hoped it was the latter.

"Thanks for the light, brother." Darius moved past them, his pendant in hand, lighting their way into the emptiness beyond.

Griffin tipped his head. "Go ahead. I'll be right behind you."

Helen did not want to walk alone, even with Darius in front and Griffin in back. She wanted a living, breathing body beside her. Something to remind her that they were still alive and not trapped in some kind of purgatory beneath the real world.

It was not so much that the tunnel was small. In fact, the ceiling rose quite far above them, the walls on either side bowing away from her in a great arc. But its barrel shape made it seem as if she were seeing everything through Mother's opera glasses. As if there were no sides at all, only Darius's back, appearing as just a pinprick in front of her.

And then there was the rubbish. It lined both sides of the

tunnel, rising and falling in heaps like vile sand dunes. She kept to the middle, breathing through her mouth to avoid the smell that was only getting worse as they made their way deeper into the underground labyrinth. She could not see much of the light from Darius's pendant and couldn't see anything in front of Darius, due to her own short stature. But Griffin's pendant illuminated the walls in the immediate vicinity and gave her enough light to see directly in front of her.

She kept her own pendant tucked inside her shirt. It was possible that she would not use her sickle at all while in the tunnels, but she wanted both hands free if she needed it. Fingering the strip of leather at her waist, she was glad she had been able to excuse herself before departing the house. The belt was crude at best, but the sickle swung securely from it, and the pouch with Galizur's darts was tied to the other side, hidden by her waistcoat.

So closely was Helen following Darius that she did not realize they had made a turn until they passed a fork in the tunnel. Darius had chosen to go right without a word. Obviously, he knew where they were going.

As they walked, her fear subsided, replaced by a morbid sort of wonder. Each curve and turn in the tunnel was notated

with markings carved right into the walls, an indiscernible form of navigation completely mysterious to her. That the tunnels were here, every day, as she walked the streets of London only increased her sense of awe. And though they reeked of things better left unsaid, the walls were crafted of neatly stacked brick, the floor alternating between more of the same, flagstone, and sometimes simply loose rock. Helen tried to imagine a contingent of men descending to work each day, smoothing over London's underground with such careful attention, knowing their handiwork would be seen by almost no one.

"It's incredible, isn't it?" Griffin's voice came softly behind her.

She looked upward at the barrel-vaulted ceiling. "It is."

They made their way through the tunnels without seeing a soul. At times, Helen heard the rubbish rustle along the sides of the walkway. At others, Darius would stop them with a wave of his hand, holding perfectly still as he listened for something only he could hear before signaling them forward once again.

Helen almost became accustomed to not knowing what was around each curve. What lay on each side of the many forks to which they came. Everything became familiar until she hardly noticed the smell, and the darkness became her uneasy friend.

Finally, Darius stopped short, shining the light of the pendant at the walls.

"What is it?" Griffin asked, catching up to his brother.

Darius aimed the light upward toward a hole in the ceiling. "We're here."

TWENTY-SEVEN

Darius ascended the ladder first, while Griffin and Helen waited anxiously at the bottom. Helen didn't know what she expected. An immediate assault on their location? The dogs that Raum had warned her about?

She didn't know, but a few minutes after Darius disappeared into the darkness above their heads, his voice cut through the darkness.

"All clear."

"Go ahead," Griffin said, looking around the tunnel by the light of his pendant. "I'll keep watch here until you're up safely."

She nodded, placing her hands on the rungs of the ladder, and pulling herself upward. It wasn't nearly as frightening as her earlier descent. Her eyes were already accustomed to the darkness, and it was far easier to work toward an escape from the tunnels than it had been to talk herself into going underground.

The light from Griffin's pendant grew increasingly faint as she continued her climb, the illumination disappearing completely just as she got her first breath of fresh air from above. It was the only indication that she was close to the top. She continued upward, the blackness so total she could not see her hands on the rungs before her. Just when she thought the climb would go on and on, Darius's voice came in a whisper just above her head.

"Almost there," he said. "When you reach the top, I'll take your hands and help you out, but for God's sake, be quiet. It looks deserted, but I haven't had time to look around."

She nodded, breathing heavily and not trusting herself to speak quietly enough for Darius's liking.

Taking one more step up, she felt for the next rung with her hand and found that there wasn't one. Instead, her hands touched something cool and dry. Leaves, she thought.

"Give me your hands, one at a time," Darius instructed.

She reached up with her right hand, relieved when Darius's strong fingers closed over hers. She had no sooner placed her left hand in Darius's than he was pulling her out of the tunnel as if she weighed no more than bag of feathers. Her feet came to rest with a crackle on the dried leaves scattering the ground.

The moon was half full. Darius placed a finger to his lips, gesturing for her to be quiet. Then he leaned down, whispering for Griffin to begin his ascent. Helen took the opportunity to look around, surprised to find the area so wooded. She had seen the trees on the schematic, of course, but had not expected their cover to be so dense. In the best of circumstances, the additional cover would help.

In the worst, it would be catastrophic.

She was untying the ribbon from her hair as Griffin pulled himself from the tunnel. He lowered his gaze to the ribbon in her hands, a silent question in his eyes, and she bent to tie it to a nearby tree. It wasn't much, but with any luck it would help them locate their escape route if they found themselves in a rush to flee Alsorta's fortress.

Griffin nodded approval. They both waited as Darius bent to lower the wooden cover over the entrance to the tunnel. When he was finished, Griffin waved them closer. They formed a small circle, their faces only inches apart as he whispered instructions.

"We need to make our way north along the tree line. Once the house is in view, we should have a better handle on how to get in. Follow me." His eyes met Helen's. "And stay close."

She nodded.

The brothers fell wordlessly into their new positions, Griffin in front and Darius at Helen's back. Despite her best efforts, it was difficult to be quiet while tramping through the dead leaves covering the ground. They rustled at her feet no matter how carefully she stepped until it seemed impossible that no one would hear them. Reaching down to the pouch at her belt, Helen pulled back the flap at the top, fingering the darts inside. So far, there was no sign of the dogs, but they still had a long way to go.

The lights near the house were visible through the trees when Griffin suddenly stopped. He grabbed Helen's hand, pulling her behind a large tree as Darius stepped silently behind another. Her back was pressed against the trunk, Griffin's body flattened against hers as his eyes darted around the vicinity. At first, she thought the brothers were being paranoid. She couldn't hear anything except the few remaining leaves rustling on the branches above their heads. But then, she heard a man's voice in the distance. Straining her ears, she tried to make out the words.

"The new one would've brought it, you know." The voice was breathless. It was obvious whoever was talking was walking or moving in some way as he spoke.

"Psh!" Another man snorted. "A woman visiting this time of night, even to deliver supper, would be nothing but a distraction. You know how Henry is with the serving girls. The old man would have a fit."

Helen rolled her eyes at Griffin. He grinned, obviously hearing the conversation as well as she could. She was aware suddenly of his body against hers, his chest pressed against her bosom, his face only inches away. For a moment, she was locked in the spell of his eyes, wishing they were anywhere but here. Wishing they were well and truly alone so that she could lean up to press her lips against his and feel his mouth open on her own. She was almost relieved to be pulled from her thoughts by the voice of the first man.

"I don't much care what Henry does when his supper's delivered," he said. "So long as it doesn't involve me freezing my hindquarters."

The man's companion said something in reply, but the voices were farther away now. Helen could not make out the words. A few minutes later, the sound disappeared completely. Still, Griffin remained against her for what seemed like an eternity.

By the time Darius appeared at Griffin's shoulder, Helen's whole body felt overheated.

"I hate to interrupt." Darius's voice dripped sarcasm. "But we should probably be going."

Griffin moved away, his eyes catching hers in a smile that made it clear he hadn't minded the delay. They followed him through the trees until they came to a clearing that led to the house. The sprawling lawn stretched from the tree line, circling the imposing house. As big as many of the buildings in downtown London, it sat on a small knoll, its brick facade rising far into the night sky. Lights winked from some of the windows, and Helen wondered suddenly if Victor Alsorta had a family. If he had a wife who did needlework by the fire and sons who played chess.

She pushed the thought away. Alsorta didn't deserve the consideration of a man. He was a monster. And he deserved to be punished.

They continued through the wooded perimeter, the tree line curving little by little, growing closer to the house until it was near enough that Helen could make out the detailed cornices around the windows. Remembering Griffin's strategy, she was ready when he stopped.

He turned to her and Darius. "This is the closest we'll come

to the house with any cover. We'll have to find a way in from here if we don't wish to run across the lawn in full view of anyone looking out a window."

A door opened at the side of the house, a young woman in a maid's uniform throwing a pot of water onto the lawn.

"God's sake! Are you daft?" A voice screamed at her from beyond the open door.

She turned toward it, lowering her head. "Sorry, ma'am. I thought I was supposed to dump the water."

An older woman appeared at the door holding a steaming pot. "Yes, yes. But not *here*. Not near the house. Take it to the woods, for heaven's sake!" Handing another pot to the young maid, she grumbled. "Tsk. Every time they send someone new, I have to start all over again."

The door banged shut behind her. For a moment, the serving girl stood, holding the pot and staring toward their position in the woods until Helen was certain they had been spotted. But no alarm sounded. No cry about an intruder. The young maid simply descended the steps and started across the lawn toward them.

"She's coming this way!" Helen whispered.

Both men looked toward the grass, watching the girl approach, the pot of water still steaming in her hands.

"I'll meet up with you inside," Darius said wearily. "Just find Alsorta and try not to do anything until I get there."

They didn't have time to protest. Darius stepped onto the lawn in full view of the girl, ambling toward her as if he were simply out for an evening stroll.

"It looks like you could use some help." His voice was like syrup, rich and sweet. Helen could hear the roguish smirk that was almost certainly on his face as he approached the maid.

"What, me?" She looked around as if there were someone else to whom Darius could be speaking.

"Yes. You," Darius said slowly. "You're far too pretty to spend your night in such drudgery. Allow me." He reached for the pot.

She shrunk back, startled. "Oh, no! I couldn't."

"You most certainly could." Darius's voice was firm but sensual.

The girl shook her head, leaning in to whisper at Darius. Helen could barely make out her words. "I'm *on trial,* you see. From the agency. I won't be able to stay if I get into trouble."

"There's no trouble to be had." Darius reached for the pot, pulling it from her with authority. Some of the water sloshed over the side. "You may be new, but I'm not. I've been working for the old man for ages. And trust me, they don't care who does it or how it gets done, so long as it does."

The girl looked nervously around. "Well . . . all right, then. But I'll have to get back soon or they'll wonder where I've gone."

Darius nodded with authority. "They don't like dumping to be done close to the house. I'll show you the best spot for this and have you back in no time. Besides, it will give us a chance to get to know each other . . ." He fished for her name.

"Maude," she said shyly.

"Maude." Darius lead her toward the trees at the back of the house. "A striking name for a striking girl."

Helen could not withhold her sigh when the girl giggled.

Griffin leaned in, speaking quietly. "Alsorta's chambers are on the second floor. We have to find a way in before the girl comes back."

Helen looked carefully through the trees, weighing their options. They shuffled through her mind like a deck of cards until she remembered her mother, leading her through one of London's worst neighborhoods on a grim February day. They didn't have an errand or any other purpose for being there. It was an adventure, her mother had said before they'd left the house in clothing borrowed from the servants.

"But why, Mother? Why will we go to the slums?" Helen asked as her mother buttoned up the too-small coat.

"Because, darling." Her mother had gazed at Helen, her eyes flashing a deep and moody gray. "It's a game. Like the games you play with your father. It will be grand, you'll see."

Helen had been afraid. The people were smelly and boisterous, shoving her every which was as she held tightly to her mother's hand. She didn't like this game as much as the ones she played with Father.

Her mother stopped on a street corner, bending down to speak softly to her. "You must act like them, my love. If you're afraid, if they see your fear, they'll know you don't belong. It is only then that they'll notice you at all."

Helen had gazed at the roughly dressed passersby. The children with dirty faces and runny noses, many of them chasing after strangers and asking for money.

"But how, Mother? How do I act like them?"

"Do what they do, Helen. Behave as they behave." Her mother had smiled secretively. "Let us pretend. It will be as a play or fairy tale. I will be the downtrodden widower, seeking work to care for my beloved daughter, who sometimes must beg in the streets for charity. None of London's richest citizens can resist the child, for she is an angel-faced beauty with sad violet eyes." Her mother tipped her head, and Helen saw, just for a second, sadness lurking in her gaze. It was gone a moment later when her mother continued. "It's a romantic, tragic tale, really."

Later, Helen knew her mother had added this last so that she wouldn't be afraid. It had worked. Helen had always loved fairy tales, and she had perfected a doe-eyed stare that, together with a plea for change, melted the most hard-hearted stranger. By the time they left the slums, Helen had gathered a heavy handful of coins.

"Well done, Helen," her mother had said as they made their way home. "Blending is the key to belonging. It's just that simple."

And with that, her mother had deposited all the money Helen had earned into a tin nailed to the wall of an old church.

"Well?" Griffin's voice brought her back to the present. "Any ideas?"

Helen's nod was slow. "We'll go in there. Through the kitchen."

"The kitchen?" Griffin shook his head. "But there are people working in there."

"Yes," Helen conceded. "But no one guards a kitchen. Just act like you belong and it will be fine."

She had already stepped through the trees and was making her way to the side door by the time he spoke the first words of protest.

He caught up to her. "Are you mad? We'll be caught."

"No," she said, "we won't. This is a big place, Griffin. I could be any one of the maids hired to serve Alsorta and you could be any one of the guards."

She marched up the steps as if she had done so a hundred times before. Griffin was right behind her when she opened the door.

TWENTY-EIGHT

The air was pungent and steamy. Dishes clattered as people shouted back and forth above the fray. Scanning the area by the door, Helen found what she was looking for in a row of pegs. She grabbed an apron from one of them and a hat from another, putting them both on in under ten seconds as she made her way deeper into the kitchen.

The blood rushed through her veins as she passed two old women doing dishes and stepped over a younger one scrubbing the floor. Helen avoided eye contact with all of them, raising her voice to a bossy shout as she hurried through the room.

"I don't care what Henry told you." She directed the words toward Griffin without actually looking at his face. "Master Alsorta needs the carriage shining like a fresh coin first thing in the morning. And maybe if you didn't spend so much of your time playing cards at the front gate you would have remembered his instructions."

"I . . . uh . . . I'm sorry, miss?" Griffin said. "I'll . . . I'll see that someone does it right away."

Helen continued her march through the cavernous kitchen, heading for a door at the end of the room. "You most certainly will. We'll get you a bucket and some fresh rags and you'll be on your way."

She was at the door, a sigh of relief already building in her lungs, when a curt voice stopped her.

"And who, pray tell, are you?"

Griffin stiffened beside her, one hand on his sickle, as Helen turned to find an older women glaring at her with shrewd eyes. She was the same one who had given Maude a dressing-down outside the kitchen.

Helen composed her face into what she hoped was a mask of serenity. "I'm Helen, of course."

"Helen?" The old woman's forehead crinkled with disdain. "And who would that be?"

"The agency sent me?" Helen looked her directly in the eyes, steadying her voice. "Earlier this evening?"

"The agency?"

Helen nodded. "Master Alsorta is quite upset about the carriage. I've been instructed to give the men washing supplies immediately."

The woman stared at her with a puzzled expression as the silence stretched between them. Helen was already marking the exits to the room when the older woman nodded.

"See it done, then. It won't do to keep the Master waiting."

Helen nodded, turning and slipping from the door with Griffin on her heels. They kept walking even after the door shut behind them. Helen held her head high until she found a shadowed alcove. Then, she stepped into it, leaned against the wall, and nearly fainted with relief.

"I cannot believe you just did that." Griffin lay his head back against the wall next to her, his voice was disbelieving. "That was . . ." He started to chuckle. "That was the most amazing thing I've ever seen."

"That wasn't amazing. Getting out of here with Alsorta will be amazing." She smiled, whispering. "But thank you."

Safe from the wrath of the kitchen crone, Helen peered out of the alcove, trying to get her bearings. A long hallway extended toward the entry in the distance, and though she could not be sure of much else, she knew they were not in servants' quarters. The rugs and furniture were far too fine.

A clatter across the hall made them jump, and they leaned back into the shadows.

"Tsk!" It was the voice of the crone, and Helen wondered that it could strike fear in even her own heart when the woman had no control over her whatsoever. "Where on Earth have you been? Do you think the Master wants to shave with cold water? You're going to hear it now! And with good reason!"

"I'm sorry," a small, familiar voice said. "I'll get it upstairs right away, ma'am."

Maude scuttled out of the kitchen with a basin of water, letting the door swing shut behind her as she headed in the opposite direction of the front door.

"Back stairs?" Helen whispered to Griffin.

He nodded.

They waited until Maude's hurried footsteps faded before daring to follow. The hallway was empty, and they made their way with haste to the back of the house. Helen called to mind the drawing they had used to plot strategy. She saw the long, central hallway in which they now stood, the various rooms set to the left and right. At the back was a large mudroom. If Helen remembered correctly—and she almost always did—the servants' stairs would be there.

"This way," she said, turning left at the end of the hall.

Griffin followed, either because he truly trusted Helen's instincts or because he didn't have a better idea. Helen couldn't be sure. But it didn't matter. The mudroom was at the end of the back hall, and just as Helen remembered, a dark, narrow staircase was set into the wall.

Griffin gazed upward into the darkness. "Ready?"

She nodded.

"Stay close," he said.

"What about Darius?"

"He can take care of himself. We'll find Alsorta and wait until Darius can join us. I have a feeling it will take all of us to bring him in."

He started up the stairs without another word. Helen followed, wondering how the servants made their way up and down such a poorly lit stairwell. Save for one flickering sconce halfway up, there wasn't a single source of illumination. She had never been in the back staircase of her own home but she found herself wondering if her family's servants had been forced to navigate the house in such conditions. She sincerely hoped not.

Helen was relieved when they arrived at the top of the steps without encountering any of the staff. There would have been no way to avoid them, and while she had been able to fool the old woman in the kitchen, Helen was willing to bet their presence would have raised suspicion with the other servants who probably knew their coworkers by name.

Griffin stopped at the top, looking both ways before waving her forward. They emerged into another hall, this one so richly outfitted that the entire floor seemed like a cocoon. The carpets were thick underfoot, the furniture ornately carved and gleaming. The effect was one of utter isolation from the rest of the world. It was almost possible to believe the house lay in a universe all its own, completely separate from the noise and crime and soot of London.

Bending to the floor, Griffin touched his fingers to a wet spot on the carpet before gesturing for Helen to follow him toward the back of the house. He led her quickly past the closed doors along the hall. She did not ask if he knew where he was going, but when he stopped at a half-open door at the end of the hall, she looked down and understood.

Droplets of water beaded on the wood floor where the carpets came to an end. Looking back, she noticed the darker spots leading to the back of the hall and knew the girl with the basin of water had come this way.

Griffin's eyes widened as voices sounded from within the room. They both leaned back against the wall, listening. They were completely exposed. There was no alcove in which to hide. No shadowed corner. If someone emerged from the room, they would be seen. For the first time since they had descended into the tunnel, Helen allowed herself to imagine what they would do if they were caught before Darius found them. There were surely windows through which they could climb, but it was unlikely that they would escape the sprawling grounds if Alsorta was still able to give orders to his men.

Griffin crossed carefully to the other side of the door frame so that they could both peer through the opening. Helen leaned toward it, Griffin's head only inches from hers as they tried to see inside without making any noise. She could only see a fraction of the room. An ornate, damask paper covering the walls. A wardrobe and washstand near a window. And a hand, dipping rhythmically into the basin, something clinking softly against the ironstone.

"Did I miss anything?"

Helen clamped a hand over her mouth, barely preventing

the scream that threatened to escape as the voice sounded near her ear.

Turning to Darius's grinning face, she swatted his arm silently, scowling but not daring to say anything aloud. Griffin put a finger to his lips, pointing his brother toward the room.

"Do we know how many are in there?" Darius whispered, close to her ear.

She shook her head, leaning toward him. "Just a maid, I think. But we can't be certain."

Before Helen could protest, Darius leaned toward the door, nudging it with his toe. To her relief, it opened a few more inches without a sound.

They leaned farther in, now catching sight of a man, sitting in a chair with his back to the door. It was Alsorta. Helen was sure of it, even from her limited vantage point. His hair was graying as it was in the photographs Galizur had shown them, and the rigid line of his back spoke to the power he was accustomed to wielding over others.

The maid stood by with a towel as an elderly gentleman silently wielded a razor. He ran it along one side of Alsorta's face before dipping it back into the water, and moving to the back of the man's head.

Running a brush in circles across Alsorta's skin, the older gentleman scraped the razor along the back of his neck. Helen leaned in a couple of inches closer, wondering if she was imagining the image slowly being revealed by the razor. But no. There was something there. Or part of something, perhaps. She waited as the barber wet the razor once more, running it smoothly over the man's neck, revealing another piece of the picture.

Helen peered curiously at it, trying to figure what it was. A . . . dragon? She thought it was a dragon etched into his skin. Or something like it. It looked to be surrounded by flames.

She was turning to ask one of the brothers about it when she noticed Darius, backing up along the hallway, still facing the room as if he were afraid to turn his back on it.

Griffin grabbed her hand, pulling her from the doorway as she tried to escape his grip, wondering why on Earth they would want to leave when they hadn't even attempted their mission.

And if all of this was not enough to give her pause, to make her heart slam against her chest like a frightened animal, the look in Darius's eyes as he backed away was.

It was not anger. Not sarcasm or bitterness or hatred. Any of these she would have welcomed. This time there was something new in Darius's face. Something she had never seen before.

Fear.

TWENTY-NINE

She shook her head as Griffin tugged her farther from the door.

"What are you doing?" she whispered, too confused to be silent. "Alsorta's right there. He's right there, Griffin."

They were twenty feet from the door, and still they were backing away carefully, as if trying to escape a rabid dog.

"You don't understand," Griffin finally whispered hotly. "We have to get out of here right now."

"But what about Alsorta?"

He shook his head. "We made a mistake. This isn't something we can do alone."

But she had hidden too many times in the past. Had kept herself safe within the walls of her home as it—and her parents—had burned around her. She couldn't hide anymore.

"The man responsible for killing our parents is in there."

She pulled her arm away from his hand. "I'm not going unless you give me a good reason."

He bent down until his face was close to hers. "That's not Alsorta."

She looked back toward the door. "What . . . What do you mean? It's him. It is. This is his house."

"This is Victor Alsorta's house and that . . . thing in there calls himself Victor Alsorta, but he's not a man, Helen. He's something else. Something far worse and far more dangerous."

"What?" She looked up into his face, not understanding at all. "What is he, Griffin?"

He spoke in a ferocious whisper. "That symbol on his neck brands him as Alastor, one of the Legion's most deadly demons and a member of the Blackguard. We're not equipped to fight him," he continued. "Not here. Not now."

"Griffin." Darius's voice was a warning from down the hall.

Griffin nodded at his brother before turning back to Helen. "We have to get out of here. We'll regroup and come back, I promise, but we have to leave now before we're discovered."

The plea in his eyes told her he was telling the truth. Besides, in the short time she had known the brothers, she had never known them to back down from a fight. That they were doing so now told her much of what she needed to know.

"Okay, but we're coming back," she insisted.

He nodded, already pulling her toward Darius, now half-way to the staircase. He was still stepping backward, his eye on the half-open door at the end of the hall, when his boot came down on a creaky floorboard. The sound cut through the silence, and they froze, looking at each other with panic in their eyes before glancing back at the door.

Helen cast a glance at the staircase. They were close enough to it now that it would be their best bet for an escape. There had been an exterior door in the mudroom. If they ran down the stairs and managed to get out the door without being caught, they stood a decent chance of making it into the woods and back to the tunnels. And maybe, just maybe, the sound would go unnoticed. Maybe it had not been as loud as it seemed in the silence of the hall and their urgency to escape.

But even as she thought it, she heard shuffling from within the room.

After that, everything happened too quickly. The sound of authoritative footsteps rushing the partially opened door, which flung open to reveal Victor Alsorta, his eyes glinting like silver disks. And then, his voice, as cold and smooth as ice as he spoke orders to someone unseen to Helen.

"Intruders! Sound the alarm."

It took less than ten seconds for the earsplitting siren to slice through the night. It seemed to come from everywhere at once, from inside her very own mind, until she wanted to stop everything and cover her ears with her hands until it quieted.

She had no such luxury. Griffin grabbed her hand and pulled, and then they were racing toward the stairs, turning the corner at a dead run, and bounding down the steps two and three at a time, Darius in the lead.

"There!" Helen pointed to the door in the mudroom.

Darius turned the lock. He flung open the door and Helen and Griffin raced through it after him. Helen barely registered the cold night air. She was too busy running for the tree line, dragged along by Griffin, still holding her hand in a grip like iron.

Where before there had been a few sconces flickering gentle light onto the grounds, now they seemed to be everywhere, lighting up the lawn so that there were no shadows. No place to hide. It was a mirror to the other activity building around them—the voices of men shouting in the distance, the sound of racing footsteps through the trees.

And the dogs.

Helen heard them in the distance. She fingered the darts,

still in the pouch at her belt, as she followed Griffin into the trees.

Once the house was out of view, she lost all sense of direction. Plunged into near-total darkness, she could only hope Darius, still in front, knew where he was going. It was all she could do to keep running, trying to avoid the gnarly tree roots protruding from the ground and half covered by the fallen leaves.

The dogs were closer. They barked ferociously, drowning out the sounds of the men shouting to one another through the trees. She heard the snarls and barks, not from the direction of the house as she'd suspected, but up ahead. She could not fathom how the animals had circled around to cut them off in the woods, but now it was a race. They would have to reach the entrance to the tunnels before the dogs found their position to avoid a confrontation.

"How much farther?" she managed to gasp.

"Not far." Griffin's voice was muffled under the barking dogs, leaves underfoot, and Helen's own labored breathing.

They ran until Helen thought her legs would give out altogether. Until her lungs burned. She was stricken repeatedly by low-hanging branches, leaving her with stinging cuts on her arms and face. But none of it mattered. Because the dogs were close. Too close. They weren't going to reach the tunnels in time. The animals would cut them off any second.

She no sooner thought it when Darius screeched to a halt just as an enormous beast flew through the trees in front of them. It landed in a flash of ebony fur, snarling and snapping at them from across the small clearing in which they had stopped.

Darius held out his hands. "Good boy."

The dog snarled, shaking its head. A moment later, two more dogs bounded through the tree line. They stopped next to the first one, growling low in their throats and baring their teeth.

"Brilliant," Griffin said. "Now what? The men can't be far behind."

Indeed, Helen heard them in the distance, saw their lanterns bobbing through the trees as they made their way to the dogs' position.

"Look to the left," Darius said, hardly moving his mouth.

Helen followed Griffin's eyes, scanning the bushes. She didn't see it at first, but then the midnight blue silk moved in the wind. Her ribbon. It was her ribbon. They had found their way back to the tunnels, even if it might be too late to actually escape into them.

"Where's the entrance?" Griffin said softly.

Darius moved his foot, ever so slowly, back and forth across the ground.

The growling accelerated, and the one in the front barked in warning.

"Darius!" Griffin said. "Stop moving."

"Just look down," Darius said, never taking his eyes off the dogs.

Griffin and Helen lowered their eyes to where Darius's foot rested, not atop the dead leaves that littered the ground, but on the wooden cover to the tunnels.

Griffin sucked in his breath. "We have to find a way to distract the dogs long enough for us to get inside the tunnel."

The dogs, as if in answer, increased their growling, inching forward to where they stood.

"Is that all?" Darius asked.

Helen marveled that he could be flip even in such a situation.

A cry from one of the men, much closer this time, prompted Helen to move. Reaching slowly toward the pouch at her waist, she spoke as calmly as she could, trying not to make eye contact with the snapping, snarling dogs.

"I'll take care of the dogs. Just get the cover off the tunnel entrance."

She felt Griffin's eyes on her face. "I'm not leaving you to the dogs, Helen."

His voice carried a finality that scared her. She had to make him understand. To trust her. Their lives depended on it.

"Listen," she said, pulling one of the darts from her belt. "I have something that will take care of the dogs, but you must open the entrance to the tunnel so that I can climb in as soon as they're down."

"As soon as they're down?" Even Darius was perplexed.

The dogs, saliva dripping from their teeth, were getting closer with every argument.

"We don't have time for this," Helen said. "I'm counting to three. And you better move and clear the ladder so that I can get in when I'm done."

"But—" Griffin began.

"One," she said softly, cutting him off. "Two . . ."

Helen was relieved to see Darius's body tense. He, at least, would do as she asked.

"Three."

Everything seemed to slow down while the blood raced through her veins. She had the oddest sense of euphoria as she pulled the first dart from the pouch. It was a signal to the dogs that the waiting was over, and they started forward, sliding a

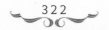

little on the dead leaves as Helen took quick aim at the one in front and let go.

She heard the tiny motor whir to life, saw a red light come on at the flight of the dart. It picked up speed remarkably fast. She was almost surprised when it hit the dog's muscled chest, just as Galizur had said it would. She was already letting go of the second dart when the first dog fell to the ground with a twitch. Helen hadn't had time to aim properly, but it didn't matter. The second dart hit its mark just as the first one had.

One more, she thought, holding the third dart in front of her, watching the last dog close the last few yards between them.

She let go, expecting to see it whir toward its intended target like the others. But something went wrong. The dart sputtered, emitting a dry cough as it flew erratically for a few feet and then crashed to the ground.

The dog was perilously close by the time she pulled the fourth dart from the pouch. So close that she could smell its hot, rancid breath. She took an extra second to level her aim, and then she let go, already moving and praying the dog would fall.

A second later, it did. Helen raced forward, bending over the paralyzed dogs.

"Helen! For God's sake! What are you doing?"

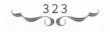

She looked over at Griffin. He had not followed Darius into the tunnel. He sat at the mouth of the tunnel entrance, his legs dangling into the abyss. As promised and despite her wishes, he had not left her.

She pulled the darts from the dogs' fur, shoving them back into the pouch on her way to the tunnel.

"I told you to go!" she shouted.

"And I told you that I wasn't leaving you here."

Helen heard in his voice that there had never been any question of his abandoning her, but there was no time to argue. That would come later. Now the men were almost upon them. She felt for the top rung, settling her foot on it and beginning to descend.

Her head had almost cleared the ground when another dog burst through the trees with lantern light just behind him. She counted the darts she had thrown.

The first dog. The second dog. The defective dart. The third dog.

Four darts used.

Reaching into the pouch, she closed her fingers around the last dart. It was out and flying through the air before the dog had crossed half the ground between them. And then Helen was climbing down the ladder as fast as her feet would allow, pulling on Griffin's legs until he, too, began his descent.

He pulled the cover over the tunnel entrance and the world fell into darkness.

THIRTY

It's an anagram," Helen said softly, looking out onto the street through a gap in the parlor curtains.

"What is?" Darius asked from behind her.

"Alsorta." She turned to face him, avoiding Griffin's eyes. "It's an anagram of Alastor."

The revelation had come to her, suddenly and without forethought, when they had arrived back at the house.

Darius took a deep breath, running his hands along the stubble at his jaw before slamming his hand down on the tea table. A silver dish and cut glass candlestick rattled against his outburst.

"I should have checked." His voice was laden with self-recrimination.

"You couldn't possibly have known." Helen was surprised to find herself sympathetic. Feeling anything other than annoyance toward Darius was new. "You thought he was a man. We all did."

She felt him seething in the silence that followed. And then Griffin spoke, asking the question that she had been expecting, however much she hoped he wouldn't.

"There's something I don't understand, Helen." He paced the room, his voice was tight with anger. "How did you know about the dogs?"

They had raced through the tunnels, following Darius and not daring to stop or look back. This time it was a blur rather than a wonder. Helen listened carefully for anything behind them that might indicate that Alsorta's men had given chase, but the tunnels were labyrinthine. Even if Alsorta's men had pursued them beyond the grounds of the house, it was unlikely they would follow the exact twists and turns taken by Griffin, Darius, and Helen.

Still, Darius had led them up through a different tunnel entirely, one far from the Channings' house, just in case. They jumped the rest of the way, barricading themselves inside the house, sickles at the ready, as they peered through the curtains. Watching and waiting.

It was only now, hours later, that they had let down their guard enough to even speak about what had happened.

Helen stood at the window, watching the sun come up over London. She had been searching her mind for an answer to the inevitable question since the moment they'd arrived back at the house.

There was no way around the truth.

"Raum told me," she said softly.

"What did she say?" It was Darius, speaking from the sofa where he had finally sprawled once they had deemed themselves safe. For the time being. "I thought she said Raum told her."

"She did." Griffin was closer, his voice at her shoulder. "Tell me that isn't true, Helen. Tell me that you have not been collaborating with the man who murdered our parents."

"I wasn't collaborating. And he didn't murder them." She knew she shouldn't say it, but she was still unprepared for the noise that followed.

Jumping back from the window, she looked at the now-empty place on the wall. Griffin had smacked it with the palm of his hand, sending the painting that had once rested there crashing to the floor.

"That . . . doesn't . . . matter." Rage simmered under his words. "We've already discussed this."

"Well, maybe it matters to me," she said hotly. "It's easy for

you. You didn't know him before. You don't have to reconcile the boy he once was with the man he is now."

Griffin became very still. "And what man is that, Helen? What kind of man is he now?"

She took a deep breath. "I don't know. I only know that he gave me information that helped us fend off the dogs. Had he not, we might very well be dead. Can't you understand why it would be difficult to brand him an enemy, despite all that has happened?"

Darius was unusually quiet, but Griffin shook his head. "No. I don't understand. And there is something else I don't understand."

She waited, bracing herself for the next question. The next accusation.

"When did you find time to meet with him, Helen? When and where was that traitor able to give you such information?"

She had to swallow around the lump in her throat. She had known it would come eventually, but she hadn't had time to tailor her answer in such a way that it would not hurt Griffin.

"Well?" he prompted.

She took a deep breath. "The first time he found me was when I went to see the ruins of my home. The day we figured out Alsorta was the one who had hired him."

She had hoped he would be satisfied, but of course, he was not.

"The first time?"

She nodded. "I saw him a second time. Yesterday. He . . ." She hesitated, trying desperately to think of a way to say it that would not sound so inappropriate. She came up with nothing. "He found me in my chamber."

He stared at her, almost uncomprehending, in the moment before he found the words to speak. "In your *chamber*? Here? In our home? You stood there, speaking to him like any gentleman, in the home owned by people he was responsible for murdering? In your private chamber no less?"

It sounded so much worse when he spoke of it. She wanted to shout, *No! It's not like that. He was trying to help. It was the only way he could find me alone, and I had to be alone because he knew you wouldn't listen!*

But she said none of it. It was exactly the way Griffin made it sound. She should have killed Raum when she had the chance—or at the very least sounded an alarm so Darius and Griffin could do it—and they all knew it.

"Yes," she said quietly.

His nod was slow. "I see."

He turned away, rubbing a tired hand over his face, but it

was too late to shield her from the pain in his eyes. Pain she had put there.

The silence sat between them until she actually wished Darius would say something. She didn't care if it was rude or sarcastic or patronizing. She simply wanted someone to fill up the space left by the hole she had just blown in her relationship with Griffin.

"These are matters you can discuss privately," Darius said, as if hearing her silent wish. "We know now that Alsorta is no ordinary man seeking greater power. The Summit is two days away. If we don't destroy him before then, it will be too late."

Helen considered his words. Turned over in her mind the players and pieces of the game. Something didn't make sense, was not lining up as it should. At first, she wasn't sure what it was, but it came to her a moment later.

"Why would the Summit matter to him?" she asked. "Why would Alsorta even bother with the Syndicate? Access to the records will give him far greater power than control over a mortal organization, even one as powerful as the Syndicate."

She hoped Griffin would answer. That he would give her some sign that he did not intend to remain silent and angry forever.

But it was Darius who spoke. "He can only have access to

the records *if* he can find the key. And that is a very big if. He's down to three Keepers, and he still hasn't found it."

"And if he doesn't . . ." Helen started.

"Then, he would need a backup plan," Darius finished. "Listen, this isn't just one demon we're talking about. Alsorta is a member of the Blackguard. They get their orders straight from Lucius, Master of the Legion. And they aren't looking for a little foothold. Not this time." He paused, shaking his head. "No. They're making a play for the mortal world, and they intend to win control one way or another. If Alsorta doesn't find the key, the Legion will bring the world to its knees through their control of the Syndicate."

"People wouldn't stand for it!" Helen exclaimed. "Not once they knew what he was. They would fight."

"Mortals wouldn't stand a chance." They were the first words Griffin had spoken since her revelation about Raum. She almost winced at the pain on his face. "Not against an army of wraiths and an organization capable of shutting down every aspect of their lives."

"But didn't you say that the wraiths are minor demons? That they're easy to defeat?"

"They're manageable when they appear in twos and threes," Darius said. "But the Blackguard controls the Legion, and those with the power of Alsorta can summon them in droves. Take a few mindless, soulless demons and multiply them by millions—all controlled by one of the most powerful, supernatural beings in the history of time—and you have an army that will overcome humanity in less than twenty-four hours."

Helen could see it. A world in which the demonic wraiths streamed from lights everywhere. All controlled by Alastor and the greater demons of the Legion.

It would be the end of the world as they knew it.

"So, he doesn't need the records at all," Helen said softly.

"They would give him control over the past," Darius said. "But if Alastor can't find the key, it seems the Legion will settle for the future."

His words rang through the room like a death knell. Finally, Darius broke the silence.

"We should rest today and go to Galizur's once it gets dark. We're going to need more information if we're to fight Alastor."

"Someone should stand guard." Griffin spoke without turning.

"I'll take the first shift," Darius said.

Helen waited, wanting to say something, anything, that would make it all right with Griffin. But it didn't take her long to realize it was an impossible desire.

She was lying on the bed, her body exhausted but her mind too busy for sleep, when a knock sounded. Crossing to the door, she was glad she had remained dressed. Although her bare feet and unlaced shirt were not entirely appropriate, it was certainly better than a nightdress.

She opened the door, both surprised and anxious to find Griffin there. She had half hoped for and half dreaded his appearance. What more was there to say?

"Come in." She opened the door wider.

He stepped into the room reluctantly, as if it was the last place in the world he wanted to be. She closed the door behind him, watching him cross to the window. His body was illuminated in the golden morning light streaming in through the glass.

"I'm sorry," she finally said, unable to bear his silence.

He shook his head, a rejection of her apology, and all at once she wasn't sorry anymore. She was angry. Angry that she should be faulted for saving their lives with knowledge gleaned from Raum. Angry that the brothers were more concerned with holding Raum responsible than bringing in Alsorta or Alastor or whatever his name really was, since he was the one who had actually ordered the execution of their families.

She crossed the room quickly, coming to a stop next to him.

"I'm sorry you're angry, Griffin. And I'm sorry I . . ." She had to swallow through her emotion to get the next part out. "I'm sorry I hurt you. But I'm not sorry for using information from Raum to get us out of Alsorta's tonight." He didn't move. Didn't even turn away from the window to look at her. She kept going, wanting to rid herself of every word she'd been holding inside. "I know you want Raum dead. That you believe he's responsible for the deaths of our parents. But it's not that simple, Griffin, don't you see? It was on Alsorta's orders that Raum hunted us. And if he had not hired Raum, he would have hired someone else. I'm not trying to excuse him—"

"Really?" Griffin interrupted. "Because that's what it sounds like to me."

"I know it does." She sighed. "It's just so difficult to explain."

"Try."

"Raum lost everything, and although we might say the Baranovas had it coming to them for their betrayal of the Alliance, Raum had no part in it."

"He could have come in," Griffin said stubbornly. "They were looking for him. He could have come in and still served as one of the Keepers."

"Maybe he didn't know," Helen said. "Maybe he didn't know they were looking for him."

Griffin turned an angry stare on her. "You don't think he would have heard? He seems resourceful enough to me."

She threw up her hands, her own anger rising once again. "I don't know, all right? Maybe he thought they were going to imprison him or kill him or whatever else the Alliance does to traitors who don't manage to kill themselves first. All I know is that he was young and alone. He had lost his parents and every semblance of the life he had. And someone came along and promised him something that would bring it all back."

Griffin narrowed his eyes. "What do you mean?"

"Alsorta told Raum that if he saw to the executions and found the key, he could have access to the records to change anything he wished."

She saw the realization dawn on Griffin's face but was not naive enough to believe it changed anything.

"He wanted to go back and change what happened to his parents," Griffin stated.

"Not just that," Helen said. "To change what they'd *done*. To make it right."

She let the silence sit between them, hoping that perhaps this new knowledge would soften Griffin's heart. Her hope died when he shook his head.

"It doesn't matter. Terrible things happen every day to people who don't use their circumstances to justify killing others."

"I'm not justifying what he did. I'm simply saying that he was just a pawn in Alsorta's—"

"Alastor's," he interrupted.

Helen waved it away. "Whatever. Raum was a pawn as we have all been. And if Raum has information that might help us bring Alastor to justice—"

Griffin turned to her with disbelieving eyes. "You're not suggesting we work with him?"

She hurried to explain. "I'm simply saying that Alastor is the greater of the evils in this situation. Raum has worked with him. Knows his grounds. He probably knows the way that Alastor operates. Raum is sorry for what he's done. I know it. I can see it in his eyes." She could not stop the words now. They were tumbling out of her mouth with hardly a thought. "He'll help us. I know he will. If we solicit his assistance, we can stop Alastor and perhaps Raum will quietly submit to his punishment at the Dictata's hands."

She knew it was a lie even as she said it. Raum would submit to no one and nothing, but she did not have time to analyze her own willingness to lie on his behalf.

"I'll never work with him, Helen." Griffin's voice was steely. "Never. Not for any reason. And if you do . . ." He shook his head.

"What?" she whispered. "What will happen if I do?"

He turned to her, his eyes aflame. "Do you have feelings for him? Is that it?"

She started to shake her head. To deny the accusation. But Griffin stepped closer to her. So close that she backed up against the wall in an effort to avoid seeing the emotion swirling in his eyes.

"Did he come close to you like this?" Griffin's body was up against hers now. She could feel the heat of him as he touched a finger to her forehead, tracing the line of her cheekbone as his eyes burned into hers. "Did he touch you, Helen? Here, in your chamber, as I have done?"

She shook her head, unable to find the words to answer.

"Did you flush with his nearness," Griffin continued, bending lower until his lips were inches from hers, "as you do with mine?"

She did not answer. They were both breathing hard, though neither was moving a muscle. She could feel the strength coiled in Griffin's body, but it was not fear racing through her veins. It was desire. His strength would only be used to protect her— with his very life if necessary. This, she somehow knew.

"It's not like that," she finally managed, pushing aside the remembrance of Raum in her chamber, his eyes seeing through her until it felt as if her every secret was laid bare. "We spoke of everything that had happened. Of his regret. And of our plans to go after Alastor. He warned me about the dogs. That's all."

"If that's all, then why do you speak of him with such affection? Why do your eyes take on a strange light when you say his name?"

"I . . . I care what happens to him." She was as surprised by the words as Griffin. Surprised by the truth of it. "I know he's done terrible things. I know he's hurt people. He's hurt *us*. But . . ."

"But?"

She exhaled. "He was once a little boy who played in my garden. Who submitted to my tea parties and gave me uncut keys as tokens of his friendship. He has suffered loss as we have all suffered, and he has borne it alone. He's still alone. I simply care for him as I would care for any friend, in spite of what he has done." She stared defiantly into Griffin's eyes. "I'm sorry if you don't understand that."

He didn't answer. Not right away. He simply stared at her, frustration and anger and something like love moving across his face.

Finally, he shook his head. "You don't understand."

"What? What don't I understand?"

His eyes took on a fiery light. "When you appeared at our door that night, I had resigned myself to a short life spent with my brother. The assassins would come for Darius and me as they had come for our parents on that dark London street. We might be able to fight them off for a time, but the likelihood of our apprehending the killer was unlikely. Not when so many others had been killed before us. I knew it all. Accepted it. Almost welcomed the knowledge of my impending death. And then . . ." He hesitated.

"Yes?"

He sighed, his expression softening as he looked at her. "And then you appeared in a nightdress with nothing but an almost-empty valise and eyes full of fear, and I knew that nothing would ever be the same. From that moment forward, I knew

I would die to protect you, and over the last few days I've found myself wanting to live. Not just today and tomorrow. Not simply long enough to murder the ones who murdered our parents, but long enough to have a future. With you."

His eyes were full of anguish. She wanted to banish it. To bring back the peace on his face when he'd slept with the kitten purring softly on his chest in the light of the fire.

She reached up to touch his cheek. "Griffin."

"Don't you see, Helen? There would be no life for me now without you in it." He covered her hand with his own, bringing it to his lips. "I need to know that you're mine. That I alone have your heart."

His eyes shined with love for her. It was a love she could see and feel. A love as certain as the rising sun. Raum was a world away. A lifetime away. The little boy she had known was gone forever. There was no changing the past, whatever Raum believed.

"I'm yours, Griffin." She spoke softly and meant every word. "Only yours."

And as he lowered his mouth to hers, she consigned Raum's blue eyes to the halls of memory, losing herself completely in Griffin's fevered kiss.

THIRTY-ONE

Something's happened! Wake up, Master Channing! Something's happened!"

Helen woke with a start, blinking away sleep and wondering if she was imagining the boy standing at the side of her bed.

"What is it? Who are you and what are you doing in my chamber?" she asked him.

The windows were black, despite the fact that the curtains were open. She and Griffin must have slept for a long time. Still, that did not explain the presence of the boy at her bed.

Something must have happened to Darius.

Panic exploded inside her as Griffin sat up and addressed the urchin by name.

"Wills? What are you doing here? What's happened?"

"It's Master Galizur," the boy named Wills heaved, out of breath. "They got him on the street."

Griffin was up like a shot.

"What do you mean?" he demanded. "Where's my brother?"

The boy gulped. Helen looked at his face and knew with certainty that the fear written there was not because of Griffin's question.

"He's already gone, Master. He told me to wake you and the miss." His eyes darted toward Helen. "And he said you both should come, sir. Right away."

Nothing that had happened thus far frightened Helen like the sight of the half-open door to Galizur's building.

She and Griffin had exited the house less than two minutes after being awoken by Wills. They jumped immediately to Galizur's, this time holding hands by choice. Whatever had happened, there was no question that it was not good. Helen drew strength from the feel of Griffin's hand over hers as they stepped under the streetlamp, slipping into the darkness of light travel. A moment later, they appeared in front of Galizur's building.

They stepped through the open door into the cold hallway

beyond. The sconces had been broken, and their feet crunched over the broken glass as they headed cautiously toward the back of the hall. Helen thought of Anna, of her diligent attention to the locks that secured the building, and hoped fervently that she was safe.

Crossing the threshold of the second doorway, they took a few more careful steps before Griffin turned to her, one finger to his lips. Helen stopped in her tracks, tuning her ears to the sound emanating from within the building. The voices were low. Under the tone of simple conversation Helen thought she heard weeping, though she could not be certain.

A moment later, Griffin waved her forward. She followed him down the hall, her anxiety building as they passed through the frame of yet another unlocked door.

Something was very, very wrong.

At last, they came to the final door. It was open as the others had been, and Griffin stopped in front of her, gesturing her back against the wall. She understood that he thought it might be a trap. That he was preparing for an ambush. Trying to get a glimpse into the sitting room before waving her through.

Placing her hand on her sickle, she took a deep breath and said another silent prayer for Anna and Galizur just as a cry erupted from within. It was followed by the sound of Darius speaking in a tone she had never heard him use.

"Anna . . . Anna," he was saying, his voice was steeped in helplessness. "What can I do? Tell me what to do!"

And then, Anna's voice, softer but with no hint of duress or threat.

Griffin sighed aloud, glancing back at her. "I think it's all right. Come on."

She followed him into the room. And though she was prepared to greet her friend—to ask what had happened and what was wrong—she was unprepared for the sight that greeted her.

"Anna?" It was all she could think of to say as she took in Anna, kneeling beside the sofa and the still, prone frame of her father.

Anna turned her tear-streaked face to Helen.

"What's happened?" Helen stepped to the other side of the sofa. "Is he all right?"

But she knew that Galizur wasn't. His face was ashen, still in a way that went beyond slumber. Something dark was spreading beneath the back of his head, creeping like a disease across the fabric of the sofa.

Anna shook her head. "He's . . ." Her voice caught in her

throat. She took a moment to steady it before continuing. "He's gone."

"What do you mean?" Helen was vaguely aware of the hysteria creeping into her voice. "What do you mean he's 'gone'?"

She asked the question even as she knew.

Griffin reached for her hand. "Helen . . ." he began.

Anna rose, smoothing her gown as she stepped toward Helen. She took Helen's hands in her own, gazing into her eyes.

"He was coming home from the corner market when they got him. He . . ." She wiped the tears away from her porcelain cheeks. "He made it home but died soon after."

"What? No." Helen shook her head, backing away as if denial alone would make it all untrue. "*No.* That cannot be."

"Was it thieves?" Griffin spoke beside her. "Wraiths?"

"I'm afraid not." Anna said softly. "It was Alsorta—Alastor's—men."

Griffin's eyes were lit with confusion. "I don't understand. Why would they come after Galizur? He's appointed by the Dictata as an intermediary. He has amnesty."

"Alastor is not playing by the rules, brother." Darius spoke bitterly, placing his hands on Anna's shoulders. "In case you haven't noticed."

"How do you know?" insisted Griffin. "How can you be sure it was Alastor."

Darius reached a hand toward them, opening his palm. In it lay one of Galizur's darts.

Time seemed to stretch into infinity as Helen stared at it. She stumbled backward, pulling her hands away from Anna's, turning her back on them all as the knowledge hit her. For a moment, she could not breathe.

A gentle hand closed on her shoulder.

"It's not your fault." Anna's voice was soft. "Father wanted you to have them. It was his task to see that you remained alive. He has always been prepared to sacrifice his life to see it done."

"But I left it," Helen whispered, turning to face Anna. She saw the animals, snarling and snapping as they inched toward them, falling to the ground as the darts found their targets. And then, the last dog, hit too close to Helen's position at the mouth of the tunnel. "I retrieved the first four, but the last dog came at us as we were descending into the tunnel. The men were right on the animal's heels."

"I understand, Helen." Anna looked into her eyes. "And so did my father."

Helen looked into her eyes and saw that Anna *did* understand.

But that didn't make it any easier.

"I'm sorry, Anna. I'm so sorry." She wanted to weep, but of course, she could not. She wanted to beg Anna's forgiveness, but it would only be selfishness, asking Anna to give her something—something she didn't deserve—at a time when it was her task to give to Anna. She leaned forward instead, wrapping her arms around the other girl in an embrace. A moment later, she pulled away to offer her the only thing she had.

A promise.

"He'll pay, Anna. We'll make him pay."

And though Anna's smile held only a remnant of its former brilliance, Helen was surprised to see that her eyes were the same serene pool that they'd always been.

"If Alastor pays for anything," Anna said, "it will be for the execution of the world's Keepers. Your safety was my father's primary purpose."

Griffin raised a hand to his forehead. "These are serious infractions of the treaty. An opening salvo to a war between the Legion and the Alliance. "

"Unless we can stop it," Darius said. "Here and now."

Griffin turned away, pacing the room. "Except now Alastor knows we're after him. We won't gain easy access to the grounds again."

"We'll storm the blasted grounds if we have to," Darius thundered.

His voice caused Helen to flinch, but despite his assertion, she knew that would not be possible. They would be cut down by Alastor's men, by his dogs, by his own power for all Helen knew, before they ever reached his inner sanctum.

"If you can find a way into Alastor's grounds, there might be tools enough for you to defeat him," Anna said, sniffling. "It's true that many of Father's creations were not yet tested and ready for use, but some were very, very close."

Griffin nodded. "It's something, but I'm afraid gaining access to the estate will be at least as difficult as defeating Alastor once we're inside."

"Unless . . ." Helen wanted to stop herself. Griffin would be angry. Worse than angry.

To say nothing of Darius.

And yet, what else did they have?

Griffin turned his eyes on her. "Unless what?"

She swallowed her fear, forcing herself to meet his eyes. "Unless we enlist Raum's help."

For a moment, the room was so silent that Helen thought she'd gone deaf. She could not even hear her own breathing in the vacuum left by her words.

Darius finally spoke, his voice low and threatening. "How dare you mention that . . . that *traitor* in Anna's presence? In our presence? I would rather die than—"

"If you would just listen, you'll see why this makes sense. Why this will help Anna," Helen broke in, wanting to stop him. To make him listen before he went so far down the road of refusal that there was no way back. She kept talking though Darius was still railing, and she could not even be certain how much of her own tirade he could hear over his own. "Raum has worked for Alastor, but that also means he knows more about Alastor's grounds than we do. Has probably met him on those very grounds. How else could he have known about the dogs? Help is there, Darius. It's right there. I know Raum will help if I ask. And if you refuse . . . if you refuse, you do so only out of stubbornness and anger, not out of a desire to protect Anna. Whatever you decide, at least be honest with yourself about that."

She was surprised to find that the room was quiet. At some point in her speech, Darius had stopped talking, though she did not delude herself into thinking he'd actually listened.

"She's right, Darius. And I think you know it." Helen could not have been more shocked to hear Griffin come to her aid. "The Summit is the day after tomorrow. We'll need all the help we can get to destroy Alastor before the Legion makes its move for control."

"You, Griffin?" Darius turned on his brother. "You would allow this? After all that has happened?"

"It isn't for me to allow or disallow, Darius. We're equals in this. We all seek vengeance for our parents' deaths. For Galizur's death. We all want to see Alastor sent back to hell where he belongs. But we're partners. We must decide together. I'm simply telling you the way I see it."

"Would Raum submit to censure by the Dictata, if he were given amnesty to aid you?" Anna asked.

Helen thought of Raum's flashing eyes. Of the straight set of his spine and the way he held himself apart from everyone in the world. She thought of it all and told the truth.

"I don't know."

Anna nodded, chewing her lower lip. She turned to Darius, taking his large hand in her small one. "If Raum can give you access to Alastor's estate and information about his power, it's worth considering."

"According to the Dictata's own rules, we should kill Raum on sight for what he's done," Darius said angrily.

"Yes." Anna nodded. "But if he agrees to appear before them when it's all said and done—assuming he even survives—I think they would agree that seeking his assistance is the wisest course of action."

"And you would agree to such a thing, Anna?" Darius's eyes searched hers. Helen looked away, trying to give them what privacy she could under the circumstances. What was passing between them felt too intimate, too personal, for Griffin and her to be party to it. "Wouldn't it pain you to see us working with the person who is, ultimately, responsible for everything? Even your father's death?"

"I think it's more complicated than that," Anna said. "We've all lost something, Raum included. I think my father would want you to rid the world—and its Keepers—of any threat by the Legion. And I don't think he would begrudge you the aid of the lost one to do it."

Helen felt the whole world hang in the balance of the silence that followed. The world in which they lived and the Orb spinning slowly below them. Both of them fighting for a chance.

Finally Darius turned to her. "How do you know he'll come?"

If you need me, I'll be there.

Helen had not realized she was holding her breath until she let it go.

"He'll come."

THIRTY-TWO

I don't much like the idea of Raum being in your chamber, despite the fact that he's been here before. Or maybe because of it."

Griffin's voice drifted to her from a corner of the room. He sat in the shadows, not wanting to deter a possible visit from Raum but unwilling to let Helen speak to him alone if—*when,* she told herself—he appeared.

And although there was shallow humor in Griffin's voice, humor likely put there for her benefit, Helen could not even manage a smile. She kept seeing Anna. Even now, there was no escaping the desolation in the other girl's eyes as she pulled a blanket over her father's face and sent word of his death to the Dictata.

"I'm sorry," Helen said. "For everything."

"Helen." Griffin's voice was a caress in the soft light of the fire. "There's no need to apologize. To continue apologizing. Anna was right. Galizur knew the risks. Ours is a dangerous task. Everyone who helps us shares in our danger. That's no secret, to them or to us."

"Still," she said softly. "What will Anna do without Galizur?"

"What we all must do." His voice was heavy with sadness. "Continue with the task our parents gave their lives for. Isn't that what they would have wanted?"

Helen thought of her parents. Of her father's laughing eyes. His patience in teaching her to fence, ride, and shoot a bow. Of her mother's gentle hands and the many wise words, handed out like so many parcels for Helen to open when she needed them.

As if her mother had known all along that she wouldn't be here to offer them herself.

Helen thought of them both and knew that Griffin was right. They would want her to fight. To rid the world of Alastor and take her place among the Keepers. To keep the Orb—and the world it represented—spinning until the Keepers would be replenished.

"You're right, of course." She directed her words to the shadowed corner. "It's what they would want. And I know Galizur would want it that way as well."

"And so we'll see that it's done." There was a pause in which the only sound in the room was the crackling of the fire. "You should sleep while you can. I'll alert you if he . . . if Raum makes an appearance."

Her feelings for Griffin deepened as he stumbled over the name. He did not like to speak of Raum. Did not want to utter his name or entertain the idea of Raum entering his home. Did not want Raum in her chamber in the dead of night. But he allowed it for the same reason he allowed Darius to take the lead. He loved them. Helen saw that now. Griffin loved his brother.

And he loved her.

His love was not selfish or prideful or domineering or full of expectation.

It simply was. And she knew now that whatever happened, she loved him as well. She would fight to protect him and would die doing so if necessary.

"Griffin?" She called out to him across the room.

"Yes?"

"You've become my friend, and I love you." It was right and true and that made saying it easy.

She heard his surprise in the intake of his breath. "And I, you, Helen. I think I've loved you since the moment you first stood on my doorstep." He paused. "But now, I really must insist that you sleep. My love will still be here when you wake up."

She smiled, though no one could see it, and then marveled that she could find a smile on such a night. It was the last thing she thought about before drifting off to sleep.

"Helen? Wake up! Someone's coming."

She didn't know how long Griffin had been calling her name when she finally came around, but she was not yet coherent when she heard scratching at the window, the scuff of boots along the sill.

She lay still, waiting to sit up until she heard the thud of boots on the carpet.

She sat up. "I knew you'd come."

It was not what she had planned to say.

"I heard what happened." Raum stepped carefully across the floor, stopping at her bedside. "I told you I'd be here if you needed me."

She felt suddenly like a traitor. She had allowed Raum to come knowing that he would be blindsided by Griffin's presence. It placed her in a precarious position, trapped in the web of her own torn allegiances and her affection for two men who were, for all intents and purposes, mortal enemies.

But it was too late to worry about that now. Raum was here, lowering himself to sit on her bed even as she heard Griffin rise in the corner.

"I think that's close enough, don't you?"

Raum froze in the moment before he stood up, backing slowly toward the window like a caged animal as he peered into the shadows.

"Who's that? Who's there?" Even now his voice was as calm as if he were inquiring about the weather. It was the voice of someone who had taken care of himself for a very long time and gotten himself out of more scrapes than Helen could ever imagine.

"Griffin Channing. You killed my parents." It was said calmly and with resignation.

Helen swung her legs over the bed as Raum turned his face to her.

"You knew about this?" he asked her. "Set me up?"

She shook her head. "It's not like that. We need your help."

"While that may be true, I find it hard to believe that one of the Channing sons would ever seek my assistance. They know what I've done."

"Yes, we do," Griffin said.

"Well, then." Helen noticed with surprise that, as he spoke, Raum had one hand on a sickle at his belt. She had thought they were only for the Keepers. "I imagine you'd like to kill me. Send my body to the infernal Dictata as proof that the executioner is dead."

Griffin's nod was slow. "I won't deny that there is a part of me that would like to do exactly that. But I'm afraid it's not that simple."

Helen jumped in. "You were right about the dogs. We would be dead if you hadn't told me. Galizur gave me tranquilizer darts to put them to sleep, but I left one behind and they . . ." Her voice broke and she cleared it before continuing. "They traced it to Galizur and murdered him."

There was regret in Raum's eyes. "I'm sorry. He was a good man. I remember his kindness when I was young."

"Now we have a problem," Griffin said.

Raum raised his eyebrows. "I thought you already had problems."

"Not the least of which has been you."

Helen heard the coiled rage in Griffin's voice and knew he was close to losing his temper. She started talking, hoping to head off an explosion between the two men that would cost them all time and energy they could not afford.

"Victor Alsorta isn't just the leader of the Syndicate," she explained. "He's Alastor, a member of the Legion's Blackguard, seeking control of the records on their behalf. He doesn't want them to increase his own wealth and power as we first thought, but to change the course of history that has led to the Dictata's rule for centuries." She looked into Raum's eyes, speaking softly. "But then, I imagine you already knew all of that."

"I did."

There was no point asking why he hadn't told her. "We think the other members of the Syndicate are planning some kind of overthrow at the Summit, which would accelerate the Legion's plans considerably. The Legion would prefer to have access to the records, but if they can't find the key in time, there's every reason to believe that Alastor will take the world by force."

Raum crossed his arms over his chest. "What does this have to do with me?"

Helen continued while Griffin brooded. "We won't be able to access Alastor's estate again. Not the way we did before. He'll be on alert. And he's going to be ready for us."

"I'm waiting," Raum said.

Griffin saved her by saying aloud what she could not. "You've

worked for him. You obviously know his security setup and probably a lot more that we don't know about. We need your help getting in and killing him before he can kill the rest of us."

Helen allowed herself to hope in the silence that followed. Then, Raum laughed aloud.

"You expect me to believe that you want my help? That you would trust me to fight beside you? After what I've done?"

His voice was incredulous, but Helen heard the self-loathing in his words.

"It's not our first choice, believe me," Griffin said. "But we don't have any other options."

Raum narrowed his eyes, looking at Griffin and Helen with suspicion. "That isn't all, is it? You won't say 'thank you very much and have a nice life' when it's all said and done."

"No, it won't be that simple," Griffin confirmed.

"Then, what?"

Helen tried to find the words to appeal to Raum. She had a feeling they would not be as carefully chosen by Griffin.

"You would help us as a show of good faith," she finally said. "When it's all over, assuming we survive, you agree to present yourself before the Dictata for judgment. In return for your assistance, we will plead with the Dictata to show you leniency."

He did not laugh or otherwise deride the suggestion. "So I'm to believe the Dictata will simply forgive me for the execution of the world's Keepers—"

"You said you didn't kill them," Helen interrupted.

He nodded. "Nevertheless, you expect me to believe that the Dictata will let me walk away, knowing I ordered the murder of the Keepers?"

"Not you. Alastor," Helen protested. She heard Griffin's snort of contempt at the rationalization and fought the urge to argue the point all over again.

Raum turned his eyes on her. "It's true that Alastor ordered it done, Helen. But I hunted you. I found you. I ransacked your homes for the key. And then I ordered my own hired killers to murder you and your families."

The sorrow in his eyes told her what the truth cost him. She knew it was a truth that he had repeated to himself a hundred times since they'd found each other, even though he was saying it aloud to her for the first time.

"And yet, if you help us set things right, I think the Dictata will take into consideration the . . . mitigating circumstances of the situation." Helen was surprised at Griffin's conciliatory tone. Perhaps Raum's regret was not lost on him after all. "It won't be a free pass, no. But it might be a fresh start."

Raum paced to the firebox. He turned away, seeking what little privacy he could find while still maintaining a visual on the room in which they all stood. Helen recognized the maneuver. They had all been taught to trust no one. Raum more than anyone.

He rubbed his jaw with one hand, his face pensive. There was no guarantee that they would prevail over Alastor even with Raum's help, but without it, they were almost certainly doomed.

He turned to face them. "I'm sorry. I can't do it."

"But, why?" Helen had difficulty speaking around the despair that rose in her throat. She stepped toward him, placing a hand on his arm. "Can't you see? We need you. This is your chance to set things right. To begin again."

"I've already had to begin again," he said wearily. "I don't have the energy to do so once more, and the truth is, I'm not even sure I care about the outcome."

She flinched at the words. "You don't care what happens to us? What happens to me?" She lifted her chin, pushing on. "I don't believe you. I know you care. I can see it in your eyes."

Her words struck him like a hammer. For a moment, there was such vulnerability, such tenderness in his eyes that she wanted to weep. Then, as quickly as it had come, it was gone.

Something slammed down over the emotion and his expression returned to nonchalance.

"I wish you well, Helen. That much is true." He brushed past her on his way to the door. "But I can't do anything to help. I have my own worries. Every low-life criminal in the city is looking for me at the moment, mortal and otherwise. It's all I can do to keep myself alive."

"I should have known that you would look after yourself first. It's what you've always done." She knew it wasn't fair even as she flung the words at his retreating back. Raum had been forced to look after himself. There had been no one else to do it. But she couldn't seem to stop herself, and she continued shouting as he reached the door. "Run away, then. Run away from the possibility of something lasting and good. It's your strong suit, after all."

He stopped in his tracks, his hand on the doorknob. Griffin stepped up next to her as if to protect her from an impending explosion. But in the end, Raum said nothing at all. He simply opened the door, disappearing into the hallway.

Gone as if he had never been there at all.

THIRTY-THREE

W hat is all of this?" Helen exclaimed, holding up a coiled metal contraption before adding it to the pile on the worktable. "I can't make sense of any of it."

They were in Galizur's laboratory, sifting through stacks of paper and crates full of mechanical remnants. After some discussion, they had agreed to see if it held anything that might aid them in a battle. They would proceed to the Alsorta estate this evening. Getting onto the grounds would be at least as difficult as gaining access to Alastor a second time, but they had little choice.

The Summit was tomorrow. They wouldn't get another chance.

Raum's refusal to help still stung. Helen had been so sure. So certain that he would come to their aid if she asked. But in the end, he hadn't cared for her at all. He would see her die at Alastor's hands before risking his own life to save her.

"Father was always at work on new gadgetry," Anna said from across the room. "I'm afraid it will take me a long time to figure it all out."

Although Darius had implored her to rest, Anna insisted that grieving would come later. At the present, she needed to keep moving. To contribute to the cause that had cost her father his life.

"We should take the new glaives." Darius held one of the small rods up to the light. A moment later, it extended into the spear Helen remembered from her second visit to Galizur's. Darius continued. "I know they haven't been tested beyond the melons here in the laboratory, but they seem to work well enough to me."

"I'm all for it," Griffin said. "Glaives, sickles . . . what else?"

"How about some new darts?" Anna rose from her chair at the table, holding something out to Helen.

"But . . ." Helen looked down, surprised to see a row of darts nestled inside a leather pouch. To her eye, at least, they looked identical to the ones fashioned by Galizur. "I thought there were only five."

"There were five *finished* darts," Anna explained. "But there were a few more that simply needed adjusting. They should be fine now, though. I've given you extras just in case."

Helen counted ten of them.

"Why don't you let me hold on to those . . ." Darius began, reaching for the darts.

Anna pulled her arm away, tying the pouch closed before handing it to Helen. "Helen did a fine job with them before."

Helen could only look at the leather in Anna's hands. She had not done a fine job. Not at all. But Anna's offer was a benediction. Forgiveness for her oversight.

"Thank you." Helen took the darts. She looked into Anna's eyes and knew the other girl understood.

"All right, then." Darius looked around. "What about fire? Wasn't your father working on a weapon that spewed fire?"

Anna shook her head. "It won't work. Not on Alastor. He's a demon—a creature of fire. And while you can fend him off with the sickle and glaive, even those things will not destroy him."

Griffin looked at her uncomprehendingly. "What do you mean? The glaive is the only way to destroy otherworldly creatures."

"Wraiths, yes," Anna said. "Even minor demons. But not those like Alastor. You can only hope to send a demon of his strength back where he came from with the sickle or glaive. Though he has been banished from this world from time to time through the ages, he has never been destroyed. If he had been, he wouldn't be able to make a stand now."

"Are you saying he's indestructible?" Helen asked, wondering why they were bothering to arm themselves if Alastor couldn't be destroyed.

Anna sighed. "Not exactly. There is one way . . ."

"What is it?" Darius asked.

"This."

Helen was stunned into silence when the answer came, not from Anna as she had expected, but from the tunnel leading into the laboratory.

The voice of a man.

Raum.

He strode carefully into the workroom, holding something long and slender in his outstretched hand.

Darius lunged for him and was stopped by Griffin, whose own arms bulged with the effort of holding his brother back.

"Think, brother," he said. "Think before you act."

Raum did not seem to take the threat seriously.

"Not exactly the welcome I envisioned," he said, stepping farther into the room. "I was, after all, invited."

Helen crossed her arms over her bosom. "You declined the invitation, if I remember correctly."

"Yes." He met her eyes. "But I've had a change of heart. Assuming you still desire my assistance."

The room descended into silence, save the sound of Darius's strained breathing as he struggled to gain control over himself. A moment later, Griffin let his brother go and tipped his head to the object in Raum's hands.

"What is it?"

Raum was still watchful, as if he expected Darius to lunge at him again and was bracing himself for the attack. Finally, he grabbed the end of the object and pulled.

Helen could not stop the intake of breath as the sword emerged, shimmering and slightly curved, from the sheath in Raum's hands. It was an object of such beauty, such perfection, that everything seemed to dim around it.

"Is that . . ." Anna stepped closer to Raum, her eyes riveted to the blade, until Darius put a protective hand on her arm.

Raum nodded. "It is."

Anna shook her head in wonder. "But how did you get it? *Where* did you get it?"

"I've had it in my possession since I realized Victor Alsorta was Alastor," he said. "You might call it an insurance policy of sorts."

"But there are only three." Anna looked up at him, obviously reluctant to take her eyes off the sword. "Only three in the whole world."

"Ahem," Griffin interrupted. "This might be a good time to tell the rest of us what it is, exactly. I realize it's a sword, but what makes this one so special? How will it destroy Alastor when nothing else will?"

"It's the Sword of the Ages," Anna said, as if they should all know to what she was referring. "One of them."

"And what is the . . . Sword of the Ages?" Helen felt almost ridiculous saying it aloud.

It was Raum who answered. "In the beginning, there was one point of entry to this world for all of your—our— kind. A place where the angels who were joining this world entered and those who were leaving it exited. When the Alliance was formed, a great fire was built there. Many, many angels had walked its ground even at that time. It was thought to be hallowed. Those who were chosen to found the Alliance gathered to forge and anoint three swords containing all of their power, concentrated for eternity in their blades. It's only with one of these swords—forged in honor of the original three Keepers—that one of the Blackguard can be destroyed."

"And only if it is used in precisely the correct way," Anna added.

"Is there a correct way to use a sword?" Griffin asked. "I've always thought it was a simple device."

"Not this one," Raum said.

"A greater demon can only be destroyed by one of the swords, and only if it is used to pierce the demon's heart at sunrise." Anna made it sound simple. As if such an extraordinary set of circumstances were commonplace.

"You cannot be serious." Darius's voice was disbelieving.

"She's telling the truth," Raum said. "The old ways are filled with rituals. Many of the terms of the Treaty are based on them. This is one of them. A way to guarantee that even the Legion have some peace in this world if they adhere to the Treaty's terms. The swords have been locked away by the Alliance to insure some semblance of order between us and them."

"Then how did you get it?" Helen asked.

"It doesn't matter." Raum avoided the question, his eyes shifting away from hers. "It will aid us in destroying Alastor."

"If we can get onto the grounds and into the house," Helen reminded him. "To say nothing of timing it all correctly and getting close enough to Alastor to actually use the sword."

"True." Raum sheathed the sword, hitching it to his belt. "How did you get in last time?"

Griffin walked to one of the worktables and unrolled the schematic of Alastor's estate. It was odd, clustering around it and seeing halls they had traversed, ground she had covered as she tried to make her escape with Griffin and Darius, as a series of straight lines and scattered markings.

"We came up from the tunnels here." Griffin tapped the area in the woods between the house and the front gate.

"And you exited the same way?" Raum was still looking at the drawing.

"Yes," Griffin confirmed.

Raum looked up at him. "That's a lot of ground to cover, especially with the dogs on your trail. I'm surprised you made it."

Looking at the drawing, at the distance they had covered from the house to the tunnel opening, Helen couldn't have agreed more, though she didn't say so aloud.

"We weren't exactly overflowing with options," Darius sneered.

Raum ignored him. "There are two other access routes, but neither of them is without risk."

"What are they?" Helen asked.

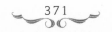

He lowered his eyes to the drawing. "There's a place in the fence here." He indicated an area to the rear of the house, as he continued. "The security is spotty. The fence is set back from the house. In the woods, actually. The guards tend to skip it every other round or so."

Darius interrupted. "I doubt they'll be skipping it now. They're probably on high alert."

"Perhaps." Raum shrugged. "But I think it's still a potential way in if we observe the schedule of the guards for a couple of hours beforehand. The problem is, it's a terrible way out. The fence is iron and topped with points. It would take some time to scale."

"Then how will we get over it to get in?" Helen asked.

Raum's answer was simple. "With effort. We'll have to aid one another and the last person over will have no help at all. But it is not impossible given enough time, and we'll probably have more of that on the way in."

Now Helen understood. "But on the way out, we may well be on the run."

"Exactly," Raum said. "Which brings me to the second option." He touched a familiar place on the map.

"The kitchen?" Griffin asked.

"There's a tunnel entrance there. In the pantry closet."

"Our plans for the tunnels don't show that entrance." There was suspicion in Darius's voice, as if Raum was intentionally trying to lead them astray.

"That's because this schematic is based on plans laid out by the city when the tunnels were originally built," Raum explained.

Griffin looked up from the drawing. "Are there a different set of plans that we don't know about?"

"Not plans, no." Raum said. "But Alsorta had a private entrance to the tunnels built directly from the house."

"Why would he want access to the sewer tunnels?" Helen asked.

"If you were a member of the Blackguard disguised as a mortal businessman, would you want your associates to use the front door?"

Griffin nodded knowingly. "So he uses the secret tunnel as an entry and exit point for members of the Legion."

"Exactly."

"How very convenient," Darius said drily. "So why wouldn't we use the tunnel entrance within the house instead of the fence to gain access to the house on the way in?"

"In the kitchen?" Raum raised his eyebrows. "Clearly, you haven't spent much time in one."

"What Raum means," Helen broke in, trying to head off an argument, or worse, an outright brawl, "is that kitchens are busy at all times of the day and night. The servants may be setting bread to rise for the morning or cleaning up after a late dinner party."

"In or out, we'll probably be seen if we use the kitchen entrance," Raum said. "It's just less of a danger on the way out, especially if we've managed to destroy Alsorta."

"Which means we climb the fence at the back on the way in, and use the tunnels to escape when we're done," Helen finished.

Raum nodded. "And there's one more thing."

They were all looking at him now, the drawing forgotten.

"What is it?" Griffin asked.

"Alsorta—Alastor—has a newfangled system of lighting. The lamps are lit by a system that pipes gas throughout the house. They're lit with a switch and put out the same way. We'll need to extinguish them by cutting off the supply from the cellar as soon as we're in the house."

"Why?" Helen shook her head. "Why take the time? We can extinguish them as we go if necessary."

"And give Alastor the chance to summon the wraiths?"

Understanding was finding its way into Helen's mind, wading through the bits and pieces of knowledge she had gleaned over the past few days.

"They'll come through the light," she finally said. "They'll jump and come to Alastor's aid if we give them the chance."

"Yes," Raum confirmed. "And while we might stand a chance of fending off Alastor and his mortal henchmen, I would not like to lay odds if we were up against the demon himself and an army of underlings, however mindless they may be."

Griffin straightened, his voice as hard as iron. "Then we won't give him the chance to summon them."

THIRTY-FOUR

How much longer?" Helen tried to keep her teeth from clattering together as they hid outside Alastor's fence at the rear of the house.

They had made their way to the estate using the sewer tunnels, this time emerging two miles from the house. Walking quickly, they arrived at the edge of the property in less than half an hour. It had not been difficult to stay hidden. They used the woods to skirt the grounds until they came to the poorly lit section of fence that Raum had shown them on the map. It had been at least three hours since their arrival, and Helen was beginning to fear that she would be too cold to scale the fence when the time finally came.

"If he sticks to the schedule he's been keeping," Griffin said from the tree next to her, "he should be by again in about ten minutes."

"And they should skip this section of the fence on the next go-round," Darius said from the shadows. "Which means we'll move as soon as he passes to maximize our time."

Raum, leaning against a tree on the other side of her, said nothing. Helen sensed his isolation in every move of his body. In the distance he had kept between them on the road to the house. In the position of his hand, on the sickle at his belt even when there wasn't a guard in sight. As if he expected them to turn on him at any moment. As if they were not to be trusted, even as they cast their lot with his and prepared to enter Alastor's lair.

"I'm going to take a look at the fence," Griffin whispered from her right. "I might be able to formulate a strategy for getting over it more easily if I can get a closer look."

Darius crouched low beside him. "I'll go with you."

"Stay here, Helen. Don't move and don't make a sound." His eyes drifted to Raum. "Unless you need help, of course."

She sighed, torn between apologizing to Raum and understanding Griffin's concern. "I'll be fine. Just be careful."

Griffin nodded. They were gone a second later in a quiet rustle of leaves.

Helen turned to Raum. "I'm sorry."

He shrugged. "No apology necessary. If I were Griffin, I'd want to protect you from me as well."

"Even still . . ." she said. "You're helping us. It seems that should count for something."

"In my experience, nothing counts for anything." Despite the words, his voice was not bitter. It carried the same resignation she had heard before. As if he knew too much of the world. Had glimpsed the future and already knew there was no point in fighting the way things were.

"And yet, you're here."

She saw him nod in the dark. "That I am."

"Why?" she whispered. "What made you change your mind?"

He picked a twig up from the ground, twisting it in his hands as he spoke. "My life. Or lack thereof."

"What do you mean?"

"It's been fine, taking care of myself these past years. Being alone." She knew from his voice that it was a lie, but she couldn't steal his pride by saying so aloud. She listened quietly as he continued. "But it's no kind of life. Not really. I think it's time I face the Dictata and be well and truly free. I'm tired of running." He paused. "And then there is the matter of you."

The last part surprised her. "Me?"

He sighed. "Yes."

"What about me?"

There was a long pause before he spoke again. "It's been a long time since someone believed in me, Helen. A long time since I've believed in myself. But these past days . . ."

"Yes?" she asked softly.

He plucked absently at the leaves on the ground. "I've felt your belief in me, and though it seems small, I've begun to wonder if that's all we really need. Just one person who knows us truly. One person who knows the darkness that lies within and believes in us anyway."

She thought about the words, wondering if they were true.

"And there's one more thing," he said softly.

"What is it?"

"I don't want to see you hurt." He turned toward her, his eyes finding hers in the dark. "It's mad, isn't it? We haven't seen each other since we were children, yet I feel the strongest desire to protect you."

The confession made it difficult to breathe. What could she say? That ever since he had found her in the factory building she had not been sure of anything? That her own loyalties were constantly in question because of the distant remembrance of a blue-eyed boy who looked upon her with affection and gave her uncut keys in the garden?

He had favored her with the truth. She would do the same.

"I feel the same way about you."

He chuckled softly in the darkness. His laughter was tense and unsure, as if he hadn't done it in a very long time. "While I appreciate the sentiment, I hardly have need of your protection. I'm a foot taller and outweigh you by a hundred pounds."

She smiled at the truth of it as something warm and familiar moved between them. It was not unlike falling into one's own bed after a long journey.

"Yes, but there are other kinds of danger," she said.

"Like what?"

"Loneliness. Guilt. Despair." She smiled. "To name a few."

"What will you do when this is all over?" Raum asked.

"I don't know. I suppose I'll learn the things I need to know in order to fulfill my duty as one of the Keepers. I'll rebuild the house I was raised in." She met his eyes. "Plant a new garden."

She couldn't pull her gaze from his. Not when he placed his hand against her cheek. Not even when he rubbed his thumb gently against her lips. His skin was callused and rough, and she reveled in the feel of it. All of her loss—and yes, all of her affection—was reflected in his eyes.

"The guard's coming." Raum dropped his hand from her face as Griffin appeared next to her. "As soon as he passes we make our move."

Helen nodded, her face afire with shame and, if she were honest with herself, something dangerously close to desire.

Darius settled against the trunk of the tree next to Griffin. A few moments later, Helen heard the boot steps of the approaching guard on the other side of the fence. She looked straight ahead, marking the guard's position by the light that bobbed over the ground, casting strange shadows in the trees. It was a cursory pass, as they had come to expect. If Alastor had put his men on alert, they had their focus elsewhere. Clearly, no one was very worried about the wooded tree line at the back of the house. It made Helen angry. Obviously, Alastor thought they were stupid enough to use the same point of entry and exit twice in a row.

They listened as the guard's footsteps faded into the distance, his light disappearing into the night. Then they all sat up and prepared to move.

"We think we have a way over," Griffin said. "Come on."

She followed him and Darius to the fence, feeling Raum's presence behind her and forcibly banishing from her mind the moment that had passed between them while Griffin had been gone. It didn't matter. All that mattered was here and now—destroying Alastor and the Legion's foothold in this world.

They came to the iron fence. Helen gazed upward, looking for its end. She couldn't find it. Whether due to its height or the black iron that blended into the darkness around them, the fence seemed to go on and on, stretching endlessly into the night sky.

The first spasm of panic gripped her. She ignored it as Griffin began unlacing his shirt.

"What are you doing?" she whispered.

"We're going to make a rope," he explained. "We'll tie our shirts together and you'll add . . . whatever it is you can add while remaining decent—"

"Wait a minute," she interrupted, certain she had not heard him correctly. "You want me to undress? Here?"

"It's the only way," Griffin continued, removing his shirt to bare his muscled shoulders. "If we knot the rope at the top, letting it hang on either side of the fence, we can use it to climb up and over. Darius will go first, followed by Raum. After that, I'll give you a boost up."

"And then what?" She was trying to imagine it in her mind, and while she thought she understood what he was suggesting, she sincerely hoped she was wrong.

He looked into her eyes. "You'll have to use the knots on

the rope to place your feet and hands, but it will be easier than trying to scale the fence itself. The bars are smooth iron and run parallel to each other. There's nothing to hold onto without the rope."

She wanted to laugh aloud at the idea of it. She could barely ride a horse without falling off. Scaling an iron fence topped by sharp points in the dead of night did not bode well.

But she knew there was no point debating the idea. This was it. Their way in.

And if the men could do it, so would she, even if it did require climbing the rope and partially undressing in the middle of the woods.

She removed her jacket and handed it to Griffin, already knotting his shirt to Darius's. A few seconds later, Raum handed his shirt to her to add to the rope. She caught the scent of something musky and warm in the fabric and flashed to the moment he had touched her lips with his thumb. She hurried to pass the shirt to Griffin before she could become even more distracted.

She had hoped her jacket, put together with the men's shirts, would be enough. But when Griffin and Darius spread out the knotted clothing, even she could see it would not get them close to the ground on either side.

Griffin turned to her. "I'm sorry, Helen." His gaze dropped to her chest. "Do you have anything on under that?"

Her cheeks burned. "Just a corset and chemise."

He inhaled deeply, his eyes apologetic. "I'm afraid we're going to need your shirt. It still won't get as close as I'd like, but every little bit will help."

She nodded, aware that they were running out of time. Pushing aside her mortification, she started on her own blouse, avoiding the eyes of the men as she removed the shirt and passed it to Griffin.

It did not take him long to finish the rope. When he did, he double-checked the knots and turned to Darius.

"Ready?"

Darius nodded.

Griffin threw one end of the makeshift rope toward the top of the fence. It didn't work, and he tried several more times before turning to them in frustration. "It's too light. I can't get the end of it over the top of the fence."

Raum chose a large rock from the ground and reached a hand toward the rope. "Let me."

Griffin hesitated a moment before handing it over.

Once Raum had the rope in hand, he created a pouch on one end, placing the stone inside and knotting it securely in place. Then, he stepped back and threw. The rock, trailing the rest of the rope, flew up and over the fence. Helen watched their knotted clothing unfurl on the other side.

Griffin looked at Raum. "Nicely done."

Darius reached toward the fence, grasping both ends of the rope and lacing them together. He walked backward, pulling them until the knot rose, bit by bit, to the top of the fence. He gave it one last powerful tug, ensuring that it was knotted securely at the top. Then, he let go, leaving one end of the rope dangling on either side of the iron fence.

Grasping the end closest to him, he glanced at Griffin. "See you on the other side, brother."

He started climbing.

He made it look easy, but Helen knew that it was deceiving. Darius was strong. He pulled himself quickly from knot to knot, using his feet to steady himself on the swinging rope. Finally, they heard the sound of boots on metal and knew he had reached the top. He dropped to the ground on the other side less than a minute later.

Darius grinned at them through the bars of the fence. "Piece of cake."

Raum took the rope, glancing once toward the top, and began climbing without another word. He was two knots up

when he stopped moving. A few seconds later he dropped back to the ground.

"What is it?" Helen asked. "What's wrong?"

He hesitated a moment before reaching for his belt. "I can't move freely with the sword swinging at my side."

He turned to the fence, his eyes meeting Darius's through the bars. A moment later, he passed the sword through with obvious reluctance, returning wordlessly to the rope. No one said anything as he rose into the darkness. His ascent was as effortless as Darius's, and nervousness built in Helen's bones as he climbed. She would have to go next, never mind her fear.

Raum hit the ground on the other side. There was sweat on his brow when he held the rope out to Helen through the fence.

"You can do this." He looked into her eyes as he said it, and in that moment, Helen believed it.

She took the rope, studying it as if it would offer a clue how to begin.

"Reach up as far as you can," Griffin said quietly. "Take hold of one of the knots and pull yourself up until you feel another of them beneath your feet."

"Then what?" she asked, her voice quavering.

"Keep doing it," he said simply. "Reach, pull, move your

386

feet to the next knot. The rope will swing a little, but you can't spend too much time in one position. Your arms will grow tired that way. Try to keep moving."

She nodded, repeating the words. "Keep moving. Right."

Griffin glanced nervously around, and she knew he was worried about time. Time she was costing them by being nervous. She approached the rope, reaching above her head for one of the knots. When she found one, she hesitated, knowing that once she started, there was no going back.

But there was already no going back. Alastor had ordered the murder of their parents. If they let him reach the Summit tomorrow, he would use his power to overtake the world—with or without the key, which he would find eventually anyway. It was inevitable.

There were only three of them left. Three Keepers. One of them had it.

Once Alastor found it, he would change the course of history to suit him. Helen might cease to exist. Worse, she might find herself enslaved to Alastor himself or someone—something—even worse. The possibilities were horrific and endless.

This was it. It had to be done.

She forced herself to acknowledge the truth and then she

pulled, lifting her body a foot off the ground, as her feet flailed for purchase against the rope.

It was not easy. Not nearly as easy as Darius and Raum had made it seem. The rope twisted to and fro, making it almost impossible to find the knot with her feet. Her arms were already growing tired when she finally found the next one. She remembered Griffin's instructions and resisted the urge to rest. To remain with the relative security of her two little knots.

Forcing herself to move, she steadied her feet and reached above her head for the next knot before forcing her feet from the rope. It was easier this time. She found the knot after only a few seconds of kicking blindly in the dark below her.

"Good!" Griffin whispered from below. "You've got it. Just keep going."

She did. The rest of the world fell away. Even their mission to destroy Alastor was put on a remote shelf in her mind. Now, there was only the rope. The rope and darkness and the velvety sky above her. She reached and pulled and moved her feet even when her arms burned with the effort.

And then, she was at the top. Pausing, she realized she hadn't asked what to do once she reached the top. Probably because there was a part of her that didn't believe she would make it that far.

Yet here she was, and it would be foolish to call down to Griffin. It was a fence. She might not be an athlete, but she knew there was only one way over it.

It was the top that scared her. Less points and more spikes, she worried about catching her clothing, or worse yet, being impaled. The thought, morbid though it was, gave her an idea.

Her right arm shook as she let go with her left, reaching through the bars for the other side of the rope. When she finally had it in her hands, she wove it through the bars, using the fabric to cushion the spikes at the top of the fence. She worked quickly, knowing her strength would not last forever. It was not perfect. Some of them still showed through when she was finished. But where before there was only the intimidating point of metal, now there was some cushion for her to use in hoisting herself over. It would mean a shorter length of rope on the way down, but she could not afford to worry about that, dangling as she was high above the ground, desperate for a way over the fence so that she could begin the descent.

She placed her left hand on the bars at the top and did the same with her right, using them to steady herself as she moved her feet up one or two more knots. Then, when her feet were uncomfortably close to her hands, she heaved a leg over the top of the fence.

She felt the bite of metal into her skin almost immediately. It was temporary. After that, everything moved necessarily fast and she could not be bothered to wonder at the extent of her wounds. Her corset ripped as she dragged her abdomen across the fabric-covered bars, throwing her other leg over at the last minute.

It was all she could do not to let go and allow herself to fall, but she forced herself to take a few seconds to steady her body before feeling with her legs for the knots in the rope. Going down was easier, though her arms shook with the effort. At least she was over the worst of it. She had made it up and over. Whatever happened now, she was getting closer and closer to the ground with every step.

Until she reached the end of the rope.

"I'm out of rope," she whispered to anyone who would listen. "I had to use it to get over the top."

"It's all right." Raum's voice came from below her. "I can see you. You're not that far from the bottom. Let go and I'll catch you."

"Are you sure?" Her hands were sliding on the rope now, slick with sweat and something she feared might be blood.

"I'm sure," he said. "I won't let you fall. I promise."

It was these words that made her let go. Raum would not let her fall. Despite everything, he had said it. Promised it.

And she believed him.

She let go, and a moment later was in his arms.

THIRTY-FIVE

He held her a few seconds longer than necessary, their breath mingling in the cold night air. Finally, he let go, and she stepped away as casually as she could.

"Thank you." It seemed too simple for such an intimate moment, but it was the only appropriate thing to say with Darius standing nearby and Griffin only feet away on the other side of the fence.

Griffin made it up and over with far less drama. He must have uncoiled her cushion at the top of the fence, because a minute after he left the ground on the other side, the rope dropped closer to the ground in front of Helen. Griffin was standing next to them in seconds.

"What about the rope?" Helen asked as Griffin caught his breath.

"We'll have to leave it," Darius said. "It doesn't matter. The guards won't be back this way for some time. Besides, even if one of them shines the lantern right on the fence, it will be difficult to see the rope through the trees.

Helen was not happy with the thought of completing their task with only a corset and chemise atop her skirt, but there was nothing to be done about it.

"What's the best way into the house?" For the first time, Darius looked directly at Raum.

"Depends," Raum said.

"On what?"

"On which maid is sneaking out of her chamber to meet a beau or which old butler left a door unlocked."

"It's all chance, then?" Helen asked. "Getting into the house?"

Raum leveled his gaze at her. "Everything is chance, Helen."

She didn't have time to decipher the message in his words.

"We still have some time before the next patrol," Griffin said. "If we're careful and keep to the trees, we should be able to get a look at the house without being spotted."

They were already moving when Helen realized Raum wasn't following. She turned back to see him standing with his arms folded across his chest.

"What is it?" Helen whispered.

The brothers had stopped walking. Raum extended a hand toward Darius. "The sword?"

Darius held Raum's gaze, and for a moment, Helen wondered if he would give it back at all.

But then he stepped toward Raum and unlaced the sword, handing it over without a word.

Raum nodded, tying it to his belt as he began moving toward the house. "Let's go, then."

They moved through the woods, slowing when the lights at the back of the house became visible through the trees. Raum pointed to the left, and they followed him without speaking. They reached a point where they could see the rear of the house in its entirety, and they looked upward, scanning the facade for a way in. A moment later, Raum waved them closer. He pointed to the house.

"There. On the second floor." They all turned to look as he whispered.

A window was open on the second floor, a trellis extending beneath it to the ground, the room dark beyond the glass.

"We can use the trellis to climb up," Raum said.

"How do we know the room will be empty?" Helen asked.

"In my experience, a late night rendezvous is the only reason a window would be open over a trellis this time of year," he answered. "But the real answer to your question is 'we don't.'"

"Wonderful." She couldn't help being sarcastic. Her arms were still numb from her journey over the fence, and she felt entirely too exposed without her shirt. But she had asked to come, and Darius and Griffin had allowed it against their better judgment. It wouldn't be fair to seek their sympathy now. She would make it up the trellis one way or another—and face whatever was in the room above them.

"Let's go." Darius was already heading for the house when Raum put a hand on his arm. Darius froze, looking down at it in shock as if he could not believe Raum dared to touch him.

Raum removed his hand. "Once we're inside, I'll head to the cellar to cut the flow of gas to the lamps. Try not to confront Alastor until they go out."

"What about you?" Helen asked. "How will we find you?"

She felt Griffin's eyes on her and wondered if it pained him to know she cared about Raum's safety.

"I'll find you," Raum said. "Don't worry about me. Just focus on the task at hand."

And then they were moving along the tree line. They waited until they were even with the open window, not wanting to break from the cover of the woods before it was necessary. Then Raum waved them forward and they were racing across the lawn, running for the trellis and the shallow shadows of the house.

As with the fence, Darius went first while the rest of them watched for guards. Reaching the top, he disappeared for a moment before reappearing at the window, waving them through. Raum went next, followed by Helen. Despite the ascension of the men, she stepped carefully at first, not wanting to push her luck with the trellis. But after a few steps, it became obvious that it was as sturdy as oak, and she climbed the rest of the way without incident, marveling that it could seem easy after the rope and the iron fence.

Leaning out the window, Helen kept watch as Griffin began his ascent. He had only gone a couple of feet when she saw lantern light moving along the edge of the house. It bounced along ahead of its source, and while she could not yet know where it was coming from, she had seen enough like it during the three cold hours they spent waiting to get over the fence to know what it meant.

She leaned farther over the sill, whispering as loudly as she dared. "Hurry, Griffin. Someone's coming."

Griffin looked away from the trellis, following Helen's eyes to the light at the edge of the house.

"I think it's one of the guards," she said.

Turning his attention back to the task at hand, he climbed furiously as Helen watched the light bob across the ground, becoming brighter and brighter with each passing second. Griffin was only five rungs beneath the sill, then three, then two. A trouser-clad leg extended beyond the edge of the house, the light illuminating the corner of grass at the man's feet. He cleared the building and Helen recognized one of the guards who had been behind the dogs as she had disappeared into the tunnels the previous night.

Now the man stepped forward, heading for the back of the property. He didn't look their way as Griffin heaved himself over the windowsill, Helen tugging on his arms as if it would make any sort of difference. He tumbled into the room on top of her with a muffled thud, and she said a silent prayer of gratitude for the thickly carpeted floors.

On his feet in seconds, he reached out a hand and helped her up from the floor.

"All right?" he whispered.

She nodded, looking around.

They were in a simple bedchamber. There was a small bed against the wall, a bureau, a wardrobe, and a night table. A muslin dressing gown was laid out on the bed, and for a moment, Helen imagined the maid who probably occupied

the room. Perhaps she had escaped into the night to meet her lover. Helen wondered if her life was simple. If she cared for one man and one man only and had a mother and father she visited on holidays.

And then, Helen saw Raum heading for the door.

"Remember," he said as he passed, "don't confront Alastor until the lamps go out. Otherwise, you'll have more on your hands than just one demon. I'll find you as soon as I'm able."

"Don't you think you're forgetting something?" Griffin called after Raum as he reached the door.

Raum turned around. "What would that be?"

"The sword?" Griffin raised his eyebrows in question. "We're the ones going to find Alastor. It seems we should be the ones with the sword."

"And give you even more of a reason to leave me behind?" Raum shook his head. "I don't think so. I told you I would help you fight Alastor and I intend to honor my word. Besides, sunrise is still some time away."

"But how will we know where Alastor is?" Helen asked.

Raum shrugged. "I have no idea."

He turned away, disappearing into the hallway.

398

It took them a few minutes to get moving. They debated whether to try the upper or lower floors first, finally agreeing to edge their way into the hall and head for the upper floor. That was, after all, where they had found Alastor last time.

Griffin stood against the wall by the door listening before he stuck his head into the hall, making sure it was clear before waving Griffin and Helen forward. They inched slowly toward the staircase, careful to stay on the carpets and tread lightly, lest any of the floorboards should squeak.

They were almost at the stairs when Darius stopped them with a raised palm.

Cupping a hand to his ear, he indicated that they should listen. Helen stood very still, trying to tune out the sound of her own breathing and the ticking grandfather clock some-where in the house. At first, she could hear nothing else, but a moment later she caught something in the air. She tipped her head, straining to hone in on the sound.

The music came to her as if on a breeze, strings and wind instruments, coming from the floor below.

Darius raised his eyebrows, pointing downward in silent question. Griffin nodded, and they began descending the stairs, Helen hoping fervently that none of the servants were wandering the halls in the night.

They made it to the bottom without seeing another soul. Darius stepped onto the landing, turning toward a niche in the wall. They were nearly to its shadowed safety when a man's voice drifted to them from an open doorway.

"Come, come," he said, his voice low and friendly. "Don't be shy. I've been waiting for you."

They froze, eyes wide with alarm.

"Yes, I'm speaking to you, my fine friends," the voice said. "Please do join me in the library. You didn't come all this way only to run, now did you?"

There could be no doubt now that the unseen man was speaking to them, though how he could know of their presence, Helen couldn't begin to fathom.

But it didn't matter. She heard the intake of Griffin's breath and knew they were caught. His mouth was set into a tight line as he stepped toward the door, pulling Helen behind him in a gesture of protection as Darius stepped up to his brother's side.

A fire snapped in the firebox, the warmth hitting Helen full in the face as she stepped across the threshold of the room. It could have been any lavishly appointed private library. Bookcases lined the walls, reaching the ceiling in all their polished glory. Catching the scent of lemon, Helen had no doubt that the wood was oiled regularly, for the shelves glowed even where they extended into the shadows.

"Ah. There you are." A man rose from a chair near the fire.

No. Not a man.

A monster, Helen reminded herself, however he may look on the outside.

"So nice to make your acquaintance." He stepped toward them, extending a hand in greeting.

Griffin and Darius ignored the proffered hand.

"As you wish." Still smiling, Alastor shrugged off their obvious disdain. He directed his gaze to the brothers. "You must be Griffin Channing. And I assume the fierce-looking gentleman at your side is your brother, Darius." He leaned around them both, his eyes grabbing hold of Helen like a starving man finding bread. Helen didn't understand the hunger in his gaze, but she didn't like it. "And this must be the beautiful Keeper, Helen, of the Cartwrights. Despite everything, I should tell you that I had quite a lot of admiration for your parents. They stayed alive far longer than the rest and kept you alive as well."

Helen flinched at the words. She didn't want to think of this thing hunting her parents. Plotting their deaths. Ordering the fire that killed them.

He turned his back on them, making his way to a drink tray

atop a cupboard against the wall. His lack of concern for their presence—and their obvious plans to destroy him—worried Helen. He was too confident for someone outmatched three to one.

"May I offer you something?" he asked, his back still turned as he poured something into a glass. "Spirits? Wine, perhaps? Or do you partake of that insipid British concoction called *tea*?"

Just above the collar of his shirt, Helen caught a glimpse of the mark on Alastor's neck. It was a dragon rising out of a great fire like the mythical Phoenix.

She moved forward so that she was even with Darius and Griffin, watching as their eyes skittered to the lamps, still licking flames behind their glass covers. She saw in their expression what she already knew; they would have to wait until the lamps were put out to make their move. Besides, Raum still had the sword and they couldn't finish Alastor without it.

"No? Nothing?" Alastor turned to face them once again. "Nothing to refresh yourselves while you wait in vain for your traitorous ally?"

Helen's heart sank, her breath catching in her throat. Alastor knew about Raum.

"What have you done with him?" she asked, trying not to panic.

Alastor's voice was calm. "Raum Baranova is of little concern to me. My guards will have him well in hand long before he reaches the control panel." He made his way to the chair by the fire. "Come. Sit. We have much to discuss."

"We don't have anything to discuss." Griffin growled.

Alastor laughed. It was cold and without feeling. "That's where you're wrong, my young Keeper."

"It was all for nothing." The words were out of Helen's mouth before she could stop them. "We don't know where it is."

Alastor turned his gaze on her. His eyes were black as a raven. "Ah, but that's where we're different, Miss Cartwright. I *do*."

"Then why haven't you taken it?" Griffin asked. "If you know where it is, you could have taken it any time."

Helen knew Griffin was stalling, still hoping that Alastor had been bluffing about Raum and the lamps would be extinguished.

Alastor nodded. "Quite right. But you see, I've only just figured it out, and given the . . . urgency of my time line, it seemed wisest to let you return to me, as I knew you would

after that fiasco last night." He took a sip of his drink. "I heard about that old codger, Galizur, by the way. Pity."

Darius stepped forward, his face tight with fury.

Griffin placed a hand on his brother's arm. "Not yet," he whispered.

Alastor laughed, rising and making his way to the fire. "I do so admire your passion, Darius! Your ridiculous hope and even more ridiculous faith in the face of certain defeat." He lifted a poker from the hearth, prodding the crackling logs in the firebox as he continued. "It's the one true mark of humanity. Even as I loathe their weakness, their suffering, I covet their conviction. Their willingness to sacrifice for the so-called greater good. Their utter faith in right and wrong." He turned to face them. "It seems the Alliance has fostered these qualities in their Keepers as well. How very sad for you."

Griffin shook his head. "We don't need your pity for being what we are."

Alastor nodded. Helen marveled that he could look so very human. That he could cross the library and place his drink on the table as if he were any man in any home in London.

"Be that as it may, it does seem a pity to waste such strength, such talent, on something so close to a mortal." He rubbed his hands together. "But enough of this. We're in opposition, as we always have been. One night's debate will not change that now, will it?" He continued without waiting for a reply. "Now, if you just give me the girl, you can be on your way."

Helen thought she had heard him wrong until Griffin spoke.

"Give you the girl?" he asked, clearly perplexed. He followed Alastor's eyes, squarely on her. "Helen?"

"That's right. If you leave Helen Cartwright, the two of you may depart unharmed." He said it simply, as if it made perfect sense instead of being utterly preposterous.

"Helen's not staying with you." Griffin took a step closer to her, his face tightening with fury. "You must be mad!"

Alastor took in Griffin's gesture of protection. Understanding dawned on the demon's face. "Ah. It's like that, is it? Well, that does complicate matters, but not by much."

"I . . . I don't understand," Helen said. "I don't have it. I don't have the key."

"Leave that to me," Alastor said, his voice cold. "Am I to assume, then, that you refuse to comply with my demand?"

"I'll tell you what you can do with your demand . . ." Darius started.

"Darius," Griffin warned.

Alastor sighed. "Very well, then."

Helen looked around as the room fell silent. Alastor's face

took on an eerie stillness, and although his eyes were still open, he seemed not to see them at all. Helen wondered if they should use his odd trance to do something, but then she remembered.

The lamps were still lit. And they did not have the sword.

THIRTY-SIX

Helen wondered if Alastor had been telling the truth. If his men had apprehended Raum before he could reach the cellar and the control panel that would extinguish the flow of gas to the lights.

She shook her head as if to rid the thought. She could not afford to lose hope. Not now when they were so close to vengeance. To victory.

And then, the lamps flickered. Helen felt a rush of relief. It was Raum. He hadn't been captured after all. He was cutting the flow of gas to the lamps. He would find them soon. They would have the sword and an additional person to aid them.

But the lamps were not extinguished.

As they flickered, Helen saw moving shadows in the pools of light. A strange rumbling sounded from the ground, and the floorboards beneath their feet began to shake. Worst of all was the sound emanating from Alastor's lips. It started as a keening. A cry of agony and rage. As if the mortal body could not contain the anguish rent from it by the demon within.

The cry built, growing louder as Alastor's eyes turned black, red rings appearing around them until they glowed like a fiery suns. He opened his mouth, and the keening grew louder, building into a roar as blue light streamed from the mouth of the man called Alsorta.

He seemed to grow. To become larger and wider. His shoulders ripped through his shirt as Helen watched, fascinated and horrified. The skin that before had been slightly papery, in the first stages of mortal aging, now became translucent. Veins appeared out of nowhere, snaking and crisscrossing the demon's body, as if it required extra blood to fuel the monstrous change. Just when Helen thought the transformation complete, she heard something move behind him. Taking a step backward, she saw the great wings—pointed and reptilian like those of a giant bat—flutter at his back.

The demon called Alastor was nearly unrecognizable as the man who had stood before them only moments before. This was no mortal. No man. This was a creature of darkness. One whose physical form existed for one purpose and one purpose alone: to destroy whatever—or whoever—stood in its path.

Which is right where Helen and the brothers stood.

The lights flickered again, and this time, Helen knew better than to hope that it was Raum. The flickering shadows in the illumination told her all she needed to know, and she was unsurprised when the first three wraiths appeared in the light streaming from a sconce on the wall.

Darius and Griffin immediately came together, turning their backs to one another as cover. They were reaching for their sickles as Helen stepped toward them, doing the same. She didn't know if she would be any help. If she would make it out alive. But she could not let the brothers fight while she stood by and did nothing. She would give her life rather than be a coward again.

Alastor roared as the three wraiths approached Helen and the brothers. She couldn't see the brothers clearly from her vantage point, but she could feel their bodies move and hear the clang of their sickles, the guttural howls as the wraiths were hit. She waited, sickle in hand, her breath coming fast and heavy, for the third one to attack her.

It didn't. It went straight for Darius, though Helen was completely unprotected and clearly wielding a weapon. She felt a flash of anger. Did they think her so little threat that they would not even acknowledge her presence?

Darius was working his sickle on two of the wraiths as Griffin fought the other. Helen ducked under the fighting, stepping away from the fray and moving up behind the third wraith. He raised his weapon against Darius as Helen raised her own. She hesitated, realizing that she would hurt, maim, or kill the wraith with her sickle. It gave her the smallest of pauses. She had never hurt a living thing in her life.

But this is no living thing, she reminded herself, bringing the sickle down on the wraith's back, using the jagged edge of the weapon.

It roared, turning to locate the source of the attack. When it saw Helen, uncertainty flickered in its red-rimmed eyes, and it moved away to attack Darius from another side.

She was still standing there, looking at the sickle in her hand and trying to figure out why the wraiths would not attack her, when both brothers deployed Galizur's new glaives. They opened smoothly, and when the brothers plunged them into the bodies of the wraiths, Helen told herself again that they were not human.

Griffin was slashing the third wraith with his sickle as Darius picked up the glaives from the floor. Helen knew the sickle wouldn't destroy the demon completely, but it was all Griffin could do with the glaives in use. A moment later the wraith faded to darkness with a shriek as Alastor roared, conjuring six more wraiths from the lights in the room. Helen stepped in front of the brothers.

"Helen, no." Griffin pulled her back, clearly unaware that she likely could not pay the wraiths to attack her, though she was standing not five feet in front of them. She already knew they would go around her, avoiding her at all costs, though she still didn't know why.

The wraiths were only inches from her position when the lights flickered yet again. Helen braced for the appearance of more wraiths and was shocked when the room was plunged into darkness. All movement in the room stopped for a split second, the fire the only source of light as everyone tried to regain their bearings.

Raum was coming. He had not been caught after all. Helen dared a glance at the curtained windows as the wraiths began advancing once again. She didn't know if it was her imagination, but she was almost positive there was a pale blue light glowing around the window frame. She looked at the mantle clock. Five o'clock in the morning. It was almost sunrise. All they had to do was hold off the six wraiths in the room until Raum arrived with the sword.

Griffin and Darius went to work. Their sickles moved so

fast that Helen could hardly see them from one moment to the next. She heard the clink of their metal blades as the brothers switched from side to side, and when it seemed they were in danger of being overwhelmed, she stepped in and slashed at the wraiths' backs and shoulders. It did not destroy them or send them back from where they came, but it caused them to howl and shriek, and the distraction sometimes gave Darius and Griffin time enough to dispatch one wraith completely before turning their attention to another. As she suspected, not one of the wraiths raised a weapon to her. She could only assume Alastor had ordered that they take her alive.

Darius and Griffin were fighting the remaining three wraiths. Helen could make out their hulking bodies in the dim light of the room. She was stepping forward to aid Darius, who was slashing at one wraith on the floor as another approached his back, when Raum appeared, his sickle, bloody and open, in hand.

Helen could imagine what had been on the other end of it.

Closing the sickle, he hung it quickly on his belt. He didn't have a glaive, but he picked up one of Galizur's, fallen to the floor during the brothers' scuffle with the wraiths, and plunged it into the back of the ambushing demon. It howled in pain as it shattered into a million tiny pieces.

The last two monsters were dispensed with quickly. They were almost automatons. They had weapons and large, muscled bodies, but that was as far as their advantages went.

When all the wraiths were gone, Darius, Griffin, and Raum turned to face Alastor. His countenance was engorged, fiery with rage. He tipped his head back, letting loose a howl so mighty the glass in the windows rattled in their frames.

Then he began moving toward them, his footsteps falling like slabs of granite on the carpeted floors. Plaster rained from the walls, the lamp shades falling to the floor in a rain of shattering glass. Helen didn't know if any of the servants remained. If they knew what their master was. But as Alastor came closer, she heartily hoped they had escaped the grounds while they had had the chance.

"What now?" Darius asked no one in particular as the demon bore down on them.

"Keep him busy with the sickles and glaives," Raum said under his breath. "It's almost sunrise."

The wings at Alastor's back cracked like a whip as they spread. Helen couldn't believe the wingspan. They could be easily swallowed in it if Alastor chose.

He didn't get the chance. Griffin stepped forward in one quick motion, throwing the glaive at the monster. The chandeliers in the ceiling rattled as the glaive buried itself in the demon's muscled abdomen and he let out a great shriek. And then the men were on him, taking advantage of their greater number, despite Alastor's greater strength. The beast swiped at them with hands that had become razor-sharp talons. He picked them up, tossing them against the walls. And always, Darius, Griffin, and Raum got back up, slashing him with their sickles, puncturing him with the glaives, trying to slow him down.

Helen watched for an opportunity to help, but there was no room for her in the fray. She kept her eyes on the curtained windows instead, watching for signs of the rising sun. A couple minutes later, the light around the frames grew brighter. Helen skirted to the window, throwing open the curtains and calling out.

"Raum! It's time."

Griffin was on the floor, unmoving and so pale that Helen's heart nearly stopped beating. She was on her way to him when Alastor lifted Darius and Raum into the air, throwing them against a far wall before stomping his way toward her. She backed toward Griffin's still form. If she was going to die, she would die with Griffin.

Her foot hit something, and she tripped, falling to the floor

as Alastor stomped toward her. She wondered if the house would come down around them before he could do whatever it was that he planned to do to her. It would be a better end than the one that awaited her at his hands. Scooting along the floor, she backed up until she hit one of the bookshelves and could go no farther. It was difficult to call the expression on Alastor's face a smile, but that's what it seemed to be as he approached her.

Looming over her, Helen could smell the stink of his breath. Feel the heat, so fiery she was surprised the house didn't burst into flames around them, from his twisted body.

"You," he roared. "You. Have. It."

She shook her head. "I don't."

"Give it to me or you will die a painful death and I will take it by force," he croaked, his voice twisted and guttural.

She swallowed, trying to think of a way to delay. Wondering if Raum or one of the brothers would regain consciousness. She kept still, allowing her eyes to dart around the room, looking for anything that might buy her time.

And that was when she saw it.

It glinted in the pink glow of the rising sun, now streaming through the opening in the velvet curtains.

The sword. That is what she had tripped on. It must have

fallen from Raum's belt during the battle, and now it lay just a few feet from her position against the bookcases.

There was no maneuver, no clever strategy that would put the sword in her hands. She would have to lunge for it, counting on her smaller size and the element of surprise to give her the couple of extra seconds she would need to reach the sword before him.

It took only a few seconds to decide. There were no other options.

She lunged forward, crawling across the floor, reaching for the sword before she got to it. She was not worried about getting Alastor into the light of the rising sun. He wanted what she had—what he thought she had. She had seen the need in his eyes.

He would follow her.

Her fingers closed on the sword as Alastor's claws came down on her skirt, pinning her to the floor. She slid the sword under the fabric of the garment, now spread across the ground as Alastor moved toward her with a strange, inhuman gait.

The sun was just two inches above her head. Just two inches.

The beast hovered over her. She saw the pleasure in his eyes. He had her and he knew it. He would eliminate every last Keeper. Rule the world with his power over time and the legion of demons at his command. It was all the motivation she needed. She flipped onto her stomach, grabbing hold of the sword and crawling for the light.

It was then, in the frantic scuttle across the floor, that she saw it.

Time seemed to slow as the rising sun hit the pendant, no longer an abstract design swinging from her neck. No longer simple filigree, fine and lovely, but something more.

Looking down into the scrolling metal, she saw the same design twisting and turning on Galizur's screen. On the ink etched onto Griffin's back.

Alastor was right. She did have the key.

He stomped toward her, his fury rising in a brutal howl. The glass broke behind the curtains. Helen heard it rain onto the floor as Alastor flipped her onto her back, his talons reaching for the pendant at her neck. She let him get close. Let his eyes light with the nearness of it.

Then she plunged the sword into his heart, twisting it for good measure to make sure she didn't miss. She watched him howl.

The veins covering his body seemed to withdraw under his skin, a look of surprise passing over his face as the wings shriveled at his back. His mouth opened, the blue light streaming from it in an eerie shriek in the moment before his mortal body burst, not in a flurry of flesh and blood as she expected, but in a cloud of ash.

She crawled toward Griffin as it rained down on her, a torrent of black rain.

THIRTY-SEVEN

$\mathcal{S}$he was not surprised to find Anna waiting for her at the door.

"Come in," the other girl said. "I saw you on the monitors."

Helen stepped into the hallway, glad to see that Anna was closing and locking the doors again.

"How are you feeling?" Anna's voice was muffled by their footsteps as they made their way through the halls, pausing at the many locked doors along the way.

"I'm fine," Helen said. "A little sore, but not nearly as sore as Darius and Griffin."

They had come to the last door. Anna closed and locked it behind them, turning her eyes on Helen. "And Raum?"

Helen looked down at her feet. "I haven't seen him. Not since that night."

She had sat in Alastor's library with Griffin's head in her

lap. At some point, she fell asleep, waking to the heat of the sun pressing against her eyelids. Darius and Griffin were still unconscious, but breathing.

Raum had disappeared.

No one came. No one inquired about the noise or the mess. It was as if all of Alastor's staff had turned to ash right along with him.

Some time later, Griffin stirred. When she looked down, it was into his mysterious hazel eyes. Darius woke soon after and they made their way back to the Channing house where she nursed their wounds before collapsing onto her bed, still clothed, beside Griffin.

"So Raum will not face the Dictata's judgment after all." Anna's voice was a murmur without accusation.

"I suppose not," Helen said.

Anna nodded, moving farther into the room. "You're not here to discuss Raum, are you?"

"No."

"You've found it, then?" Anna asked.

Helen nodded. "How long have you known?"

"Almost since the beginning." Anna gestured for her to sit. She poured water from a steaming pot into a delicate teacup, handing it to Helen. "Well, I suppose I should say that we were fairly certain Darius and Griffin *didn't* have it, which left you by process of elimination."

"Why didn't you tell me?" Helen whispered, staring into her cup as if the tea at the bottom held the answer.

Anna sighed. "It's a burden, being the Keeper of the key. We thought it better—safer—that you should not know in case you were questioned. Those from the Legion have . . . methods for extracting information. None of them pleasant. We simply wished to protect you and the key until such a time as the executions could be put to a stop."

Helen looked into her eyes. "Why me?"

Anna smiled, shrugging. "I suppose the Dictata knew you were the best person to have it. The most worthy."

Helen's laughter was bitter. She stood, pacing to the mantle. "I am far from worthy. I let my parents burn. Enlisted the help of the man who ordered them murdered. Came, even, to see him as a friend."

"A friend?" Anna prodded.

Helen could not meet her eyes. Friend was hardly a strong enough word to describe her feelings for Raum.

Anna stood, crossing the room and touching Helen on the arm. "Come with me."

Helen was puzzled, but Anna was already making her

way to the staircase, and Helen followed her into the now-familiar recesses of the cellar laboratory. They traversed the tunnel, immaculate in comparison to the sewer tunnels beneath London, in silence. When at last they reached the laboratory, Helen's eyes were drawn to the Orb, the strange connection she'd felt to it still present. She didn't know if it was her imagination, but the Orb seemed to move slightly quicker than it had just last week. Gazing up at it, she thought it a beautiful world. That one and the one on which she stood as well.

"They have already begun appointing new Keepers," Anna said with a smile. "The Orb will grow stronger, day by day, as will the world it represents. But that's not what I want to show you."

Helen followed her to the Orb, staring down into the tiny point of blue light that was the only access to the records.

"Try it." Anna tipped her head at the lock.

"What? The key?"

Anna nodded.

"But . . . isn't it against the rules or something? I thought I was simply supposed to keep it safe."

"You are," Anna said. "But I don't think anyone will mind its Keeper having a quick look from the door. Besides," she added, "my father's authority is bequeathed to me, and I'm quite sure he would do the very same thing."

Helen removed the pendant from around her neck. She held it close to her face, looking again at the pointed, scrolled filigree at its end. It seemed impossible that it should open anything. That it should fit the pinprick of light at all.

She lifted her eyes to Anna's. "What do I do?"

"Place the pointed end of the crown against the keyhole."

"But it won't . . . It won't fit."

"Trust me. Place the point at the end of the crown against the point of light on the floor," Anna instructed.

Helen lowered herself to the floor, sitting back on her knees as she studied the light. Such an innocuous-looking light, and yet she could feel the energy, the power, flowing from it, reaching upward and enveloping the Orb that spun above her head.

Part of her didn't want to confirm what she already knew. It was the last vestige of her denial. Once she placed the end of the pendant in the keyhole, her ability to unlock the records would be confirmed. There would be no turning away from her place in the Alliance.

And yet, she found that she didn't want to turn away. The Alliance and her role in it had come to matter to her. It was a legacy of her parents, a way in which she would be forever connected to them and to the people that they were.

And to Griffin, Anna, Galizur, and yes, even Darius.

She had barely settled the end of the crown against the point of light when it expanded, a mini-explosion rippling outward before collapsing in on itself. The other end of the pendant grew hot in her hand. Helen held tight to it, not wanting to lose it and not sure what would happen if she let go.

And then, the strangest thing happened.

The scrolled end of the pendant, once an elaborate, hollow crown, flattened itself against the light, the two merging as one, expanding into the floor in a familiar design of overlapping circles, tiny flowers forming in its geometric design, until both the pendant and the symbol it had invoked disappeared in a flash.

Helen was still staring, still trying to understand what had happened to her pendant, when a doorway of pure light opened in the floor before her.

"Don't worry." Anna's voice was soft. "Your pendant will come back when the door is closed."

The light that emanated from the door was pure and golden. It shone like the light of the sun. Not as on the hottest of days when Helen feared her skin would grow pink, but as on the days when she would sit in the garden, her head tipped to the gentle warmth of it.

Through the door, Helen could see a staircase, descending far beyond into the light.

"The records are in there?" she finally asked.

"Yes." Anna took a deep breath. "It's an awesome responsibility, Helen, to be the Keeper of the key. To the past, present, and future."

"That's why I don't understand. Why me?" Despite her awe at seeing the entrance to the records, that was still the question that burned in Helen's mind.

Anna stuck a hand into the light. It disappeared in a flash, narrowing to a tiny pinpoint until it looked just as it had before. Helen's pendant dropped into Anna's open hand.

"Helen." Anna tipped her head, a gentle smile playing at her lips. "Don't you see? The Dictata has access to the records. They have looked into the past. Into the future. And they have chosen you." She pressed Helen's pendant—the key to everything—into Helen's palm. "Perhaps it's time to trust in their judgment."

THIRTY-EIGHT

Helen didn't mean to end up at the burned remains of her home. It was daylight. She couldn't jump back to the Channing house, which was just as well. She wanted to walk. To think upon everything Anna had told her and everything she had learned.

She aimlessly traveled the streets of the city. The brothers, it seemed, finally trusted her to take care of herself, though Griffin would still worry if she was gone too long. She waited for a carriage to pass before crossing a street, heading toward the scent of fresh bread. A moment later she looked up to see the ruined facade of the home she had shared with her mother and father.

She smiled at the creak of the iron gate. She would not hear it again. The next time she came to this place, it would be to give orders for new construction. She couldn't live with

the Channings forever. Whatever happened between her and Griffin, she did not want to be beholden to anyone. Not even him. She wanted to stand on her own. To have a home that was hers. Most of all, she wanted to see it all again.

The parlor. The library. The garden where she had held tea parties with a blue-eyed boy.

It was this she was thinking of as she stepped through the front door, making her way down the front hall. She entered the ruined parlor, and for a moment, it was just as it was. There was Father with his paper, grumbling about the state of affairs. Mother was at the piano, playing so beautifully that it made Helen's heart ache. She turned in a circle to take it all in. Remembering.

She was surprised to feel wetness on her cheeks. Lifting a hand to her face, she touched the tears with wonder. They were proof that it had all been real.

And that maybe, she was real, too.

"It was lovely," a voice said from the door. "I can still see it."

She turned, realizing she had expected Raum all along. Had hoped he would find her here.

She turned her gaze back to the room, seeing it all one last time before it faded into the ashes around her.

"I can see it, too."

They stood in silence. Raum stepped carefully toward her. He touched a gentle hand to the cut on her brow, a reminder of her battle with Alastor.

"Are you all right?"

"Do you care?" she asked softly.

He nodded. "I'm afraid I do. Too much for my own good."

"Then why did you leave?"

He took a deep breath. "I wanted to face the Dictata on my own terms."

The words startled her. "You've . . . you've seen the Dictata?"

He nodded.

"And what . . ." She was afraid to ask. Afraid to know what they would do to him.

He chuckled. "Well, it's a funny thing. It turns out they aren't going to do anything at all. Unless you count indentured servitude as punishment. And it may be."

She shook her head. "What do you mean?"

A hesitant smile turned his mouth up at the corners. "It seems the Dictata wants to be more proactive in the future. Get them before they get us, you might say."

"I'm afraid I still don't understand." Helen felt daft, but it was true.

"They're expanding the existing corps of assassins to form an elite battle group that will be able to act on threats like the Blackguard before they reach such dire proportions. It will provide Descendants an opportunity to serve, if they so wish, though I think it will be most fitting for those of us with less . . . conventional talents."

Helen looked into this distance, trying to imagine this new world in which she would take her place as Keeper and others like her would hunt for demons to keep them—and their world—safe.

It would be a dangerous task for all those involved.

She looked into his eyes. "And they've agreed to let you be a part of this new corps?"

The grin came more easily this time. "You might say they insist. I think returning the sword went a long way toward proving my allegiance."

She smiled up at him, knowing there was more, and knowing she would not like the next part at all. "What will happen now?"

He looked away before turning back to her. "Now I prepare to leave."

She nodded. "Where will you go?"

He shrugged. "Wherever they need me, I suppose. They're still recruiting. Still puzzling it out. But the general idea is that we'll travel to the site of possible threats and go undercover to investigate them. If they're real, it will be up to us to destroy anything from the Legion before it can do significant damage to the Keepers." He hesitated, his voice softening. "To you."

His eyes burned into hers, and she turned away. She could not afford to be lost in those eyes again. "When do you leave?"

"As soon as I have my orders. Probably tomorrow."

She felt his hand on her shoulder. "Helen, look at me."

She swallowed hard, trying to banish her emotion before turning to meet his eyes.

"Come with me," he said.

She shook her head. "I can't do that."

"Because of him?" His voice was bitter and she knew he referred to Griffin.

"Because of many things," she said. "I'm one of them. A Keeper. They need me now more than ever."

"You don't have to renounce your role as Keeper. They live all over the world." He took her shoulders in his hands.

"Just come with me, Helen. Be with me. I can keep you safe."

His eyes burned into hers, the strange, indefinable shock wave moving between them.

She wanted to deny it. To push the idea away without a thought. But for a split second, she saw it all. She saw herself in Raum's arms, traveling the world with him. Loving him.

He leaned toward her, his mouth inches from hers. His lips were smooth and supple. She could imagine them on hers. Imagine the warmth flowing between their bodies as they kissed. His mouth was so close to hers she could feel the heat of his breath. She put her hands flat against his chest.

"No."

He stopped, hovering near her mouth.

"I can't, Raum." She paused. "I won't."

He leaned away slowly, the space between them growing cold as he turned from her.

"Do you love him?" he asked in a broken voice.

"I love you both." And as she said it, she knew it was true.

He spun on her, his eyes full of anguish. "Then, why not?"

She crossed the empty space between them, looking into his eyes. "There's more to it than love. Too much has passed between us, Raum. Too much sadness. Too much death."

He nodded as she said these last words, as if he had known all along.

"I'll always have . . . affection for you." Her eyes stung with unshed tears. She marveled that after so many days of not being able to find them, now she could not keep them at bay. "But the things that have happened—"

"The things I've done," he corrected her.

She shrugged. "What does it matter which words we use? It can't be wiped away."

He nodded. "You're right. Of course you're right."

Remembering something, she opened the bag dangling at her wrist. She found what she was looking for a few seconds later and held her hand out toward him.

"This belongs to you."

He took the object, his eyes full of questions. When he opened his palm, it held an uncut key.

He shook his head. "Where did you get this?"

"It's the one you dropped in the factory that first night." She hesitated until her curiosity got the better of her. "Why did you leave them? At the murder scenes."

He took a deep breath. "I don't know. I suppose part of me wanted the Dictata to know that it was me. That I could steal from them as they stole from me, though of course,

that isn't the way it is, is it?" His voice was bitter and full of shame as he closed his fingers around the key, letting his hand fall to his side.

She reached for his hand, cupping it in hers. "Perhaps you'll remember me and all we've shared when you look at it. Perhaps you'll remember that serious girl with soft hands who cares for you still."

They stood in the ruins of the house, staring into each other's eyes. There was nothing else to say, and Helen braced herself for the moment when he would leave. The moment when he'd say good-bye forever.

Instead, he said something unexpected. "There's one thing I must ask you before I go."

She nodded.

"Do you forgive me? Well and truly forgive me for everything I took from you?"

She thought for a moment, not wanting to give him empty reassurances. There had always been honesty between them. That was something, at least.

Looking into his eyes, the blue sky of her childhood, the answer was as plain as day. "I do. Well and truly."

He lifted a hand to her cheek. "And what about yourself, Helen? Will you ever forgive yourself?"

She swallowed the emotion that rose in her throat. How could he have known that of all the enemies she had fought, it was this foe that haunted her most?

She tried to smile. "That might be more difficult."

"It shouldn't be," he said quietly. "Forgive yourself as you have forgiven me. As we all must forgive our own failings. I don't think we can be free otherwise."

His words rang through her mind.

Was it really as simple as that? Could she give herself the benediction of forgiveness that she had given Raum? She didn't know the answer. But as she leaned on tiptoe to kiss Raum's cheek, she knew she would try. She would try to remember the girl from the garden and her friend Raum. Their innocence and kindness to one another in the giving of small trinkets and simple friendship.

She would remember it all and grant that love and acceptance to those around her.

And maybe, just maybe, to herself.

She made her way out the door and down the path, closing the creaking gate behind her. She thought of Raum's words in the darkness outside Alastor's estate and wondered if perhaps he had been right. If perhaps each person simply needed one other who believed in them.

She didn't know. But as she walked away from the house and toward her future, she knew she had all that and more.

Two men who knew all her darkness and believed in her—loved her—still. And though she cared for both of them, there was only one who was her best friend. Only one who represented all the love and honor and sacrifice to which she would aspire.

And he was waiting.

ACKNOWLEDGMENTS

As with a child, it takes a village to raise a book. I have been very, very fortunate to have so many people in my corner. It seems only right to thank them if given the opportunity.

First, a big thank-you to to my editor, Nancy Conescu, at Penguin/Dial. We have made quite a journey together. I can honestly say that I wouldn't have it any other way. You continue to make me a better writer through a unique kind of alchemy that combines a firm hand with a gentle touch. I don't know how you do it, but I've learned so much from you and I've enjoyed every minute of it. I couldn't ask for anything more.

Another thank-you my agent, Steven Malk, who always, always has my back. By dealing with all the stuff that makes me crazy and stresses me out, you make it possible for me to write my very best. I trust you implicitly, Steve, and there are very few people in this world who have heard those words from me.

Thank-you to Don Weisberg and the Dream Team that is Penguin/Dial for making me feel so welcome and for giving me—and my work—a new home. You are not only incredibly astute and innovative, you are also some of the nicest, warmest people I have ever met.

To Lisa Mantchev, Jessica Verday, C. Lee McKenzie, Jon Skovron, Stacey Jay, Saundra Mitchell, Carrie Ryan, Daisy Whitney, and the 2009 Debutantes who have shared this journey with me through good times and bad. We've come a long way.

A special thank-you to Tonya Hurley, Juliette Dominguez, and MJ Rose, who have become friends and confidantes. In this world, neither is to be underestimated.

To my mother, Claudia Baker, for teaching me the lesson of unconditional love.

And to my father, Michael St. James, for teaching me the lesson of self-acceptance.

To Morgan Doyle, whom I love like a daughter, and to all the teens who talk to me on Facebook, let me be a part of their lives, and listen in on their conversations. It's because of you that I feel so connected to teens everywhere. Most importantly, it's because of you that I'm able to write for them.

To the many, many readers who e-mail me and talk to me online, reminding me why I do what I do, why I love doing it, and why it's so important. Each of you means more to me than you could possibly know.

Lastly, to Kenneth, Rebekah, Andrew, and Caroline. There is nothing without you.